ISOLATED

Matt Rogers

ISBN: 9781519090126
ISBN-13:

"Man is the cruelest animal."

— *Friedrich Nietzsche*

PROLOGUE

Officer William Brandt of the Jameson Police Department unlocked his front door and stepped into a cozy living room furnished with a plain couch, a small flat-screen television and a glass coffee table. Ordinarily at the end of the work day he would relish the peace and quiet of the evening's final hours. Then he would head to bed, alone. Just as he had for the last year, ever since he and Georgia had parted ways. Ready to repeat the process the next day.

But tonight was different.

An hour ago he'd seen something he wasn't supposed to.

With a pounding heart he crossed to the kitchen, small and white and decorated just as sparsely as the living room. He snatched the landline phone off its cradle and held it in a sweating palm. Usually the silence of the empty house had a calming effect. Now it unnerved him.

He stood staring into space for what felt like an eternity, listening to the sounds of the forest outside. The eerie chirping of crickets. The pine branches rustling in the mountain breeze.

Jameson was a small town buried in the never-ending woods of the Australian countryside, far from the twenty-four hour bustle of the city. The isolation gave Brandt room to breathe. At least, that's what he told people.

In truth, he fucking hated the place.

Hundreds of square miles of nothingness in every direction meant there weren't many places to make new acquaintances. Or find a girlfriend.

It also meant there was a lot of room to bury a body.

If they got to him, he knew no-one would ever find him.

Clutching the phone in his grip, it sunk in that he had stumbled upon something sinister, a secret that those responsible would kill to protect. He found himself plagued by the unshakeable feeling that he was in way over his head.

A spontaneous detour after leaving the station had led him down a road he didn't normally use. He'd seen floodlights in an area of forest he believed to be deserted. He'd decided to check it out. Even though he was off-duty, curiosity got the better of him.

He'd been spotted.

Now he began to punch in a number, unsure if he was making the right decision. Before he landed in the dead-end career of a small town police officer, he'd done some time in the military. The defence force advertisements had influenced him enough to serve three long and uneventful years in the

Royal Australian Navy Reserves. They'd stationed him up in Sydney at Fleet Base East, where he'd made a few friends in the Special Operations Command.

They were who he needed right now. Special Forces were the only body capable of addressing an incident of this magnitude.

Especially after he stressed the importance of what he'd seen.

A floorboard creaked in the corridor connecting to the kitchen. It was almost inaudible, but the silence amplified the noise. He froze halfway through the process of dialling. He put the landline back on the wall and reached for the holster at his waist. Jameson's crime rates were virtually nonexistent, which meant he'd never used his firearm in the line of duty. He was inexperienced in these situations. He struggled to suppress his nerves.

Before he had time to draw his weapon a man stepped round the corner. It sent a pang of shock through his chest. The intruder was a little taller than him, his expression steely. His eyes were cold and hard. Emotionless. He seemed perfectly calm, as if breaking into houses was an activity performed for leisure. Were it not for the enormous handgun in his palm, safety flicked off, Brandt would have trouble believing the man had hostile intentions.

The intruder levelled the pistol at his head.

'You know why I'm here?' the man said.

Brandt nodded. 'I swear, I won't say anything to anyone. I'll pretend I never saw anything.'

'But you did see.'

'I know. Please. You can trust me.'

'Maybe I can. Maybe I can't. No way to know for sure.'

'I won't talk.'

'You've got that right.'

It only took one shot.

The round exploded out of the barrel, deafening inside the confined space. It entered through Brandt's temple and blew out the back of his head amidst a spray of blood and brain matter. The intruder had chosen an IMI Desert Eagle to kill the officer because it left no room for speculation. Surviving a direct impact to the forehead from one of its cartridges was impossible.

Brandt's lifeless body spun away. He landed heavily on the kitchen floor and lay still.

The intruder took one look at the corpse and knew nothing further was necessary. He tucked the handgun away, then shrunk back into the shadows. He had no time to linger. He would get his men to dispose of the body later.

There was work to be done.

CHAPTER 1

Just a few short miles away, Jason King took a single glance around the country-town bar. He saw five men. After a beat of observation, he concluded that three were inebriated locals and two were workers temporarily residing in the countryside. He had spent thirty-two minutes sitting at the thick oak countertop of the bar. Timing the duration he spent in one place was something instinctive, ingrained into his subconscious from past experiences.

'Can I get you another round, bud?' the bartender said, motioning to King's empty glass. He was a burly man with a beard that fell past his neck and thick long hair tied back into a bun. His heavy-duty clothes reeked of beer and tobacco.

He was no threat.

'Sure.'

The man took King's glass and placed it under the tap. A stream of ale ran into the bottom, creating a thin layer of froth as the glass filled to the brim. It was his second glass and he couldn't help but admit it was good.

He took the time the bartender spent on the refill to shoot another look at his surroundings.

One could never be too careful.

Nothing had changed. A roaring log fire on the far wall cast a pale orange glow over the room. Wooden tables covered most of the floorspace, each cut from the trunk of a single tree and polished and smoothed to perfection, adding to the gritty outback feel of the decor. The three locals sat together in the far corner near the fire. Giant mugs of beer rested on their table, each at various stages of completion. They talked loudly, cackling at each other's comments. The pair of workers were still dressed in their high-visibility vests. Both their outfits were covered in dried concrete stains and their faces sported the weary expression of labourers finally resting after a long day's work.

The bartender laid down a fresh round in front of King, full to the brim. 'Here you go.'

'Thanks.'

'Can't help but notice your accent, mate. American?'

King nodded. 'Born and raised.'

'What brings you all the way out here?'

'Recently retired. Decided to travel for a while. See the world.'

'You look too young to be retired.'

'I made use of the time I had. Got a lot of work done.'

‘Well, you’re a lucky man.’

King shrugged and sipped his beer. ‘That’s debatable.’

‘Why here?’ the bartender said. ‘There’s a million places you could have gone. I can’t say we’re the most attractive tourist destination on the planet.’

‘It’s quiet out here,’ King said. ‘I needed to get away from all the trouble.'

'Trouble?'

He paused. ‘Life gets chaotic sometimes.’

‘I get it. Sometimes you need to put all the shit behind you.’

King nodded.

‘How are we treating you so far?'

‘I like it here.’

There was a moment of silence. King adjusted his khaki trousers and took another mouthful of beer.

'Tell me,’ he said. ‘What’s it like?'

The bartender raised an eyebrow. 'Huh?'

'Running a bar in these parts. Must be peaceful.’

'Well, I can’t complain, mate. Like you said, it’s quiet out here. I stay afloat from loyal customers. People keep coming back. It’s never more than steady, but I do alright. I don’t need to pay to have a drink. It’s the little things you take pleasure in.' He paused, surveying the room. Quietly proud. 'Sorry, I’m rambling.'

King shook his head. 'No, it's nice to hear. Gives me some insight into a different type of life to mine.'

'A future career prospect, maybe?' the bartender said, chuckling.

'I doubt it.'

'You don't seem like much of a talker.'

'I'm not.' King paused again. 'Sorry, I'm more the solitary type. Don't do well with small talk. But I appreciate your company, don't get me wrong.'

'Likewise, bud. I'll leave you to it. Enjoy the rest of the trip.'

The bartender moved to tend to the table of the three locals. They had exited the bar in unison a minute previously, exchanging waves with him. King slid the cuff of his leather jacket up his forearm and checked his watch.

Almost midnight.

The abrupt departure of the locals signified that the place would be closing shortly. The two workers seemed oblivious to this fact. Definitely out-of-town folk. They lounged back in their chairs, deep in conversation, blissfully unaware. Then again, King often saw what others did not. He'd learnt to notice small details.

This time of year the temperature dropped to almost zero in these parts. He zipped his jacket up to the collar. It would be a cold walk up into town.

'Wrap it up, gents,' the bartender announced to the room. He scrubbed away at the tabletop with a wet sponge, cradling three empty beer mugs in his other hand.

King slid a twenty out of his wallet and dropped it on the countertop, even though the two beers were only six each. From across the room the bartender spotted the red note and assumed he wanted change.

'Be right there, mate,' he said.

'Don't worry about it. For the service.'

The bartender smiled. 'Ah, of course. Tipping. You lot are too generous.'

King raised a hand in a gesture of farewell and headed out into the night. He stepped down into an outdoor dining area housing empty tables and full ashtrays. All coated in a thin layer of frost. Ahead, a deserted mountain road twisted around a bend, turning steep as it ascended up the hill into Jameson. He tucked his hands into his jacket pockets as a wave of cold washed over him. The temperature had dropped to near arctic. With each exhale, a cloud of steam rose from between his lips. Most would baulk at the thought of walking through the night in such conditions.

Not King. He found the solitude calming.

He crossed the road, feeling the asphalt crackle under his boots. Thick trees with pine branches boxed him in, stirring a slight sense of claustrophobia in his chest. He let his thoughts settle, finding a rhythm as he strolled across the mildew coating the side of the road.

He found a particularly large pine jutting out from the tree line, almost touching the asphalt. Acting on an urge, he sat down against the trunk. The ridges and bumps of the wood pressed into his back, but he didn't care. He decided he would spend a moment resting, observing his surroundings. There hadn't been much time for that in his life.

The dirt was cold. It soaked through his khaki trousers. He let himself enjoy the sudden quiet. There were still sounds, of course. Close by, a cricket chirped somewhere under the dirt, and overhead the trees rustled in the alpine breeze. He remained unperturbed. His career had taught him to blend into his surroundings and he did just that. Shortly after he sat down, the night wrapped around his figure. He breathed in the cold air. Enjoying the tranquility.

The faint glow of a pair of headlights broke the darkness. King assumed it was the pair of workers from the bar. Their battered old pickup truck came into view a few seconds later, the engine chugging throatily as it tackled the steep mountain road. He knew he was invisible to them. He watched the vehicle approach until it drew parallel with him, moving fast, heading for Jameson.

Then a figure stepped out of the woods further up the road.

CHAPTER 2

The silhouette had come from the opposite side of the forest. King watched as the pickup slowed to avoid a collision. Its headlights lit up the figure. A man dressed in simple clothing. He wore a plain blue windbreaker and a pair of jeans. His hair was cut short, almost to the skull. His face was sharply defined and clean. It bore a look of restrained panic.

King sat completely still. Something about the situation felt off. He saw the driver's side window roll down.

'Can I help you?' a voice from inside called out.

The voice was curious. A little hesitant. One of the workers, surprised to see another soul in these parts.

The man from the woods stepped out of the pickup's path, moving to the driver's side.

'I'm lost,' he said, his voice quivering.

'You want a lift into town?'

'That'd be great,' the man said. 'Me and my buddy have been walking in circles for hours.'

'Your buddy?'

A second man emerged from the trees, dressed similarly. His face was also clean. Both men's clothes were brand new. There wasn't a semblance of dirt on either of them. King knew for certain they were not telling the truth. They had not been lost in the forest for hours. In fact, he was sure they knew exactly where they were.

They'd been waiting.

The second man walked over to the passenger's side window. It rolled down too. Now both workers were exposed.

'Thanks for this,' the second man said.

'No problem. You boys okay?'

'I think so.'

'Cold night to get lost.'

'Tell me about it.'

'Anyway, jump in the back tray. We'll get you into town.'

Neither of the men moved. The man by the driver's side visibly stiffened.

'Are your names David Lee and Miles Price?' he said, his tone now firm and authoritative. Demanding an instantaneous response.

'Yeah,' came a voice from inside the truck. 'How'd you know—'

That was what killed them.

The correct response to realising a couple of strangers from the forest knew your name would be to stamp on the accelerator and get as far away as possible. As soon as the confirmation came, both men slid guns from their belts in unison. There were suppressors attached. King couldn't ascertain their exact make in the low light, but they were fearsome-looking pistols. He guessed Glock 17s.

There was nothing he could do to save the workers. It only took one shot through each man's skull to silence them forever. The two discharges were muffled, but no suppressor fully silences the noise of a gunshot. Instead, a pair of vicious coughs echoed down the road. Without a soul around to hear.

Except Jason King.

He watched the pair of killers move with calculated efficiency, each sliding a corpse out of the respective doors. They dragged the bodies along the road and heaved them into the rear tray. They constantly checked for cars, but the road was empty at this time of night. When they were done they straightened up and slammed the tray closed.

'We need to get rid of this before anyone sees. Take our payment and get the hell out of here.'

'You didn't see anyone?'

'No.'

'Take a quick look. I need to clean the blood off the seats.'

King remained motionless. He clenched his fists. Perhaps he would be spotted.

The man lit up a flashlight and scanned it quickly over the surrounding trees. The yellow beam passed briefly over King. He remained motionless, resting against the tree trunk.

To most men, he would be invisible.

Not this time.

'*Hey!*' the man screamed to his friend, immediately producing the same pistol from his holster.

King exploded into action. He got his feet underneath him and scrambled around the trunk, disappearing from sight. From the road he heard the familiar sound of a suppressed gunshot. The bullet grazed past the space he had occupied moments earlier. He felt the displaced air, close by. They were good shots.

Most men would panic and run. King stayed deathly still on the other side of the trunk, his pulse barely rising, remaining calm. This would confuse his assailants. He knew exactly how to play mind games.

There was silence from the road. Then voices.

'Where did he go?'

'What the *fuck* are you talking about? What are you shooting at?'

'A … a man. He was sitting against that tree.'

'You're sure?'

'Yeah, I'm sure. Scared the shit out of me.'

'And he ran away?'

'He was so fast.'

'You couldn't shoot a guy sitting on the ground?'

'What do we do?'

'We make sure there's no fucking witnesses.'

King smiled. They were panicked. The one with the buzzcut seemed to be in charge, and a little more under control. But they were both amateurs. Compared to him, at least. They spoke loud and fast. Adrenalin rushed through their veins, scrambling their instincts. King could hear it in the tone of their voices. They could kill when they were the ones with power, but now he had made them uncomfortable. They would make mistakes.

They would die.

He heard noises. Footsteps on the asphalt. Inaudible to the average person. But King picked up every little nuance of the pair's movements. The man with the buzzcut was on the left. He made less sound. The man on the right had been startled by the sudden appearance of a witness. His impatient footsteps showed it.

King stayed where he was, pressed against the trunk. They would assume he had taken off into the forest when in reality he had moved no more than a few feet. He let adrenalin flood his own system. The added boost of energy was useful to someone who knew exactly what to do with it. He didn't allow himself to get jumpy.

His hands grew warm, despite the freezing night air. He rolled his wrists and took a deep breath. The footsteps had moved from the road to the forest floor. The two men were unable to walk quietly on the dirt surface. Leaves crunched underneath their heels. They quickened their pace.

The panicked man passed the tree first, moving fast. In his haste, he failed to take a look at the trunk where he had first seen King. He stared ahead, eyes wide, searching for the slightest sign of movement amongst the trees. He thought the witness was long gone.

Now.

King darted forward and wrenched the suppressed pistol from the man's outstretched arms as effortlessly as plucking a dandelion from the grass. After all, he was six-foot-three and packed with muscle and his attacker was a slight man shaking with nerves. For a moment he almost felt sorry for how unfair the situation was on the smaller man. Nevertheless, he had still tried to kill him. Which, unfortunately, was unforgivable in King's book.

He slid a finger into the trigger guard the moment he had control of the weapon and drove the barrel up under the man's chin. He fired a single shot through the base of his skull. It sliced through the guy's brain and exploded out the top of his head. He dropped like a rag doll. Death was instantaneous.

Just then, the second man with the buzzcut rounded the tree trunk.

King spun and fired a shot but suddenly Buzzcut was no longer there. He had ducked away, assessing the situation and retreating with lightning speed.

King heard scurried footsteps on the road. The man had fled. He rounded the tree trunk and saw the muzzle flash of an ejected round. A loud metallic *bang* echoed off the surrounding trees. The noise took King by surprise. He ducked back instinctively and paused for breath, confused. He glanced down at his left hand. A second ago, it had been firmly clasped around the dead man's Glock.

Now it was empty.

Buzzcut's warning shot had miraculously struck the handgun, blasting it out of King's palm. Wild luck. Completely unintentional. Nevertheless, the man was smarter and faster than his dead partner.

He would be more of a problem.

King listened until he was sure it was safe, then stuck his head around the trunk.

He saw nothing but a slight rustle of leaves as Buzzcut disappeared into the woods on the other side of the road.

CHAPTER 3

King powered through the scrub, having shed his leather jacket long ago. He knew he was keeping pace with Buzzcut. Every few moments there would be a sign of movement up ahead. Nothing more than a fleeting glimpse of a limb, but it was enough. He flew past pine trees with decaying branches, some torn clean off near shoulder height. Deep boot imprints were stamped into the muddy surface of the forest floor at random. The man had little interest in stealth. He was in a hurry.

The woods were silent at this hour. Chirping crickets and nearby critters had fallen quiet as the pursuit raged around them. King kept a consistent pace. He made sure his mind was calm and his lungs were full of air. Ahead he could hear the panicked breaths of the man who had tried to kill him. The guy was an amateur in every sense of the word. Perhaps he was gaining distance temporarily, but in the long run King would catch him. He could keep this pace up for hours. He doubted Buzzcut could.

It was difficult terrain to traverse. He hurdled fallen logs and twisted roots that lay in his path. This section of the forest lay on a steep mountainside, which Buzzcut was in the process of rapidly descending. King made sure to take care in his descent. It would only take a twisted ankle to incapacitate him. Then his target would get away and he would have no answers.

He knew the man was out of ammunition. Buzzcut's footsteps were loud and fast. He'd seen what happened to his partner. The pair hadn't been anticipating a fight. They must have only had a clip each. Otherwise, King would have bullets cutting through the air around him.

Five minutes into the pursuit and he was already gaining. Buzzcut's sharp inhales became longer, drawn out. The man wheezed for breath. Panicked.

Rookie mistake.

King could see him now. He made out the silhouette just ahead, darting between trunks and tripping on obstacles. He could hear King behind him, his pace measured and even. The woods began to thin, the trees growing further apart as the steep ground evened out. Large areas of grass and undergrowth filled the spaces between the trunks.

They had reached the bottom of a valley.

King saw Buzzcut burst out into an open area devoid of trees. He pressed on. Inhaling through the nose, exhaling through the mouth. Measured breathing was the key to preserving his gas tank. Buzzcut was panting and stumbling up ahead. He had run for his life and exerted all his energy in the process.

The forest disappeared behind King. He found himself in the middle of a large expanse of overgrown grass. It was not a natural clearing. The trees had been cut down to make room for what lay ahead.

An abandoned metal work factory towered over the rest of the forest, constructed in the centre of the clearing. It was a behemoth of a facility, easily surpassing the tops of the tallest surrounding trees. Twisting rusted pipes snaked their way around the exterior of the structure. That was as much as he could make out in the darkness.

For a moment, he reconsidered his previous decisions. He could have just run blind into a slaughterhouse. There could have been dozens of reinforcements within the factory waiting as he jogged obliviously into open ground.

He could have been exposed.

Could have.

But he wasn't.

There was no-one waiting.

Buzzcut seemed just as surprised as King was to have happened upon the factory.

King sensed an opportunity and broke into a sprint. He gained ground fast. His quadriceps strained under the exertion.

Then Buzzcut spun, raised his Glock 17 and fired.

A muzzle flash lit up the clearing and King recoiled, shocked by a white hot burning sensation in his left arm. He reeled away. The shot had taken him completely by surprise, and now he was hit. Because Buzzcut had held off on firing for so long, King had assumed he was out of ammo. He'd paid the price for such a foolish mistake. He wouldn't make the same error again.

Instantly he could tell it was just a graze. His nerve endings screamed and his skin bled, but his arm was fully functional. It moved without obstruction. He took nothing more than a quick glance down, glimpsing a thin trail of crimson running down his bare arm. The wound was difficult to make out in the soft moonlight. There was no time to focus on it. He was still on open ground, with no idea whether Buzzcut still had a round in the chamber.

As if on cue, a hollow click echoed across the clearing.

King recognised the sound all too well.

An empty magazine.

He charged forward with a newfound energy. He saw on Buzzcut's face the same expression that he'd seen on countless men in the past. Eyes widening, arms shaking, skin paling. The look of a man who had wasted his one opportunity to remain in control and would now pay the price for blowing it.

Buzzcut took off into the darkness. King watched him run into the bowels of the metal work factory, vanishing from sight.

The night became absolute as the moon dipped behind a low cloud. The structure loomed ahead, nothing more than a black outline against a black sky. King slowed his pace and stopped to listen. Crickets in the grass. The occasional creak of a rusty pipe. No sound of the man he was chasing. Buzzcut had done well to disappear.

There was no point in giving up now. King decided he would take a look inside the factory before calling it off. He knew that by now Buzzcut could be on the other side of the clearing. If it was his goal was to escape, then King would never find him. But he had a sneaking suspicion that there was something else on his mind. The guy had just witnessed his partner's gruesome death.

King wondered if Buzzcut wanted revenge.

He hoped so. Revenge meant it was personal, and making it personal led to making mistakes.

He jogged lightly through an enormous set of double doors and into the ground floor of the factory. The space was cavernous, once home to enormous industrial machines. He could feel the grooves in the concrete floor under his feet, where they'd used to rest. It was silent in here. There was no moonlight. He couldn't see anything. He relied on touch and sound alone. His footsteps echoed off the walls. Every now and then, he splashed through a small puddle in the cracked concrete.

He made just enough noise to be heard.

Thirty seconds after he entered the factory, he picked up a sound. Behind him. Not an effect of his movements. Something else.

He smiled.

Buzzcut was still here.

King was quietly impressed. The man had been almost completely silent in his movements. He had tracked King across the factory floor without making a sound, avoiding all the puddles, all the obstacles. Then he had made a fatal mistake.

King heard a soft *thunk* that to any other man would have been inaudible. But he was paying attention. Twenty feet back, he'd sensed something next to him and softly ran his hand over a hollow metal tank, fixing its position in his mind. Buzzcut had just scraped against it. King recognised the noise.

He turned and exploded back in the other direction.

Buzzcut would hear him coming.

But it was too late.

In the darkness they crashed into each other. King stuck his shoulder out, bent his knees and drove the bulk of his weight into the other man's chest. He heard a surprised gasp and a wince of pain. He could sense Buzzcut's horrid surprise. One second he had been stalking his prey, and the next he was on the ground, winded.

King still couldn't see. But he didn't need to. He clamped both of his huge hands around Buzzcut's head, one on either side. Before the man could regain control of the situation King slammed the back of his skull against the concrete. A crack echoed off the factory walls.

It was a formidable, crushing blow. King was two-hundred-and-twenty pounds of muscle, yet even stronger than he appeared. His strength had been something of legend in his former life. Now, he used it to devastating effect.

Buzzcut went instantly limp. There was every chance he was dead, but King made sure by winding up and slamming a closed fist down against his windpipe. He put his entire bodyweight behind it. Bone and cartilage gave under the strike. Buzzcut gave a final pathetic wheeze before joining his partner in death.

CHAPTER 4

King rolled off the body, panting with exertion. His blood boiled and his skin tingled. An unavoidable reaction after killing with his bare hands. This kind of adrenalin was impossible to control. No amount of discipline would reduce its effect. There was nothing to do but ride it out.

He let the stillness wash over him. The silence was oddly calming. Slowly, his heartbeat began to return to a normal rate.

As soon as he stopped shaking, he set to work.

It seemed he would never know what David Lee and Miles Price had done to deserve a pair of bullets in their skulls. But now both their killers were dead. What occurred had entered all kinds of muddled grey areas, both morally and legally. King had four dead bodies on his hands, and it was his job to hide the evidence. He certainly didn't care for a murder trial, and if it came to that he would probably be found guilty of something. Chasing an attacker through thick woods to cave their throat in would certainly tarnish his reputation in a courtroom.

He much preferred natural law in situations such as these.

It took him twenty minutes to make his way back to the main road. A tough trek through steep, rugged terrain. He stepped out of the woods with sweat dripping off his brow. The pickup truck's murky headlights lit up a section of the asphalt, carving twin paths of soft yellow light through the darkness. Insects buzzed in the glow. An eerie silence lay over everything, something that often occurred in the aftermath of sudden violent conflict.

Everyone in earshot of this place was dead.

As he passed across the road in front of the truck he saw blood splattered across its windscreen. The contents of the cabin were blocked from sight. No signs of tampering. If any traffic had passed by, no-one had stopped.

He crossed to the opposite side of the woods and headed deep into the scrub. It didn't take long to find the other man's body. He lay face down, slumped into the undergrowth. Despite the dim light, the gunshot wound through the top of the guy's head was clearly visible. A fat gaping hole. King hefted the body onto his shoulders and carried it back to the ute. He threw it in the rear tray alongside the workers' corpses.

'I wonder who you two pissed off,' he muttered under his breath.

King went round to the driver's door and climbed inside the cabin. The interior smelled like alcohol and death. A half-empty packet of cigarettes lay in the centre console alongside a small satchel of marijuana. There was a helmet in the passenger's footwell, coated in flecks of concrete. The glove box held receipts dating back eight days, each for meals at the bar down the road. These men had lived simplistic urban lives. Work hard, eat a full meal, rest, repeat.

Sometimes King wished his own life had been so straightforward.

Droplets of blood covered the windscreen. He fished a box of tissues out of the back seat and cleared away a portion of it. He slammed the door shut and drove off quickly. Waiting any longer in the middle of the road would only increase the risk of being seen.

He spun the vehicle around and lifted a Navman GPS out of the driver's footwell. He switched it on. A robotic female voice greeted him in a monotonous tone. He entered the rough co-ordinates of where he expected the metal work factory to lie, knowing that there had to be some kind of vehicular access to the site. It highlighted a track leading down from the main road. A pop-up message warned him that the road was unsurfaced. He dropped the GPS back to the muddy floor of the cabin and drove off.

As he took the truck round the steep mountainous bends, he weighed his options a final time. Going to the police would be the most noble course of action, but there was no way to explain what had happened without getting dragged into a lengthy legal battle. With no witnesses and four brutalised corpses, he didn't like the odds of defending his innocence.

Two workers were dead. King didn't know why. Maybe they were in debt. Maybe not. The men who had killed them were also dead. They'd tried to shoot him, so he'd fought back. He'd succeeded. In the grand scheme of things, that was fair. There was nothing else to consider, nothing to mull over. Best to remove the evidence and forget all about it. Everything about the past hour had brought back memories of a darker, violent past. A past he was desperately trying to forget.

The pickup handled the unsurfaced road easily, its thick tires eating up the gravel. King heard the three corpses bouncing around the rear tray. An unsettling sound. He grimaced. The headlights illuminated the track ahead, casting long shadows across the ground. The cold breeze sent a chill down his spine and he shivered involuntarily. He hadn't bothered to roll the windows up.

The trees melted away as he pulled out into the clearing. The abandoned factory lay ahead. The twin beams of light emanating from the pickup gave King a better idea of the structure's form. A multi-level building, built with no symmetry or pattern, like several warehouses had been stacked on top of each other. Metal tubes and walkways ran along the exterior walls. Most of its features had long since rusted away. The factory looked forlorn and ready to collapse. No-one had touched it in years.

King swung the wheel around and drove through the large entrance on the ground floor. The headlights revealed the enormous space, proving to be almost exactly how he'd pictured it in the darkness. Largely empty, save for a few dilapidated tanks and broken machines scattered across the floor. Near the centre of the floorspace, lying limp next to a dirty puddle of water, was Buzzcut. Unquestionably dead.

King got out and eyed the nearest machines, rundown from years of lying dormant. Each had a slightly different design. One looked something like an oversized inverted cone, with a rusted dial on one side. It would serve the purpose King needed it for.

He dragged the bodies out of the rear tray one by one, piling them beside Buzzcut until the four dead men were positioned side-by-side. He moved quickly. It was unpleasant work. First, he searched the pockets of the construction workers, and came up with a pair of leather wallets and a couple of cigarettes. The wallets had nothing more than loose change, identification and workers permits in them. King tossed them over the lip of the cone, then did the same with each of the bodies. Due to excess weight, David Lee proved a little more cumbersome to manhandle than Miles Price, but King got the job done.

Next, the hitmen. He knew they wouldn't be stupid enough to carry identification on them, and he was proved correct after a quick search of the bodies. But deep in one of Buzzcut's pants pockets, King came up with something.

A keyring. It held a single silver key and a tag labeled '*Jameson Post*'.

He knew he should throw it away, just as he had done to the two construction workers and their wallets. It would be foolish to keep anything that could link him back to what had happened. But an irresistible urge overcame him. He slipped it into his pocket. It couldn't hurt to poke around.

Buzzcut and his partner followed David Lee and Miles Price into the cone. When his work was done King took a moment to rest against the side of the pickup. He mopped a bead of sweat off his forehead. Despite the cold night, lifting deadweight proved tiresome. But the corpses were out of sight and it would take an inquisitive soul to discover them. He couldn't have imagined anyone setting foot in this place for years, let alone searching for bodies.

He retrieved a heavy set of pliers from the rear tray of the pickup truck and set to work destroying the vehicle. It only took a light blow to shatter each window in turn. Then he swung hard and fast at the chassis, gouging huge dents in the metal until it matched its surroundings. Nothing but broken junk. Lastly, he used the pliers to lever off the plates. He tossed them in with the bodies. The pliers themselves followed suit.

A twist of the keys in the ignition and the engine died. The headlights flickered out, plunging the factory back into darkness. He threw the keys in the general direction of the cone and was rewarded with a resounding *clang* as they struck home.

Then he turned and headed out of the factory, determined to forget that the ordeal had ever happened.

CHAPTER 5

It took thirty-eight minutes to reach Jameson. By the time King strode into the town's outer limits it was close to two in the morning. He came up the road into the main street. Murky halogen streetlights lit the way. There was a big brand supermarket on the left, vast and physically imposing in comparison to the rest of the stores. He eyed a convenience store, a chemist, two restaurants, a cafe, a pair of motels, a tourist information centre, a hardware store, a petrol station and finally, at the very end of the road, a post office. The sign above the door read '*Jameson Post*'. He retrieved the key from his pocket and stared at its tag long and hard. After a moment of thought, he put it away. He would decide tomorrow if it was worth chasing up.

The two motels faced each other off on either side of the road, clearly in direct competition. One was devoid of lights, completely enshrouded in darkness. The other had a small front light glowing above the entrance to its office. That was enough for him to make up his mind.

He trudged across to the motel that was lit and rang the bell to the office twice. Then he stood in silence and waited. He was used to waiting. His whole life had revolved around the art of patience. Long stretches of waiting, with occasional bursts of massive instantaneous action.

Finally the door swung open, revealing an elderly European lady in her night-gown. Her hair was dishevelled and thick bags sat under her eyes.

'I'm sorry to disturb you ma'am,' King said. 'I was wondering if you had a room available. Just for one night.'

Despite the hour, her face lit up at the sight of a customer. He wondered if she struggled to stay afloat in such a remote region.

'Of course we do. Come on in.'

He stepped through into a small room with white plasterboard walls and a desk piled high with loose sheets of paper. The woman scurried around behind the counter and fished a document out of the mess. She placed it in front of him along with a pen.

'Name and signature here, please. Usually we charge eighty-nine a night, but since you're only spending half a night I'll give it to you for fifty.'

'No problem. Thank you.'

'Why so late, may I ask?'

'I misjudged my timing. The walk took longer than I expected.'

'Where did you walk from, dear?'

'Queensbridge.'

'You walked from Queensbridge? That's more than fifteen kilometres.'

'Yes it is.'

She fell silent. King knew he was being uncooperative, but there was nothing he could say. He scrawled out a signature and slid the paper back across the counter, along with a fifty-dollar note. She took it and handed over a key. As he reached for it, she let out a gasp.

'Oh my god!' she cried. 'You're cut real bad.'

King looked down and swore internally. The blood had caked dry on his exposed arm. A thin, jagged gash ran the length of his tricep. Adrenalin had forced his mind off the wound in the heat of combat. Now that he was paying attention to it a dull ache appeared in his upper arm. Funny how the brain worked.

'The trees along the road are deadly,' he said. 'Caught my arm on one of the branches and it ripped all my skin off. Terrible luck.'

'My goodness. Do you need me to ring Jonas? He can open up the medical centre for you.'

'No need for that. If you have some bandages and antiseptic that should do me until the morning.'

She gave him a strange look before opening a drawer and taking out a bottle of Dettol and a thin roll of gauze.

'You remind me of some of the farm boys around here,' she said. 'They all play the tough guy until it's too late. Last year Terrence dropped dead of a fever. Doctors said it was a bad batch of pneumonia and he'd have been just fine if he hadn't tried to tough it out at home. I don't want that happening to a strapping young man like yourself.'

King smiled. 'I'll be okay.'

'You sure won't be in that T-shirt. Aren't you freezing?'

King recalled throwing his leather jacket away before he'd chased Buzzcut into the forest. He had never bothered to retrieve it. 'I guess I didn't prepare for this weather.'

'Well, we can't have that…' she trailed off. Hesitated for a moment. Then made up her mind and retrieved a large grey windbreaker from underneath the desk.

'Take this,' she said, holding it out.

King paused. 'I can't do that. It looks expensive. I'm just a stranger.'

'It was my husband's.'

'Is he around?'

'Not since a month ago,' she said, bowing her head.

'I'm awfully sorry to hear that.'

'So you have it,' she said, composing herself and looking back up with a warm smile. 'I'd rather it be put to use.'

He took the windbreaker and looped it over his arm. 'Thank you. I appreciate it.'

'Now, you be careful. Go to the doctor's tomorrow. Double checking that cut can't hurt.'

'Thank you, ma'am. Have a nice night. Sorry to disturb you.'

'Not a problem, Mr…'

'King.'

'I'm Yvonne. Goodnight, Mr. King.'

He left the office and checked the tag on the keyring. There was a small '4' scrawled into the plastic in permanent marker. He headed up a flimsy set of wooden stairs and unlocked the door to room 4.

A simplistically designed room, as almost all motel rooms were. Nothing out of the ordinary. King had seen a hundred just like this. A thin double bed in the corner, a small television opposite a set of plush chairs and a kitchenette. The door set in the far wall led to an adjoining bathroom and toilet.

King dropped his only possessions — his wallet and the 'Jameson Post' key — on the bed and made his way through to the bathroom. He removed his shirt and studied the graze in the small mirror above the sink. The bullet had barely touched him, but it had drawn a large amount of blood. There was nothing to worry about. The skin would heal in a few days. He had been lucky.

He took a shower to wash his arm clean. As usual, the nozzle barely reached past his shoulders. The water stung as it crept into the damaged skin. He grit his teeth and squashed the pain back down. After turning the water off he dried himself and trickled a stream of the antiseptic down his arm. It dripped into the wound, flaring his nerve endings. He let out a soft grunt to manage the burning sensation.

He wrapped the gauze Yvonne had provided around his arm, barely managing two loops. She hadn't given him much, and he was a big guy. The bandage would stop the bleeding for now. He could stitch it up later, if need be. He walked naked to the bed and slid under the covers.

It didn't cross his mind that he had killed two men earlier in the evening. He had overcome that feeling years ago. He didn't kill recklessly, but if someone aimed a gun at his head, he couldn't stop himself from reacting. Two hitmen were dead, and the world was no worse off.

He closed his eyes and was asleep in seconds.

CHAPTER 6

The sun woke him at seven in the morning after a undisturbed night's sleep. He had left the curtains open specifically for that purpose. When it was daylight outside, there was no use sleeping. Five hours was more than enough to refill the tank.

He rolled out of bed and went through an exhausting hour of calisthenics. A gruelling routine, but King had long ago mastered his mind. When there was no gym available this was what he did to stay fit. He no longer saw it as an option, or a chore, or enjoyable. It was simply nothing. It just happened, and there was no disrupting the routine.

Agility was important, so he finished off the workout with a set of vinyasas. It didn't matter how strong he was. If he wasn't fluid with his movements, all the raw power in his frame would be useless.

Dripping with sweat, he took a second shower in the cramped tub, dressed in the same clothes from the night before, then tugged the windbreaker over his massive frame.

Surprisingly, it fit well enough. Yvonne's late husband must have been a big guy too.

He headed out of the room and down to the main street. By now the early risers were up and moving, drinking coffee outside the cafe and preparing themselves for a hard day's work. Scanning the community, he noted that the majority of the town's occupants appeared to be farmers.

Jameson Post was open. King had nothing better to do, so he crossed the road and walked in. There was nowhere he needed to be. He could spend as long as he liked in Jameson. It was worth checking if Buzzcut's key led to anything suspicious.

The door jangled as he opened it, but none of the customers turned to look. They were concerned with their own matters, busy sealing envelopes and scrawling letters in freehand. The man behind the counter was in the process of serving a long queue. Too preoccupied to notice King. He had a few moments to himself.

He made for the row of PO boxes on the far wall. Two thirds of the wall was taken up by the small rectangular slots. King tried the key in one, but it was too large. That eliminated the majority of the work. He eyed the last third of the boxes, each larger and more thickset, designed for a greater amount of storage. Definitely more expensive. He slotted the key into the first one.

It didn't turn, but it fit.

It only took King five more attempts to find the right one. He moved fast, trying to prevent unwanted attention. On the sixth and final box, the key twisted and the small metal door sprang open.

It was empty.

King had to make a decision now. He could leave the key here, move onto the next town and forget any of this ever happened. Or he could continue prodding. He pondered for a moment.

There was no reason to hang around. A pair of construction workers were dead. It meant nothing in the grand scheme of things. There were four roads leading far away from this little town and it didn't matter which one he took.

A croaky voice from behind said, 'Morning.'

King spun on his heel. Standing behind him was an elderly woman, dressed in an olive green blouse and white slacks. A white sunhat rested atop her head. She looked to be in her seventies. Her face was wrinkled with age, but her expression was jovial. As if she was simply happy to be alive.

'Good morning,' King said.

'Are you from around here?'

'No, I'm from out of town. Just passing through.'

'Oh, well, that's nice. Don't see many of your type around here, dear.'

'My type?'

She made a long, sweeping gesture, bringing her hand from the floor to the ceiling. Indicating King's height. 'You know. The tall, handsome type.'

King chuckled. 'I wouldn't go so far as to say that. How long have you been here?'

'All my life, dear. Most folks who live out here grew up in these parts.'

'I'm Jason, by the way.'

'Pleasure to meet you, Jason. Suzanne.'

There was a pause.

'Well the reason I bothered you, young man, is because my box is just under yours. I hope I'm not rushing you.'

'Not at all,' King said, swinging the small door closed. 'I was just leaving.'

He motioned to move past Suzanne.

'Your key, dear,' she said.

King turned round and looked at the key he had left on top of the postal box. It still bore the same 'Jameson Post' tag. He'd hoped Suzanne wouldn't notice, so he could move on with his life. It seemed fate had another idea.

'Ah, thank you,' he said, feigning foolishness. He reached up and snatched it back.

Suzanne let out a gasp.

King looked down and saw the hem of his shirt had risen over his belt as he'd reached for the key, exposing a thin line of bare skin at his waist. There was a tattoo visible, inked into his pelvic area. A steel triangle, half of which resembled a lightning bolt, with a serrated knife slicing through the centre.

'I know that symbol,' Suzanne said.

King knew he should have walked out of that post office right there and then. This wasn't something to talk about with a complete stranger. But he relented.

'You do?'

'Delta Force.'

King couldn't help but admit he was surprised. To be fair, it only took a Google search to find the unit's insignia. Yet the last thing he had assumed was that the old lady in front of him would have knowledge of such a fact.

'It is,' he said. 'I spent some time in the Force. Not long though.' There was no need to share the complete truth.

'I noticed the accent, dear.'

'Quite a few people have told me that.'

'Look, the only reason I ask is because I have a relative ... and, oh — I'm not sure I should be talking about this. I'm terribly sorry.'

King hesitated. Then he made up his mind. 'Go on.'

'Well, my nephew ... his name was Lars ... he ran off to America twenty years ago. My sister and her husband — they didn't go too easy on the kid, if you know what I mean. Beat him up very badly a few times. I always got on with him, though. He was a good child. I know it's a long shot, but I was wondering whether you came across Lars during your time in the military. He always said he wanted to become a soldier.'

'I'm sorry, ma'am, but that's not something I can talk about. The Delta Force is very different to the Army. Everything's classified.'

Suzanne raised an eyebrow. 'Is that so, love?'

'I'm afraid it is.'

She leant in closer. 'Well, if you choose to help me out, I might not tell anyone what I know.'

'And what exactly do you know?'

'That's not your postal box.'

'How can you be sure?'

'A pair of men opened that exact box yesterday, dear. I watched them do it. You weren't either of them.'

King motioned to the box he had just unlocked. 'You saw two men use this?'

'I sure did.'

'Do you have any information about them you could give me? Any descriptions?'

'Do you have any information about my nephew?'

He hesitated. It was against protocol, but what was a little old lady going to do? Especially with the answer he was going to give.

'I'm sorry, ma'am, but I never met anyone called Lars during my time in the Force. I wasn't supposed to tell you that, but I just did. I wish I could be of more help.'

'And I wish I could be of more help too, Jason, but there's not much I have to say either. I was in here yesterday morning, and two men came hurrying in. One of them had real short hair, and the other had medium length hair. They were both white. And they were … oh, I don't know, about average height. I wasn't paying them much attention.'

'Seems like you can remember a lot about them for a couple of passersby.'

'Jameson doesn't get many passersby. Everyone knows everyone here.'

'So you hadn't seen them before?'

She shook her head. 'Never.'

'They were new in town?'

'I guess so. Haven't seen them since though…'

'That's odd,' King said, though he knew she wouldn't be seeing them anytime soon. 'So that's all they did — unlock the box?'

'Yes, and they took out a parcel. A big box of some kind, all wrapped up in brown paper. I remember this clearly, because they looked all jittery. Like they were … not nervous, but on edge. I don't know. When you see the same people day in and day out, anything different spices up your day a little.'

'I can imagine. You don't know who put the box there?'

'I'm afraid not, dear.'

'No problem. Thank you very much for your help, Suzanne.'

'Are you going to tell me what this is all about?'

'Maybe if I run into you again.'

She shrugged. 'Doesn't bother me. Old age makes you care less. You have fun with your adventures.'

And with that she turned and strolled out of the post office. King noted that she had completely forgotten to check her postal box, and went to call her back. But he decided against it.

There were a million questions he needed answers to.

CHAPTER 7

'I'm sorry, mate, but there's nothing I can do.'

'This is urgent,' King said.

'I can see that. But it's about privacy. I can't ruin the integrity of the store.'

The man behind the counter was unrelenting. King spun in a circle, surveying the occupants of the post office. There were none.

'All I need is one glance at the security cameras,' he said. 'There's no witnesses. You can pretend it never happened.'

The man — whose nametag read "Billy" — visibly stiffened. 'I've said no, buddy. And you won't change my mind on that. You'd better quit talking about witnesses and the like. I could ring the police.'

King pressed a pair of fingers into his eyeballs. 'Look, I know what you're thinking. Big imposing guy who you've never seen before asking to look at tapes. Sounds bad. Looks bad. But I can assure you I'm doing the right thing.'

'Alright, mate.'

'You don't believe me.'

'Why would I?'

'Because you saw two men who you've never seen before in your life collect a package from that postal box yesterday.'

King pointed to the empty box.

Billy paused a beat. 'How'd you know that?'

'You were suspicious. You'd never seen them before, but they had a key. Someone had given them a key. But they were in and out before you could react. Correct?'

'How the *hell* did you know that?'

'I'm a private investigator. I just talked to an old lady called Suzanne — I take it you know her — who told me all about two men collecting a package. Now I'm assuming they didn't rent the box; firstly, because they were collecting something, and secondly, because I know for a fact they're involved in some shady business. So unless you want to take the blame for withholding evidence, I suggest you show me the tapes so I can find out who put the package there.'

It was a long spiel, filled with authority and impatience, designed to confuse. It was the most King had spoken in months. But it worked.

'Alright,' Billy said. 'Let's go out back—' He turned. 'Nicole!'

A girl strode out of the back room. She was young. Maybe only just turned eighteen. She sported dishevelled hair and a drab, mousy complexion. She wore attire that matched Billy's. A faded pair of jeans and a polo whose logo read "*Jameson Post!*".

'What, Dad?' she grumbled. 'Stop fucking yelling.'

'You're up front for half an hour. I need to look at some tapes in the back room.'

Nicole looked King up and down. 'Who's this?'

'A private investigator.'

Her eyes widened. 'Bullshit. The fuck have you done?'

'Nothing. Just stay here.'

What a pleasant relationship, King mused.

He followed Billy behind the counter and through a narrow doorway. He crouched to avoid smacking his forehead on the doorframe. This building was obviously constructed decades ago. The back room was old and dilapidated. Paint peeled off the walls and paperwork lay scattered across three trestle tables, each with some variation of broken appendages. King eyed one of the tables, sporting three legs taped firmly with multiple layers of duct tape. Clearly a post office made just enough money to get by. There seemed to be a budget of zero for repairs.

Billy collapsed into a tattered leather armchair and wheeled it up to an ancient computer. A few clicks of the mouse and the screen displayed a grid of four separate security cameras, two on the exterior of the building and two inside. The lower left screen showed Nicole behind the counter, absent-mindedly chewing gum. Billy squinted at the monitor and perused slowly through the different options. Pause, rewind, skip. He clearly hadn't found the need to study security footage in years.

'Now it's here somewhere...' he tutted under his breath.

King waited patiently. He took the time to scrutinise his surroundings. Trying to get a sense of how Billy lived.

Frugally, he concluded.

The whitewash bleakness of the decorum suited the contents of the room. Nothing — save stacks of paperwork — was there that did not need to be. There was no room for trivial possessions.

'Here we are,' Billy said, leaning so far forward on his chair that his nose hovered barely a centimetre from the screen.

King stepped closer, studying the footage. Billy had pulled up a replay, about thirty seconds long. It appeared to be from two days ago, judging by the timestamp along the bottom. He touched a single finger to the space bar and the clip began.

For the first five seconds, there was no movement. Just a continuous shot of the row of post office boxes. Then, a brief blur of activity on the side of the screen. Someone walking past the frame. Another five seconds of nothing.

Then a figure stepped into frame, heading for the box King had found empty. A woman. She appeared to be in her late twenties. The cameras were ancient, meaning the footage was blurry, but he could make out her long brown hair and lithe frame even through the horrid resolution.

'She's cute,' he said.

'Oh, gosh, that's Kate Cooper,' Billy said, shaking his head. 'What's she doing getting herself into this mess?'

'Who's Kate Cooper?' King said. 'Because this could turn out very, very bad for her.'

'She's a nobody. Definitely not one to get wrapped up in all this shit. She's lived around Jameson for maybe a year now. Runs odd jobs, that sort of thing. I think she's from England. Got a bit of an accent. Nicest person you'll ever meet…'

'You got an address?'

Billy paused. 'You're not going to hurt her?'

'I'm a private investigator,' King said. 'I'm just trying to find out what's going on.'

Billy scrawled on a scrap piece of paper. 'If you do find out, be sure to let me know.'

'Will do.'

'Will you give me a call later? To fill me in?'

'I don't have a phone. At least, not for now.'

A pause. Billy looked at him. He looked back.

Billy said, 'You're the weirdest private investigator I've ever met.'

'You meet a lot of private investigators?'

'No. But you're still strange.'

Billy motioned to hand King the scrap of paper, then recoiled, then leant forward again. Contemplating something.

'Spit it out,' King said.

'I don't quite know how to put this.'

'Put it however you want.'

'Well, I feel like I have an opportunity here.'

'An opportunity?'

'To fix a problem. I feel like you're the man to help.'

'Elaborate.'

'Look, it's not exactly legal. I don't want to get into trouble.'

'Don't worry. I'm not working with the police.'

'No shit. You're not a private investigator, either.'

King shrugged. There was no point continuing to lie. He had everything he needed. 'Name's Jason King.'

'Who are you, Jason King?'

'Someone who has nothing better to do than snoop around when they see something fishy.'

'You're American.'

'You're observant.'

'You're some kind of soldier. Or were, at least.'

'How'd you know that?'

'I overheard you talking to Suzanne.'

'Good hearing.'

'I'm not deaf. It's a quiet place. Listen, mate, I'm willing to help you out with all this investigative stuff. I can tell you've got no ill intentions. I'll give you Kate's address. And I have a lot of money saved up. I can give you that, too.'

'What do you need?'

'You told me you're trying to do the right thing.'

King raised an eyebrow. 'If you're suggesting I'm some kind of hero, I'm not. I'm just curious.'

'Look around,' Billy said. 'What do you see?'

King glanced left and right. 'A shithole.'

Billy smirked. 'You're honest, too. Anyway, I've got nothing. It's taken me years to save what I've got hidden away without anyone finding out.'

'How much?'

'About twenty grand.'

King whistled. 'Not bad.'

'Yeah, well, it's yours if you can help. You heard of the Iron Rangers?'

He shook his head.

'Then you're definitely not from around here.'

'They sound like bikies.'

'You bet. Batshit crazy too. They've got a clubhouse a couple of dozen k's out of Jameson. And the little police station here has either been paid off or doesn't give enough of a shit to try and intervene. They make every small business around here pay them a wage each week. They call it protection, but everyone knows what it really is.'

‘They’ll beat you up if you don’t pay?’

‘To say the least. They’re a toxic bunch.’

‘How many?’

‘Four.’

‘Are they tough?’

‘They seem so.’

King paused, trying to think of another way to put it. ‘Are they from around here?’

He nodded. ‘All local boys. Fell in with the wrong crowd.’

‘Small town thugs,’ King said, nodding.

‘All the minuscule profits I make go straight to them. The money I’m offering you is all I’ve managed to store away.’

King remained silent.

'You’re a strong guy,’ Billy said. ‘I bet you could kill me with one hand.'

Still no response.

'I need you to make them stop.’

'You think I can scare an entire motorcycle gang by myself?'

‘Like you said, they’re local thugs. I feel like you’re something else.’

King raised an eyebrow. ‘Am I? That’s a wild assumption.’

'Look, just go have a look around. You said yourself that you’re curious. I can see it. This postal box shit has nothing to do with you. You could be out of here in a heartbeat, but you’re hanging around.'

'This is some action-hero crap you're asking me to do, Billy.'

'Just rough a couple of them up, mate. It's twenty thousand dollars. I bet you did a hell of a lot more for a hell of a lot less in the past.'

'You're just full of theories.'

'And you're not stupid. You can see when an entire town is getting fucked over.'

'At the moment I can't see anything.'

'They're horrible people, man.'

'I've got no evidence.'

'Ask anyone around here. That's your evidence.'

A pause. King weighed up what he had heard. It was time to make a decision.

'I'm not promising anything,' he said.

'I don't want you to promise me shit,' Billy said. 'Just go ask around. You'll see something needs to be done.'

King waited a few moments. 'You going to give me that Kate girl's address?'

'You going to help me out?'

He could feel the stress leaching out of Billy's bones. The man was gaunt, plagued by exhaustion. There were deep rings under his eyes.

Someone had to do something about this.

And who else was going to?

He made up his mind to act a second before he decided he wasn't going to go about it in a half-assed way.

'Stay here,' he said. 'Tell me exactly where these Iron Rangers are. Keep Kate's address until I get back. I'll have a look around.'

Billy's eyes lit up. The despair dissipated into excitement. 'Thank you!'

'Don't thank me yet. Like I said, no promises.'

'Fine by me.'

King looked at his watch. 'I'll be back in a couple of hours. Around lunchtime. If I'm not, call the cops.'

'Don't talk like that, mate, you'll make me nervous,' Billy said. 'What are the odds of something bad happening to you?'

'To be honest,' King said, wrenching open the door, 'very slim.'

CHAPTER 8

The battered old sedan drifted to the left unless he battled to control it.

At least it was better than walking.

King kept one hand on the top of the faded steering wheel. The other clutched a rudimentary map Billy had drawn on a scrap of paper. It led him out of Jameson and down a winding road to the bottom of a gully. He was halfway there. The thick forest flashed past on either side, stirring eerie memories of the previous night. It was approaching high noon. The sun battered down on his forearms, glaring in through the open windows.

He knew Billy was desperate. A man had been driven to his wits end if he decided to lend a total stranger his car. Billy had zero reassurance that he would get the vehicle back.

But he would.

The gesture made King trust him. For better or worse.

Up ahead the forest cleared on one side of the road, making way for a small inlet packed full of buildings. The main clubhouse stood out amongst the group. A long low shack, positioned in the centre of the inlet. An enormous garage sat adjacent to it. The roller door had been raised, revealing several gleaming motorcycles propped up undercover. On either side of the main complex there were a scattering of small houses, each no bigger than an apartment flat. The whole place looked rundown and dirty.

Just from assessing the exterior of their complex, he knew there would be no reasoning with these men. He'd seen their type before. Sheltered thugs, blissfully unaware of the outside world. Wrapped up in the fantasy that they were the toughest sons-of-bitches around. He pulled the sedan softly into the lot. The tyres crunched under the gravel, but even from this distance away he could hear heavy metal music blasting inside the clubhouse. They wouldn't hear him.

Good.

He got out of the sedan and looked around. No sign of life. Two pairs of motorcycles in the garage, meaning everyone was home. Four-on-one. Not the worst odds he'd ever faced.

As he stood completely still, inhaling deep lungfuls of air, an inkling of his past began to surface. The adrenalin. The shivers. The unsettled stomach.

Signs of approaching conflict.

He had no evidence that these bikies were involved in any kind of wrongdoing. Therefore, massive overwhelming force was not justified. Not yet. After pondering for a few seconds, King realised he looked like a fool loitering in front of the building. He decided to simply knock.

He walked up onto the wooden deck. Faded planks creaked under his feet, but the din from inside only increased in volume as he got closer. A mixture of pounding drums and heavy guitar riffs pounded out of what sounded like an expensive sound system. One of the windows facing the front of the clubhouse lay ajar. The smell of weed and booze and tobacco seeped out. All the curtains were closed. He couldn't see in. There was no knowing what he was up against.

He knocked. Three sharp raps, loud and firm. Then he waited. The seconds ticked by. There came a grunt of exertion from somewhere inside. But no response.

He knocked again. This time louder. Hard enough to rattle the doorframe. Still no answer. The music was deafening, drowning out all other sounds. They wouldn't be able to hear him.

Screw it, he thought. He didn't have to be here.

And he didn't have to be polite.

The door was made of flimsy wood panelling, with hinges that had rusted in their brackets long ago. Paint flaked off the frame. It was an old, rickety thing. Weak. King took a single step back, pinpointed the exact spot where the most force would be applied liberally to each support, and rammed a boot into the door.

It was weaker than he had anticipated. With a *snap* like breaking bone the entire door ripped from its hinges and fell inward. It hit the dusty floor of the clubhouse and came to rest, surrounded by a halo of splinters.

King stepped back again and waited patiently for a response.

It didn't take long. The music stopped instantly. At the same time, a cacophony of swearing echoed out onto the patio.

'What the *fuck…*'

'*Fucking—!*'

'Bloody hell.'

But surprisingly, still no response. No-one barrelling out onto the deck, pumped full of aggression.

They were hesitating.

King had a strange feeling. Something wasn't right here. He leant forward and stuck his head round the now empty doorframe.

Bare skin. A flash of movement. A slight figure running into an adjacent room. Four beefy men scrambling for clothes. The musk of testosterone.

He took one glimpse at the situation and saw blistering, flaming red.

Someone was about to get hurt, and no-one was going to stop it.

First, he had to confirm his suspicions. He strode fast and hard into the clubhouse. At six-foot-three he was an imposing figure to most, and right now there was unmistakable fury plastered across his face. It made all four men freeze up. He was in their midst before one of them could react. He made to move past them, to check the room he had seen someone enter.

Suddenly a barrage of reactions, all at once.

'Who the *fuck* do you think you are, mate?'

'What are you doing?'

King wondered who would make the first mistake. Then the man closest to him got in his way. Blocking his path to the room.

Without breaking stride, King reached out and seized him by the throat before the poor guy even had time to assess the situation. With the other arm he wound up and thundered a fist straight and fast, like a whip being released. It slammed directly into the man's forehead, a crushing blow that rattled his brain around inside his skull and knocked him instantly unconscious. King released him and he fell back, hitting the ground like a limp sack of shit. This wasn't the movies. The guy's head would not stop throbbing for the next week.

He made it across the length of the clubhouse without any further confrontation. Shocked by a stranger interrupting their private matters and effortlessly incapacitating their friend, the other three stayed frozen to the spot. He took one look around the doorframe of the adjoining room and saw all he needed to see.

A young girl, no older than thirteen, desperately wiggling into a pair of jeans.

King turned back to the three men still standing.

'You have one second to explain this,' he said.

A single moment of pure silence.

One of the bikers walked forward, suddenly regaining confidence.

'Mate you'd better get the fuck outta here before—'

King exploded. It was a technique he had practically perfected; feigning complete calm one instant and charging like a raging bull the next. It had its intended effect. The man who had stepped forward to confront him almost jumped out of his skin in fright. King extended two hands and used all the strength in his frame to give him a double-handed shove, square in the chest. The guy had already been in the process of backtracking and the added push sent him toppling back off his feet.

There was a pool table in the corner. Before the other two men could react, King dashed over and lifted a cue off its surface. In a split second he sized up his opponents. One was fat and beefy and would be hard to handle in terms of sheer strength.

Him first.

A step forward. A fake swing from the left. Beefy flinched. King reversed his grip, swung back and sliced the cue through the air faster than the eye could see. It splintered across Beefy's head, shards flying everywhere, a loud *crraaaaack* echoing off the walls of the clubhouse. The man dropped like a stone.

The last guy on his feet was skinnier than the rest, to the point where he looked emaciated. He was high on something, jittery and gaunt. His bony limbs shook in the sudden quiet.

'Come on 'en,' he jeered. 'I'll knock ya fuckin' teeth out, mate. I'll fuckin'—'

He didn't get to finish. King charged him, bundled him up against the wall and delivered a staggering right uppercut into the man's solar plexus. The guy let out a guttural noise somewhere between a cough and a dry heave. Shaking with adrenalin, King seized two handfuls of his tattered singlet. Spun him around. Built up momentum. Then let go with a colossal heave that sent him shooting like a dart into one of the flimsy windows. The pane shattered and he tumbled straight through, landing heavily on the porch outside amidst a downpour of broken glass.

Momentary quiet. Two men were unconscious. One was hurt bad on the outside deck. The only man yet to be incapacitated was the one King had pushed. He had only just made it back to his feet.

King turned to face him. He saw confusion, apprehension, fear in the man's eyes. Sure, he was a biker, but there were few people King had come across in his life who were *true* tough guys. This guy was used to preying on vulnerable shopkeepers. He didn't know the heat of combat or the smell of lead or the sight of death or the sound of an enemy convoy approaching.

He'd never experienced anything like this before.

Anyone like King.

CHAPTER 9

'W-w-w—'

The biker couldn't even manage a comprehensible sentence. Shock was plastered across his face.

'Bet you're not used to being on the other end of a beatdown,' King said.

The guy's aggressive instincts had become non-existent. He leant on the arm of one of the chairs, reeling from the rapid brutality of the fight.

'Who are you?' he said, his voice shaky.

'Friend of Billy's.'

'Billy … the fuckin' post office guy? Jesus Christ. Why'd you kick our door in?'

'You wouldn't answer it.'

'We were busy.'

'Evidently.'

'Look, uh — you're a decent guy, right? You've taught us a lesson, or whatever. We ain't gonna bother Billy again. I get it. Now just leave us alone.'

'I might have.'

'Huh?'

'I might have just given you the message, if I didn't see what I did.'

'It was consensual.'

'I'm sure it was. How old is she?'

'Nineteen.'

'Bullshit.'

'She is…'

King took a single step forwards. 'How old is she?'

'She's nineteen! And it's none of your fuckin' business, anyway.'

Another step forward. 'What's your name?'

'Jed. Now fuck off.'

King got closer, and Jed became more aggressive.

'Did you hear me? I said *fuck off!*'

Jed made a slight move, as if to lash out. King put a stop to that immediately. He kicked Jed square in the gut with a thick-soled boot, putting heavy forward momentum into the blow. Jed doubled over, gasping and retching. It would knock the fight out of him for the next few seconds, at least.

King strode over to the far wall and ripped the thin television off its cabinet. Cables disconnected or tore as he yanked it loose. The flat-screen was roughly the size of a small tabletop. Its hard plastic casing made it light and easy to yield.

He walked back and swung the flat surface of the screen in a wide arc. Jed was still hunched over, holding his aching gut. The television cracked across the top of his skull. The screen shattered at the same time as he dropped. His legs gave out and he began to topple to the floor, knocked off balance by the colossal impact. King dropped the broken television and kicked out again. This time he aimed for Jed's ribs. The toe of his boot hit Jed in the side just as his fall picked up momentum. Another *crack* echoed through the clubhouse. Jed tumbled away, shrieking in agony. King guessed two or three ribs were broken.

'That was rude, Jed,' King said. 'You're going to apologise for telling me to fuck off.'

No response. Jed looked pathetic lying on the floor, moaning and cradling his wounds. Blood ran from the top of his head and dripped onto the dusty ceramic tiles. King was surprised he had remained conscious.

'No apology? Fair enough.'

He wrenched the man up by the scruff of his neck and dragged him outside. From the far end of the porch he heard a moan of distress. He glanced across and saw the skinny guy lying on the deck amongst a scattering of glass shards. He was cut bad. He wouldn't be a threat.

'You,' King said. 'Get up and come with me, or I'll break both your arms.'

Sniffling, the man scrambled to his feet as fast as his shaky legs would allow him. The threat of further violence obviously trumped the pain he felt.

'Follow me,' King said.

Still dragging Jed, he stepped down off the porch and strode to the open garage next to the clubhouse. The sun beat down overhead. Jed was in bad shape. He stumbled forward, struggling to stay upright. King had to hoist him up by the collar. When they finally reached the garage he let go. The biker collapsed in a heap in the dirt.

'These your bikes?' King said.

Jed didn't answer. The skinny guy trailing meekly behind said nothing.

King spun toward the man with a burst of speed. It gave him such a fright that he fell back on his rear in the dirt, still clutching his wounds.

'I said … are these your bikes?'

'Y-yes.'

'Yes what?'

Skinny looked at him, perplexed. 'Whaddaya mean?'

'You're going to call me sir, or I'm going to give you another beating. Are these your bikes?'

'Yes, sir.'

There was nothing more to be said. King stepped into the garage. It was a creaky tin building with cracked concrete flooring. Rusty tools adorned the walls. The whole place reeked of fuel. The wooden shelving running along the right-hand wall looked as if it would fall apart at any second. Several metal cans of petrol lay along the top shelf. King walked over and hefted one into his arms. It was heavy. He could cope.

He made his way over to the first of the four motorcycles, a matte-black Harley Davidson complete with custom fenders. A real nice piece of work.

'How much did this cost you?' King said as he ripped the lid off the canister.

'My life savings, man,' Jed whimpered. 'Please…'

'Even better.'

King upended the can over the Harley, making sure to empty its last dregs before throwing it aside. The bike gleamed in the sunlight. It had a new coat.

'Anyone here got a light?' he said.

Sheer perplexion crossed Jed's face. Either shock, denial or stupidity kept him from putting two and two together. Skinny seemed to be aware of what the question meant.

'Nah, man,' Jed said.

'If either of you have one, and I find it,' King said, 'I'll beat you to within an inch of your life.'

'I've got one,' Skinny said.

'That's what I like to hear.'

The man fished around in his pocket before producing a compact silver Zippo. King snatched it out of his fingers. Flicked the top off. Slid his thumb over the spark wheel. A small flame leapt up.

Jed realised what was happening.

'No!' he yelled. 'You prick. Fuck off!'

He took a step forward in a hopeless attempt to scare King away from the bike. King lashed out hard, twisting at his waist, putting all his bodyweight into a right hook that cracked across Jed's jaw and sent him tumbling back onto the dirt. He'd put more power into it than he usually would. That shot had sent a message.

Don't ever try that again.

'Please don't hit me,' Skinny helplessly spluttered.

King spun on his heel and threw the open lighter into the garage. It landed squarely in the thin puddle of petrol spread across the concrete underneath the Harley. The entire floor lit up like an inferno. Flames enveloped the bike, licking away the matte paint, eating away at its frame. A whimper sounded from the ground behind King. He turned to see Jed watching the blaze unfolding. There were tears in his eyes.

Skinny began to shake as the fire spread to the rest of the garage. The tin shed spurred the blaze on until all four bikes were swallowed. The heat was astonishing. King took a few steps back to ease the burning sensation against his skin. He found himself between Skinny and Jed.

'That's a shame, isn't it?' he said.

Jed was in too much pain to move, but Skinny took a step away. King sensed he was about to run for it. He couldn't have that.

Two handfuls of the shirt and a vicious knee to the gut put the gaunt biker on the gravel alongside his buddy. The placement of the blow had taken every ounce of wind out of him. King was sure that neither of the pair would have the energy or the motivation to move for the next half hour.

He left them on the ground and re-entered the clubhouse. He took a moment to survey the scene. Half the furniture in the place had been either overturned or destroyed in the carnage. The two bikers left in the room were in the process of recovering from concussions. They swayed on the floor, attempting to get to their feet.

King wasn't the type to kill needlessly, so he left them both where they were and crossed to the room where he had last seen the girl.

She was still there, sitting in the corner of a single bed, her knees tucked up to her chin. She trembled as King entered the doorframe.

'Are you okay?' he asked.

'Who are you? What's going on?'

'I'm just a passerby. I did what I could to help.'

'They're the scariest guys I've ever met and y-you just beat the shit out of all of them,' the girl said, stumbling over her words. 'Please don't hurt me, please…'

'I'm not going to hurt you. I'm going to take you home. Where do you live?'

'Back up in Jameson.'

'I've got a car.'

The girl said nothing. She stared at the floor, still shivering.

King walked over to the bed and crouched down by its side. The girl shrank back.

'Look, you've got nothing to be afraid of,' he said. Comforting wasn't his forte, but he gave it a shot. 'I'm not going to hurt you. Those guys out there wanted to hurt you, and look what I did to them. That's what I think of people like that. I'm really sorry about what happened to you but you need to trust me.'

'Okay,' she said in a voice barely above a whisper. 'What did you do to them?'

'What did they do to you?'

'They touched me. Took my clothes off and they all started to touch me. I think it was going to get worse but you showed up.'

'Was there anyone in particular who did more?' King asked.

'The big guy. The really fat one. He started it all, and everyone else kinda … followed.'

'Stay here.'

A thin mental barrier kept King from exploding with rage as he headed back out into the main area of the clubhouse. Conveniently, the beefy guy had just come out of his stupor. He sat bolt-upright, staring around the room with a look of utter confusion spread across his features. He had no idea what had happened. Then he turned and saw King's giant frame striding at him.

'Who the f—'

King came within range and stomped down hard on the man's hand. He felt multiple bones crush under his heel. A horrendous scream echoed through the room.

'Do you have money here?' King said slowly and clearly.

'W-what?'

'You guys definitely have cash. You extort every shopkeeper in Jameson. Where's your money?'

'I don't know.'

'If you don't tell me I'll break every single bone in your other hand.'

'Um … kitchen cupboard. Top left. Fuck…'

King nodded his approval. Then he crouched down so that his face was inches from Beefy's.

'I was in the Special Forces,' he said. 'I'm not sure if you realise what that means. It means that you four may think you're the toughest, scariest men to walk the planet … but you know why you think that? Because you come from the middle of nowhere. You're fucking hillbillies. You have no idea what the rest of the world is like. You know how to bully local shopkeepers, and that's about it. Now, I'm going to take this girl back to her parents. If I hear a fucking whisper that any of you four have shown your face in town, I'll come back here and I'll tie you all up and kill every single one of you. Nod if you understand.'

Beefy nodded.

'Look into my eyes,' King said. 'Look right into them. Now listen. If you ever try anything like this again, I will slaughter you. Do you think I'm bluffing? Does it look like I'm making this up?'

'No.'

'Do you doubt me?'

'No.'

'Will you do everything I say without a hint of protest?'

'Yes.'

'When your buddies wake up, you tell them everything I just told you. And you get the fuck out of this place. I'm coming back tonight to check whether you're still here. Got it?'

A nod.

King knew he had Beefy exactly where he wanted him. The man gave off clear signs of a mentally broken individual. The shivering. The wide eyes. The inability to make eye contact. The unmistakeable smell of piss. His previous aura of macho invincibility had just been torn to shreds.

King would not be returning that night. There was no need. The four of them would be in another state by then.

He called for the girl and she tentatively emerged from the room. Her eyes boggled at the sight of the destroyed clubhouse. He ushered her through the mess and out onto the front deck. On his way out, he threw open the top left kitchen cupboard and seized an enormous wad of hundred-dollar bills from the top shelf. He went outside and placed a reassuring hand on the young girl's shoulder.

'See those two,' he said, motioning at Jed and Skinny. Both men were flattened out on the dusty ground, cradling their wounds and staring with pale faces at the crumbling garage, still ablaze.

The girl nodded.

'They don't look so tough now, do they?' he said.

She shook her head. 'Thank you so much for helping me.'

'Not a problem.'

They set off towards the car.

'What's your name, by the way?' he asked.

'Amanda.'

'I'm Jason. Ready to go back home to your parents, Amanda?'

'Yeah. I just want to see Dad.'

'What were you doing out here anyway?'

Her slight shoulders slumped. 'They grabbed me in town. Look, I'll tell you all about it in the car … just … please … get me out of here.'

King opened the door for her and she slipped into the passenger seat, weeping. He crossed to the other side, started the engine and pulled out onto the main road. He took a final look back at the clubhouse. Two severely injured bikers trembling in the dirt, a third still out cold inside. The beefy guy would be nursing his injuries for the next six months.

As he drove away, the garage's supports reached their breaking point and the entire structure fell inwards, sending flames sky-high.

'Hell of a morning,' King muttered under his breath.

He took the rundown sedan round a corner and the clubhouse disappeared from sight.

CHAPTER 10

Amanda remained silent for the next fifteen minutes.

King didn't bother her. She had been through a lot. He couldn't imagine how violating the experience must have been. To think if those men had gone any further…

'Are you okay?' he asked again as the sedan cruised into the heart of Jameson. There was less activity than when he had first woken up. He guessed most residents were farming. Only a couple of pedestrians could be seen on the footpaths.

'I guess so,' she said. 'I'm just thinking about what could have happened.'

'They won't be doing anything like that again.'

'To me?'

'To anyone. Trust me.'

'I've never seen you around.'

'I'm from out of town. Where do you live?'

'Ten minutes out of Jameson. I'll direct you. Just keep driving.'

The shops and main roads slowly disappeared, replaced once again by the uneven surface of potholed country tarmac.

'So, Amanda, what were you doing there?' King said.

'I've been hanging around town a lot lately,' she said. 'Dad's looking for work so he's not around to keep an eye on me. I just roam the streets some days. Probably not the best idea.'

'I'd say it's not.'

'This morning I was walking back from Gemma's house. Those guys pulled up on their bikes. They were really rude. It's pretty clear I'm young and they were still jeering and catcalling me.'

'How old are you, exactly?'

'Thirteen.'

King shook his head in frustration. Barely a teenager. 'Did they kidnap you?'

'Not exactly … well, I don't know. They just told me to get on the back of the bike and that they would take me home. They were forceful. I was scared. I thought they'd hurt me if I didn't do what they said.'

'Don't worry,' he said. 'I understand.'

'But they didn't take me home — they took me to their clubhouse. They said they wanted to show me around. I didn't know what to do. I had no idea where I was, so I couldn't run away. Then they locked the door and the big guy said he wanted to have some fun and…'

She trailed off. King reached across the centre console and rested a hand on her shoulder.

'It's okay,' he said. 'I'll get you home.'

'How can you be so sure that they won't do that to someone else?'

'I saw it in their eyes. I broke them.'

'Who the hell are you?' Amanda said. 'Where did you come from, and why did you help me, and how did you do what you just did?'

'I'd be confused too,' King said. 'Look, I can't really go into details, but I used to be a very dangerous man—'

'Pretty sure you still are.'

'Okay, I still am. My job used to involve using those skills, and now I don't have a job. So I help people out when I see things I don't like.'

'And you can't say what exactly you used to do?'

He shook his head. 'That's not something we should get into.'

Amanda shrugged. 'Well, you sure helped me. Thank you, Jason. Left here.'

For the last ten minutes they had coasted along winding roads, boxed in by undergrowth and towering tree trunks on either side. Now, Amanda pointed at a small dirt track that ran off the main road and cut through the trees. King spun the wheel. Billy's sedan made the transition from uneven asphalt to gravel. Its suspension struggled to handle the off-road track. He saw Amanda tense up and shrink back into her seat. He wasn't sure if she was recalling memories of the morning, or simply had not been expecting the jolts and bumps of the new road. Whatever it was, King would have a stern talk with her father. To be left to her own devices at such a young age was bound to lead to trouble sooner or later.

It only took half a minute for the path to branch out into a wide clearing, dead in the middle of the forest. The woods surrounded them on all sides. A thin, well-kept layer of grass covered the clearing floor. In the centre of the space lay a sprawling one-storey house. It looked similar to a lodge. Long and large and homely.

'This your place?' he said.

Amanda nodded.

'It's nice.'

'Dad's home,' she noted, pointing to a thin trail of smoke rising from the chimney. She sounded surprised, King noticed.

'I'm not sure how he'll feel about this,' he muttered under his breath.

'Huh?'

As if on cue, the front door burst open and a man came bounding out into the clearing floor. He was thickset and squat, with curly black hair and a full beard. He wore a cheap plaid shirt and jeans. His feet were bare.

'Who the fuck are you?!' he yelled.

King turned to Amanda. 'See?'

He swung the driver's door open and stepped out into the clearing. Amanda's dad recoiled slightly as he saw King's size. But it didn't stem his anger.

'What are you doing with my daughter? Amanda, honey, come here…'

King twitched slightly. Something about what the man had said struck a nerve with him.

'What are you doing *without* your daughter?' he said.

The man froze, perplexed. 'What?'

'You should be on your knees thanking me.'

'The hell are you talking about?'

'Do you know where your daughter was this morning?'

'With you, I presume. And you have ten seconds to explain this.'

King raised an eyebrow. 'Actually, I have all the time in the world to explain this. But don't worry, it'll only take me ten seconds. I saved Amanda from being raped.'

The man had not been expecting that. Instantly, the aggressive demeanour faded. 'W-what?'

King turned to Amanda. 'Why don't you head inside? I've got to tell your dad a few things.'

She nodded knowingly. She stepped up onto the porch and marched through the open front door without saying a word.

Her dad sank onto the front steps, sporting a blank ten-thousand-yard stare. 'What are you saying?'

'What's your name?' King said.

'Richard.'

'Richard, do you know the four bikers that hang around town? One of them's called Jed.'

'I've seen them around. You're not telling me—'

'Looks like they offered your daughter a lift home. She was walking back from Jameson this morning. They ended up ignoring her directions and she ended up trapped in their clubhouse. I was passing by, knocked on their door, and by then they had all her clothes off.'

Richard's face had turned to a pale sheet. Shock does that to a person. His mouth stayed shut for a long fifteen seconds.

'I'll kill them,' he finally blurted out.

'I don't think that's a good idea.'

'I don't care. I'll go there with a crowbar and I'll … I'll fucking beat them to within an inch of their lives.'

'No need for that.'

'Why not?'

'I dealt with them.'

Richard looked up. 'Huh?'

‘Recognise that car?’ King said, pointing to the battered sedan.

‘Isn’t that the post office guy’s ride?’ Richard said after studying the vehicle for a moment.

‘It is.’

‘What are you doing with it? Is he okay?’

‘He’s perfectly fine. In fact, I’d say he’s never better.’

‘He put you up to it?’

‘He let me know what was going on around town. Are you aware?’

‘Of course,’ Richard said. ‘But this is a tiny town. There’s nothing they could do to stop it.’

‘I stopped it. I got a bit angry when I saw them with your daughter and I trashed the whole place. Badly injured them all too. I don’t think you’ll ever see them around again.’

‘W-who are you?’

King sighed. ‘Seems like everyone’s asking me that question lately.’

CHAPTER 11

King gripped the small mug of steaming black coffee that Richard had given him and hunched further over the dining table, which was a thick slab of polished wood. It reminded him of the bar from the night before. Back when this whole thing started, just over twelve hours ago. He certainly hadn't been expecting such madness in a small country town off the beaten track.

Beside him, a large open fire crackled. Richard sat on the other side of the table, sipping at a coffee identical to King's.

'I can't thank you enough,' Richard said. 'Is there any way you can explain who you are? Because without you, I don't know where my daughter would be.'

'I really can't say much,' King said. 'But you're welcome.'

'You can bet your life I won't let anything like that ever happen again.'

'Let's hope not.'

'It's so hard to keep an eye on her at all times. I didn't realise what a mistake I was making until now.'

'Amanda said you're looking for work?'

Richard nodded. 'I was laid off a month ago. So many of us were. There's a place twenty minutes out of town that's been there forever. Owned by a couple of locals.'

'What happened?'

'Came under new management. Overseas buyers kicked all the old workers out.'

'Seems a bit harsh.'

He shrugged again. 'It's how things are these days. No job safety.'

'How's the employment search going?'

'Terribly. Have you seen where we are? Jameson's not rife with opportunities.'

'Well,' King said, 'this should get you through until you work out what to do.'

He reached into his jacket pocket and withdrew half of the bills taken from the clubhouse kitchen. It looked to be well over ten thousand dollars. Richard's eyes widened at the sight.

'This is too much,' he muttered.

'Take it. Just promise you'll keep an eye on Amanda as best you can.'

'Of course I will.'

King slid the money across the table.

'I really don't understand what's going on…'

'I'm not asking you to understand,' King said. 'I'm just telling you that you won't get any more problems from those bikers. And giving you some of what I found there. Use it to stay afloat until you get employed. And take care of your daughter.'

'I promise.'

King rose from the table and took one last look around the place. It was a house that had been meticulously furnished as a labour of love. The art on the walls, the rugs on the floor, the large open fireplace, the beat-up armchairs, the smell of the forest all around. Nothing expensive, just a collection of bits and pieces saved up over the years to create the thing that King never had; a home.

'This is a really nice place,' he said to Richard.

'Thank you.'

'I mean it. You're a lucky man.'

'You got a place?'

King shook his head. 'I've never really lived anywhere. Always been on the move.'

'You moved around America? You've still got the accent.'

'Every single person feels the need to bring that up over here.'

Richard laughed. 'Foreigners. They always spark interest.'

'Yeah, I moved around America. But also all over the world.'

A pause. 'Were you in the Army?'

'Kind of.'

Richard sighed emphatically. 'Well, Jason, you're a hard man to crack. That's for sure. But I'll always be in your debt, mate.'

He offered a hand.

'To be honest, I'll probably never see you again,' King said, grasping it and shaking. 'But I appreciate the thought.'

Richard pulled an unprofessional-looking business card out of his pocket and handed it over. It had nothing but his name and mobile phone number handwritten on the front.

'Just in case you find someone looking for workers on your travels,' he said. 'Tell them to give me a call.'

King nodded his understanding and tucked the card into his jeans. 'I'll be sure to keep my eyes open.'

Amanda emerged from one of the doorways, her brow furrowed. 'You're going already?'

'I don't tend to hang around too long in one place,' King said.

'I think you should settle down,' Richard said. 'Something about this house has grabbed you, I can tell. Go find a home somewhere. You don't need to move your whole life.'

'I know. But for now, it's what I'd prefer.'

Amanda stayed leaning against the doorframe. 'Good luck with whatever it is you're going to do.'

'Thank you,' he said.

King moved to the front door. Opened it.

'Take care of yourselves,' he said, nodding to Richard and Amanda.

They nodded back.

King strode back to Billy's sedan. He swung the door open and climbed in. Started the car with a quick twist in the ignition and pulled the wheel in a tight arc, heading back the way he had come.

The trip to Jameson passed in silence. All the action of the last hour had put his mind to rest. Ashamedly, that life was all he had ever known. When there was conflict, he was at peace. He hated to admit it, but it was the truth. The day-to-day happenings of ordinary life had almost become too monotonous to handle, even though he slept somewhere different every night. He knew if he was to move on from that life he should avoid situations like what had happened at the clubhouse. It did nothing but bring back old memories.

He parked the sedan in front of the post office after sixteen minutes of driving.

It's useless to time everything so meticulously, he thought as he slammed the door shut. Another old habit he would do good to forget.

By now it was high noon. In the city, this meant stores would be at their busiest, bustling with white-collar workers on their lunch break. Here, everyone was now farming. The morning rush had all but subsided. King spotted two people on the main road as he made his way into the post office. Jameson was a ghost town.

'Jesus Christ!' a voice proclaimed as the door jangled upon his arrival.

He saw Billy standing behind the counter at the other end of the store. There wasn't a single customer in sight. Even from this distance King could make out the beads of sweat trickling down his forehead. He was beaming.

'You're certainly happy to see me,' King said.

Billy visibly relaxed. 'I thought you were some nutter, King. I thought you'd go in there all high and mighty and get shot in the head, and then they'd find my car and come back here and kill me.'

'Far from it, my friend.'

'Come out back. *NICOLE!*'

'What?!' came a shouted reply from the back.

'Need you up front again.'

Billy led King past the same disgruntled young employee that had eyeballed him the first time.

'You're back,' she noted in a sardonic tone as they passed.

'Congratulations,' King said. 'You have eyes.'

She shot him an icy glare. Then they walked through into the back room and Billy slammed the door shut with the intensity of a man desperate for answers.

'Tell me everything,' he said.

CHAPTER 12

By the time King had finished explaining the events that had transpired, he wasn't sure Billy's jaw could fall any lower. The man sat deathly still in his chair, almost shellshocked. At the same time King noticed a faint glimmer of emotion in his eyes. He knew the look. Pure, utter relief. Like an enormous burden had finally been lifted off his shoulders.

'You seem stunned,' King said.

It took a few seconds for Billy to gather his thoughts. 'When you showed up here I thought this was all too good to be true. Like I said before, I thought you were a crackpot who thought he'd stir up trouble in a small town.'

'I'd say I did stir up trouble.'

'Only the best kind of trouble. I'm still not sure if I believe everything you just told me.'

'Feel free to head down and take a look for yourself.'

'Nah,' Billy said. 'I'll take your word for it. But what if they come back for me?'

'They won't.'

'You can't be sure of that, mate. From what you told me, you completely fucked them up. They're going to want to take out their anger on someone. And they know you're tied to me. You took my car.'

'They won't,' King repeated.

Billy stood up and laid a hand on his shoulder. 'How do you know?'

King allowed the corners of his mouth to turn into a wry smile. He reached out and gripped Billy's shoulder, returning the gesture. 'If you knew half the things I've done in my life, you'll know to take my word for it.'

'All this cryptic talk,' Billy said, exasperated. He sat back down, shaking his head.

'Okay Billy, you want the truth? I've seen people break hundreds of times. Mentally. Over the last ten years I've seen many sport the same expression those bikers did this morning. It's the look of total defeat. They don't want anything to do with me, they don't want anything to do with you, they don't want anything to do with Jameson anymore. I watched them crumble. I'm very good at doing that. How's that for an explanation?'

Silence.

'Well…' Billy said after a long pause. 'That certainly scared the shit out of me.'

'So you believe me?'

'Oh yes. I believe you. I'm sure they're very far away from here by now.'

'You're correct.'

'But still, you can't be one hundred percent certain.'

King shot him an icy glare.

'Kidding, kidding,' Billy said, running a hand through his curly hair in exasperation.

He rose off the chair again and crossed the room to a thin filing cabinet tucked away in the corner. King hadn't even noticed it was there. Billy withdrew a key from one of the pockets in his shirt and unlocked the bottom drawer with a swift twist of the lock. It sprang open to reveal a thick row of manila folders, all crammed into the cabinet with not an inch of room to spare. He reached to the very back and shimmied out the final folder. This one was a little thicker than the others, King noted. Billy opened it up and grabbed its contents.

A thick wad of Australian currency. All yellow. Fifty-dollar notes.

Billy crossed the room, hand outstretched, gesturing for King to take it.

'I'm a man of my word,' he said.

King didn't move. 'That's all yours, Billy.'

Billy froze, perplexed. His brow furrowed in confusion. 'But I said I'd pay you if you helped me out.'

'And I'm telling you it's all yours.'

'Then…' Billy stared at the floor, gathering his thoughts. 'Then why did you help me?'

'You looked desperate. And I hate people like those bikers. Besides, I found some of their cash at the clubhouse and took it. I gave half to Amanda's dad. I'll use the other half to keep myself afloat for a while.'

'Do you want a lift anywhere?'

'I'll be fine. Thanks Billy. But I never would have taken your money. You worked hard to earn that. You deserve it.'

'So you did all that for nothing? You put your life in danger.'

'I wasn't in danger.'

'Do the tough guy act all you want, you still took a big risk for someone you didn't know.'

King paused. 'I guess I did.'

'So thank you.'

'Not a problem.'

King could tell nothing further needed to be said. Billy appreciated what he had done. And that was that.

'So this woman,' he said. 'Kate Cooper. Can I get her address?'

'You can have whatever the hell you want.'

'Will I need to borrow your car again?'

Billy shook his head. 'You seem fit enough. It's a twenty minute walk from here. Think you can manage?'

'I can handle that.'

King waited patiently as Billy scrawled a few words on a scrap of paper. He sat the pencil down and passed the note across. It read:

12 Walbrook Drive.

'How do I get there?' King asked.

'Turn left when you leave and follow the road. Eventually you'll see the street sign. It branches off the main road.'

King followed him out into the post office, which was still just as empty.

'Been busy?' Billy said.

Nicole raised an eyebrow. 'You kidding?'

'Of course.'

They walked past her and stepped outside. Wind feathered through the surrounding trees, blowing a cool mountain breeze along the main strip. King shivered in the sudden cold. The drone of a small plane passing overhead made him look up. He spotted it, nothing but a tiny speck in a sky full of thick clouds.

He looked at Billy and held up the scrap of paper. 'Thank you for this. Helps me out.'

'Just don't go assaulting her or anything. She's a nice girl. Works hard. I wouldn't forgive myself if you turned out to be some psycho.'

'I think you know you can trust me.'

Billy nodded. 'This still all seems like a dream. If you're a man of your word and I never see those bikers again, I'll owe you for the rest of my life. Will I see you again, King?'

'Depends, Billy. Good luck with your business. I hope everything works out.'

'You too … with whatever the hell it is you're doing.'

And with that King was off. He shook the man's hand and turned on his heel. It was a calm day in rural Victoria. The middle of autumn. None of the blaring horns or constant murmur of pedestrians or sharp noises of the city. Out here there was just peace and solitude.

A nice day for a walk.

He set off at a brisk pace, channeling memories of hikes he'd made long ago. Those walks had been far worse. Often, he had no idea what he'd be heading towards, or if he'd come out unscathed on the other side. Here in civilian life, he was confident of any encounter. There were thugs and gangsters in society. But these ordinary crooks paled in comparison to the enemies of his past. Even the hitmen from the night before had failed to rattle him. They were simply irritating. He wondered just how different he was to the rest of the population. Perhaps it was irreversible, burnt into his subconscious. Guns and murder and clandestine activity were nothing out of the ordinary. In fact, he felt more at home dealing with these problems than handling daily life.

Forget about it, King, he told himself. *Try to move on.*

So he listened to the sounds of the world around him as he walked, concentrating on nature. On normality. The buildings on either side grew further and further apart. Before long it was simply the asphalt beside him and scruffy brush all around. Nothing to do but follow the road, which twisted through uninhabited woods.

He thought briefly of the two men he had killed the night before, unable to keep his mind off it. Their bodies would soon decompose in the machine he'd left them in. Wildlife would find them. Or they would rot away. Neither image bothered him in the slightest. They had chosen to shoot at him. He hadn't deliberately involved himself. He'd done nothing but retaliate.

He dwelled on the altercation, replaying it over and over again in his mind. Before he knew it a gravel path appeared ahead, just wide enough to fit a lane in each direction. It spiralled off into the forest. Sections of the woods had been cleared out to make room for houses. All small and plain and comfortable. Hipped roofs. Wide open yards. Pine trees on all sides.

Kate Cooper was number twelve.

King set off down the path. His boots crunched over the gravel surface, making more noise than the asphalt. It was so quiet in these parts. He felt as if his footfalls were disturbing the residents. Every now and then a bird call would break the silence. Apart from that it was nothing but the sound of his own shoes scuffing against the gravel and the soft whirring of crickets and grasshoppers in the surrounding forest.

There was no-one in their yards. King wondered what these people did with their lives. They weren't farmers, and it seemed like that was the only thing anyone did around here. Maybe these were the homes of the store-owners.

Maybe one of these houses was Billy's.

A car sat idly in the driveway of number twelve. King checked the letterbox to see if he had the right place before he approached the front door. He took a look at the vehicle as he passed. Another sedan, similar to Billy's, this one a Subaru. Another beat-up vehicle on the throes of collapse. King couldn't remember the last new car he'd seen. Not since the city, which he had left weeks ago.

He stepped up onto the deck and rapped on the door three times, short and sharp. He heard a sudden bustling inside. It seemed he had startled someone.

There was a long pause, longer than it usually takes for someone to answer the door. He waited patiently. He assumed it was odd to have unannounced visitors around these parts. Strangers were rare. Everyone knew everyone.

Finally, he heard the sound of a latch sliding. The door swung open a crack. He could see the chain still firmly attached, preventing an intruder from forcing their way inside. One could never be too cautious. A woman's face appeared in the gap.

Kate Cooper.

She was slim. Somewhat tall for a woman, maybe five-ten. Five-eleven even. In person she was even more attractive than the brief glimpse King had seen on the cameras. Brown hair, shoulder-length, a freckled nose, skin slightly pale, deep green eyes. He remembered Billy mentioning something about her being from England.

'Can I help you?' she said, her accent slightly British.

Her voice was assertive. Confident. King admired that. Through the narrow slit of the door he could see her standing with her chest stuck out. Not timid. Like she was the one in control. Impressive, considering a six-foot-three stranger had just come knocking on her door.

'Afternoon, ma'am,' he said.

'Ma'am?' she said. 'What's ma'am? Who calls people ma'am anymore? Who are you? What do you want?'

For a split second King hesitated, taken aback. 'Well, I'm awfully sorry. Just wanted to be polite so you didn't get any bad ideas.'

'Bad ideas?'

'I'm a stranger.'

'No shit.'

King couldn't help smiling a little. 'Straight to the chase. I like it. Anyway, are you Kate Cooper?'

Silence. The door stayed firmly where it was.

'Hello?' King said.

'I heard you.'

'Oh, that's good. Are you going to answer?'

'Yes, I'm Kate Cooper. Once again, who are you?'

'I'm Jason King. I'm a tourist, passing through here. Anyway, I was at the post office earlier this morning and I...'

The door slammed shut in his face.

CHAPTER 13

At that moment, King knew he was onto something. The very mention of the post office had caused an instantaneous reaction. He considered leaving. Kate clearly didn't care for a conversation.

But this was too significant to just let go. Four men were dead already.

'Kate!' King yelled at the door. 'This is serious! Open the door right now.'

'Fuck off!' she yelled back, her voice muffled. 'Leave me alone.'

'I don't know what you're so hostile about!'

'Go away!'

'Do you want me to get the police involved? I'm just looking for an explanation.'

'I'll get the police involved right now. I'm calling the station as we speak.'

'How do you think they'll react when I tell them four men are dead from what you did?'

There was no reply. King waited on the porch, poised, ready for the door to open and Kate to comply. But no such event occurred. In fact after thirty consecutive seconds of silence he heard the sound of the back door swinging open.

'Son of a bitch,' he muttered.

He took off in a run along the porch. Kate's house sat in the centre of a wide lot, which meant the deck looped all the way round the structure. He rounded the corner at breakneck speed and made it to the rear of the house in seconds.

Too late.

Kate had retreated to the opposite side of the patio deck. There was enough outdoor furniture in the space between them to make reaching her a cumbersome task. Wooden bench seats surrounded a glass table in the middle and a lattice trellis covered in vines blocked the way. If he charged at her she would have more than enough time to escape. She had a cellphone pressed against her ear, speaking rapidly. Out of the corner of her eye she saw him and lowered the phone.

'Police on their way,' she said. 'You'd better get out of here and leave me alone.'

'Why?' King said. 'I've got nothing to hide. Police can ask me whatever they want. I'll tell them the truth.'

'I don't know what you're talking about.'

'The package you delivered to the post office.'

'It was just a package. You're talking about four people dying. You're out of your mind.'

'Hang on…'

Then King saw it. Fear in her eyes. At that moment everything clicked. She wasn't part of this. She was just a messenger. Hired help. She thought he would blame her for said deaths, which she had no knowledge of.

'Don't kill me,' she said, barely audible from the other end of the patio. 'I did everything I was instructed to do.'

'I'm not trying to kill you,' he said. 'I'm trying to help you. What are you so afraid of?'

'You're with them, aren't you?'

'With who?'

Before she could respond, King heard the screeching of tyres and the squeal of a police siren from the end of the street. The noise scythed through the forest like a knife. An unnatural sound for these parts.

Kate ran.

One second she was ready to answer King's questions. The next she had turned and bolted for the front of the house. He watched her go, his stomach sinking. The situation had just become a great deal more complicated. He was no closer to discovering any semblance of truth. And there was no doubt that he would be arrested shortly.

The sirens reached a crescendo as the police pulled into Kate's driveway. King had an idea of what he was in for. He guessed an arrest in these parts was a freak occurrence, something the locals talked about as folklore. Jameson was certainly not the crime capital of Australia.

He knew it would do good to make the arrest as uneventful as possible. Heightened tensions were beneficial to no-one. So he walked back the way he had come. Toward the front deck. Toward the police.

'Whoa, whoa, whoa!' a voice shouted as he rounded the corner. 'Stay right there!'

King stopped in his tracks and raised both hands. Palms out. Demonstrating that he wasn't armed. 'I am staying right here.'

The police car parked in the drive looked to be just as old as Kate's sedan. Its paint had half rusted away and the big black logo on the side reading 'JAMESON POLICE DEPARTMENT' was missing letters. The passenger door and the driver's door both lay open. An officer stood behind each door.

The two of them were far from imposing. A man and a woman. He was just under six foot and scrawny, his uniform at least two sizes too big. She couldn't have been far over five foot, with an athletic build and brown hair tied back tight. And she looked angry. Far angrier than the guy. She'd been the one to shout at King as he came into view. King didn't blame her. He was an imposing sight to anyone, let alone someone attempting to arrest him.

'Mr. King, is it?' the female officer said.

'How do you know that?'

'Ms. Cooper here told me.' She motioned to Kate, who stood alongside her near the vehicle, sporting a thousand-yard stare. Like she had just looked death in the eyes. Whoever had employed her to deliver the package must have truly terrified her.

'I don't know what's made Ms. Cooper so distressed,' King said. 'I simply knocked on her door to ask her a few things.'

'We can sort that out at the station, I think.'

'There's a station here?' King said.

'Yeah,' the male officer said. 'It's not on the main road.' His tone was far less aggressive. Like he hoped it was all a mix-up.

King waited through a moment of awkward silence. The officers had refrained from drawing their guns. Either to reduce the tension of the situation, or because using their pieces was a foreign concept. He could tell they were unsure as to what this was. They'd received a call from a distressed woman, as if she was being abducted. They'd raced here, ready for confrontation. But here was her supposed stalker, standing calmly on the front porch. Waiting for someone to speak.

It was clear they were rusty in the serious-crimes department.

'Would you like me to come with you to the station?' King finally said.

'That would be good,' the man said.

'We should cuff him,' the woman said.

'Don't worry,' King said. 'I'll play by the rules.'

'How do we know we can trust you?'

'Because I'd be a mile away from here by now if I wanted to be.'

The pair of them had trouble responding to that. King headed for the car. As he got closer he made out the badges pinned to the breast pocket of each officer's uniform. The man's read "Officer Dawes", and the woman's read "Officer Kitchener". Kate stood nervously off to the side, shuffling from foot to foot.

'Back seat?' King asked as he passed them.

Kitchener nodded.

'No problem.'

He opened the door and settled his bulk into one of the seats. The car smelt like cheap air freshener, covering the standard scent of an old musty interior. He watched as Kitchener spoke to Kate for a moment. The window muffled her voice but her manner was reassuring, like a parent telling a child that everything would be alright. He guessed she was promising that they would sort King out at the station. That all would return to normal soon enough.

He guessed things in Jameson never strayed too far from normal.

Dawes lowered himself into the driver's seat as the two women finished their conversation. He glanced back momentarily, checking King's position, then started the vehicle.

'Busy day?' King said.

He smiled. 'Chaos around here, mate.'

Kitchener got in the car and the smile vanished.

'Back to the station,' she said. 'Then we'll question him.'

'Just to clarify,' King said, 'am I under arrest right now?'

'No, you're not. But just co-operate with us here. You've certainly scared the shit out of that poor woman. Let's sort everything out when we get to the station.'

'I don't think I was the one that scared her,' King said. 'Something certainly has though.'

Neither officer responded to that cryptic message. Dawes started the engine and pulled out of the driveway. The car handled the gravel well. Far better than Billy's old sedan.

The trip passed in silence. King decided not to speak. They were heading to the station to speak.

No use wasting words in here.

Dawes turned right out of Kate's street and headed back to the town centre. They passed Billy's post office. King got a brief glimpse through the open doorway. He saw Billy standing rigid behind the counter, staring directly at him. For a brief instant the two made eye contact. King knew what the man was thinking.

What an idiot.

As they left the shops behind, passing the pair of motels at the very edge of the main strip, King noticed an asphalt road he had previously overlooked branching away into the woods. The police car turned down it. It led to another small cluster of residential houses, these a little more modern than those in Kate's street. He guessed this area had been recently excavated and developed.

At the very end of the street there was a rectangular brick building the size of several houses put together. Large lettering above the entrance read 'JAMESON POLICE DEPARTMENT', the logo the same as the one adorning the side of the car. Dawes pulled into an adjoining four-car garage connected to the station. It housed two identical sedans and a police motorcycle.

'Follow us,' Kitchener said, her tone authoritative.

'What else am I going to do?' King said.

They led him into the station through a narrow door in one wall of the garage. He followed the pair through blank white-washed hallways, each as stale as the last. He caught a quick glimpse of a lobby with identical white walls and a bored-looking male officer sitting behind a reception desk before they ushered him through a thick steel door into a square room, also white. It was furnished with a metal table and four chairs, two on either side.

'Sit,' Kitchener instructed.

King sat.

'So I'm not under arrest,' he said. 'Therefore this isn't an official questioning. What is this exactly?'

'We're just talking,' Dawes said.

He shut the steel door behind him and the pair sat down on the opposite side of the table. King rolled his sleeves up and rested his burly forearms on the surface. The steel was cold to the touch.

'This is all very informal,' he noted.

'You don't stop bringing that up, do you?' Kitchener said.

'I'm used to order. I guess a town as small as this does things a little differently.'

'Were you a cop?'

'No.'

'You were something, that's for sure. I can tell from the way you speak.'

'I can't say what I was.'

'The military?'

'Sort of.'

'Ah, U.S. military,' Dawes said. 'Big macho man. What are you doing all the way out here?'

'I retired.'

'Retiring doesn't usually mean travelling halfway across the world and ending up here.'

'I wanted to see the world.'

'Your standards have hit the ground floor if you've resorted to exploring Jameson. Especially harassing local women.'

'I wasn't harassing her.'

'That's not what she said.'

They knew nothing about the package she delivered, King thought. Kate had decided not to inform them of anything he had asked her.

'She's very reactionary,' he said. 'I simply knocked on her door to ask her something. She panicked.'

'What did you ask her?' Kitchener said.

King hesitated. It would not be wise to divulge anything he knew so far. A slip-up could lead to the location of the bodies in the metal-work factory. He wanted prying eyes as far away from there as possible. If they were discovered, things would turn serious very fast.

'I was chatting to Billy earlier today…' he started.

'Post office Billy?' Kitchener interrupted.

'Are there multiple Billy's in this town?'

'I don't think so.'

'That's a dumb question then.'

She gave him the evil eye. 'Continue.'

'We talked about a lot of things. He told me that Kate was a regular at his post office. He told me she was single. I thought I'd head over and introduce myself. That's all.'

'You realise how that might intimidate people?' Dawes said. 'Especially someone of your size.'

'I do. But I was nothing but pleasant. I apologise if my actions were taken out of context.'

'That's a weird thing to do,' Dawes said. 'Knock on a total stranger's door because one of the locals mentioned her.'

'I'm sorry if you think that.'

'I don't know if I believe it.'

'I couldn't imagine why.'

'It seems like there's more to you than that,' Kitchener said. 'Where have you been staying?'

'Last night I stayed at the motel. I don't know what it's called. The one on the left when you come into town.'

'Where did you come from?'

'I walked from Queensbridge.'

'That's a long walk.'

'I stopped at Ale House. The pub near here.'

'How late was this?'

'Around midnight.'

'Late to be walking through the woods,' Dawes said.

'I can handle myself.'

'Did you run into anyone?' Kitchener said.

'Not a soul.'

She stood up from the table. 'I think we're done here. Ms Cooper seemed more spooked than scared for her safety. We'll let you go, but we have to note that we brought you in. Give us five minutes to sort that out. Okay?'

'Not a problem.'

'Just to make her comfortable, please don't go back there,' Dawes said. 'Makes this whole thing easier.'

'Not a problem,' King repeated. 'I'll be on my way soon anyway. I don't like to spend too long in one place.'

Dawes nodded.

They shuffled out.

Silence.

King took the time to ponder over what he had so far. Two construction workers murdered by hitmen. A terrified local woman who had delivered a package to the post office and then panicked when questioned about it.

So far, that was it. Kate was the only lead he had, and the likelihood that she would open up to King about her experience was dangerously close to zero. It was a reluctant conclusion to come to, but he began to accept that there was not enough information he could acquire about the situation to achieve anything meaningful. Not without resorting to desperate measures.

It was time to move on.

He made up his mind to leave Jameson when the steel door of the interview room opened and a man stepped in. A police officer King had not seen before. His features were plain. Black slicked-back hair, a pale complexion and wider-than-usual eyes. His beady pupils flicked around the contents of the room, taking everything in. He sat down opposite King, where Dawes had previously sat.

Then everything changed.

CHAPTER 14

'Afternoon, sir,' the man said. His accent was strange. Australian, but slightly off. As if he were disguising his natural voice.

The breast pocket of his blue uniform was bare. No name badge.

'Afternoon,' King said. 'Who are you?'

'I'm Officer Brandt. I've just got a few questions for you.'

'Okay.'

'I've heard that you were picked up outside Kate Cooper's house. Is that correct?'

'Correct.'

'May I ask what you were doing there?'

'I already explained this to the other two.'

'I'd like you to clarify it to me, please.'

'Why?'

A scornful smile spread across Brandt's face. King had never seen an expression so fake.

'Just for procedure, sir.'

'I stopped in to say hello.'

'Is that it? Nothing else?'

'That's it.'

'What were you doing at the post office earlier today?'

King kept his mouth shut. Something was off. Kitchener and Dawes had talked informally. They had said they were letting him go. Their general demeanour did not align with the man sitting across from him, who was re-iterating many of the same questions King had heard a minute earlier.

'*Hey!*' he roared. He screamed the word at the top of his lungs. It reverberated around the walls of the small room. Deafening. He was sure the entire station heard it.

Instantly, Officer Brandt panicked. His pale skin turned a shade paler. His eyes boggled in their sockets. Like a deer caught in headlights. He kicked his chair back in one visceral motion, wrenched the door open and disappeared from sight.

Gone in seconds.

King sat still, waiting for movement. It didn't take long. He heard urgent footsteps in the hallway outside, from the opposite direction Brandt had fled. Then Kitchener and Dawes burst into the room. They knew something was awry. King could see it in their eyes.

'What?' Dawes said instantly.

'Who just came in here?' he said.

'What are you talking about?' Kitchener said.

'One of your officers just tried to question me.'

The pair exchanged a glance.

'We haven't talked to any of the other officers since you got here,' Dawes said.

'Then who's Brandt?' King said.

The pair visibly froze.

'What the fuck?' Dawes said, his professional demeanour gone. 'How do you know that name?'

'A man just came into this room and started asking me questions you two had already asked. Said he was Officer Brandt. Seemed like he was doing his own investigation. He left when I caused a commotion.'

'Brandt didn't show up for work yesterday,' Kitchener said. 'We haven't been able to get a hold of him since.'

'Well, he's here now.'

'Why would he come back without showing his face?'

'Oh, shit,' Dawes said, coming to the realisation at the same time as King.

'That wasn't Brandt,' they said in unison.

From the end of the hallway came the sound of a door slamming. It echoed through the station. An urgent noise. The sound of someone fleeing.

Kitchener went pale. 'Stay here.'

She and Dawes turned and bolted out of the room. The steel door swung shut behind them. King heard it click closed.

He stood up and reached for the handle, but it didn't budge. Locked. He was trapped until someone came to get him.

Which would prove disastrous if Brandt's imposter killed everyone in the station.

King felt his pulse quicken. He realised that the conspiracy in Jameson was significantly larger than he had originally thought. The man who'd just questioned him had worn the uniform of a missing policeman. That meant the two hitmen from the night before were merely pawns. A single cog in a larger machine. He knew this feeling all too well. He had felt it many times before.

The revelation that he was onto something.

And it was in that moment he knew he would not leave Jameson until he had answers.

He sat back down at the table and waited for activity. Attempting to break through a locked metal door would achieve nothing.

Movement outside. His ears picked up the sound faster than most people. Being prepared for combat put King into a mental state of heightened senses and constant readiness. Every slight sound was amplified tenfold. That was how he heard the footsteps before the door opened.

Brandt's imposter stepped into the room. King registered the man's wide eyes and the determined, icy look on his face. Then a millisecond later his gaze darted to the pistol in his right hand. He wasted no time mulling over possibilities. As soon as he saw the weapon he exploded with the force of a raging bull.

He tensed his legs and powered up off the chair. Brandt started to flinch. He'd been in the process of raising the gun, and the burst of movement from King made him jolt. King got both his hands underneath the metal table and wrenched it off the floor.

Lifted by the inhuman power that comes with a surge of adrenalin, one end of the table rocketed off the ground and hit the man clean, accompanied by a dull *thunk*. The impact threw him back across the room. He maintained balance for less than a second, then toppled out the open doorway. King heard the clatter of a handgun skittering across concrete and knew he had disarmed the man.

The table landed on its side and slid for a moment, spurred on by the momentum of the heave. It came to rest on one side of the room. King stepped over one of the table legs blocking his path and moved out into the hallway.

Kitchener and Dawes were nowhere to be seen. The imposter was unconscious, knocked senseless by the massive power of the contact. He would come to soon. And he would have a headache for a week. King stepped over his body, picked up the pistol he had dropped and tucked it into his own waistband. A Beretta M9, he noted. American. Not the standard issue for the Victorian Police, that was for sure. This wasn't Brandt's gun. It was the imposter's … whoever he was.

I have to leave.

The events occurring in the shadows of Jameson were serious. Incredibly serious. Whoever was behind this had just broken into a police station to try and get answers out of him. When that had failed, they'd attempted to kill him. He was now in significantly more danger than before. They knew who he was. The two officers who brought him here were good people, but they wouldn't get answers. Not within the boundaries of the law. That much he knew.

It was time to do something drastic.

He knew other officers would arrive any second. Whether it be the man in the lobby, or Kitchener, or Dawes. He turned right out of the interview room and moved fast and quiet down the hallway, leaving the imposter knocked out cold on the linoleum floor. He did not care who found him there. Or what they did with him.

There was no sign of life in this section of the station. He guessed the Jameson Police Department was short-staffed as it was. Perhaps there were only four officers in the whole place. It was a reasonably large building.

King knew he could vanish effortlessly.

He glimpsed natural light in the gap underneath a wooden door. A way out. He tried the handle. It opened, leading to a evidence room almost entirely devoid of evidence. He saw empty metal shelves lining the walls and a bare concrete floor. A rectangular window was positioned high at the far end of the room.

He could fit through.

He strode past the shelving until he was directly underneath the window. Suddenly, he heard muffled voices from the centre of the station.

Female: 'Holy shit. This guy's wearing Brandt's uniform.'

Male: 'Where'd King go?'

Female: 'I don't know … what the hell! Who moved the table?'

Male: 'Fuck, what's happening?'

Kitchener and Dawes. Even from the other end of the building King could sense their panic. Their inexperience. Small-town cops weren't supposed to deal with situations such as these. They were supposed to take care of speeding tickets and unpaid rent and other menial tasks. Nothing to the degree of missing police officers, and mysterious strangers, and assassinations.

They meant well. But they could not help. King accepted the fact that he would have to deal with this matter himself.

He reached up and tried the window. Locked. He took a deep breath, wrapped his fingers around the handle and gave it a vicious pull. Accompanied by the sound of a flimsy bolt snapping, the window pane flew up. There was just enough room to fit a man through. He gripped the bottom of the windowsill and levered himself up, utilising his upper body strength. In one swift motion he shimmied head-first through the open window and outside the building.

It was a sizeable drop to the dirt. King squeezed one leg out and let go of the ledge, falling silently to the ground. He landed like a cat and straightened, getting his bearings.

He was somewhere around the rear of the police station. The back of the building was nondescript, made of brick and entirely flat. The window he'd escaped through seemed to be the only one on this side of the station. The area was small and claustrophobic, like a prison yard. It didn't look like it had been tended to in years. Weeds sprouted from the base of a high wooden fence and the grass itself was overgrown and brown. On the other side of the fence, the tall pines of the forest cast shadows across the ground.

It was late afternoon. The chaotic events of the day had made time pass quickly. It shocked him to think that less than twenty-four hours earlier, he had been trekking the road from Queensbridge with not a worry on his mind.

But he would not leave these questions unanswered. Not now. He was in too deep. There was one person who could at least fill in some blanks, which would hopefully result in an explanation for the deaths he had witnessed last night.

Kate Cooper.

As he scaled the fence and dropped down into the woods behind the police station, he came to the grim conclusion that she would not give him answers voluntarily. Especially since she had seen him taken away in a police car not an hour earlier.

He sighed. Desperate times called for desperate measures.

He would have to kidnap her.

CHAPTER 15

'Absolutely fucking not,' Billy said, standing on the other side of the same familiar back room. An empty paper plate sat on the table in front of King, previously piled high with chicken cacciatore. He'd graciously accepted the offer of leftovers and wolfed the meal down without hesitation. It had been necessary after the afternoon hike.

The trek back to Jameson had taken hours longer than he'd anticipated. Not long after heading into the forest he'd considered doubling back to the police station. The endless rows of pine trees had begun to induce claustrophobia, to the point where he thought he would never make it out of the forest. Sticking to the main roads would have been a better option, even if it ran the risk of discovery by the police, or a group of furious bikers, or whoever the hell else wanted him dead. That number seemed to be increasing exponentially with each passing day. King wondered how many enemies he would have by the time he left Jameson.

If he could leave.

'Billy, I need your car,' he repeated. 'And I might need to keep it this time.'

'It's all I've got, man.'

'I know.'

'Like, I appreciate everything you did for me. For all of us. But I can't.'

'And normally I would just accept that and move on.'

'Normally?'

'There's something going on in this town. I don't know exactly what, but people are dying.'

'Dying?' Billy said. 'The hell are you talking about?'

King pondered for a second. *Could he trust this man?* He took one look at the post office owner, scared out of his mind, desperately seeking answers. He could.

'I didn't tell you this when we first met, but I saw something on the way into town last night.'

'What?'

'A couple of construction workers. They were shot.'

Billy's jaw visibly loosened. 'This is Jameson. Nothing goes on here.'

'Something is. And the more I think about it the more worried I get.'

'What if you take my car and end up getting killed? I'll never get it back.'

'That would end up a little worse for me than losing your car would be for you.'

'I know, but…'

'If I make it through this alive, I'll return it.'

'Why don't you just leave?'

King cocked his head. 'Leave?'

Billy waved an arm in the air, gesturing to his surroundings. 'This town. Whatever's going on. It has nothing to do with you. You live off the grid anyway. Just keep walking. Forget you ever saw anything.'

'I can't do that.'

'Why not?'

'I just can't. It's hard to explain.'

'You take it upon yourself to help people. It's not your responsibility.'

King snatched a set of keys off the table between them. 'I know it's not. But I'm still doing it.'

'What exactly are you doing with my car?'

'I really can't say.'

'Why?'

'You wouldn't approve.'

Billy nodded, refusing to probe any further. King figured the man was taking effort to distance himself from the situation. The less he knew, the better.

'Alright, King,' Billy said. 'I'm only doing this because of what you did for me.'

'I know.'

'Will I see you again?'

'Maybe. Depends what I find out.'

Billy crossed the room and outstretched a palm. Despite his best efforts to appear calm, his hand trembled ever so slightly. King looked at the man and knew he was confused. Terrified, even. He lived a simplistic, uneventful life that had been upended by King's arrival.

'I'm sorry, Billy,' he said.

'Sorry?'

'Maybe if I hadn't shown up, none of this would have happened. I'm sorry I involved you. I'm sorry you got wrapped up in all this. I'll do my absolute best to fix this situation, but right now I have no idea what I'm walking into. It could be anything. So I can't promise that I'll be back with your car.'

Billy shrugged. 'It's just a car. You're risking a lot more than I am.'

'It's your future.'

'Yeah, and I might die if you don't work out what's happening. So go right ahead. It was dumb of me to complain.'

King reached out and shook Billy's hand. 'Thank you.'

'You're the one who needs thanking.'

King paused. 'Actually, I need one more thing.'

Billy looked at him. 'And that is?'

'You have video footage of the two men picking up the package, right?'

Billy nodded. 'You want a copy?'

'Please.'

He sat down at the desktop computer, looking relieved. King guessed Billy had been expecting a greater favour than a video. Especially after giving away his only vehicle. He slotted a USB drive into the computer and navigated through an array of folders on-screen. Once he found the file he was looking for he dragged it across. Ten seconds later, he handed the stick over. King tucked it into his back pocket.

'I hope that helps,' Billy said. 'Good luck with everything, buddy.'

'I think I'll need it this time,' King said.

He pocketed the car keys and headed for the entrance. He passed Billy's daughter manning the register, sporting the same dismal expression. Like working at a post office was the worst job imaginable.

'When will you be back next?' she quipped as he moved past. 'Seems like you live here now.'

'Maybe never,' King said. 'You keep up that charming smile of yours in the meantime.'

He left her to scoff at the remark and exited the building. By now it was late afternoon. The walk from the police station had carved out a sizeable chunk of the day. The buzz of wildlife from the surrounding forest reached a crescendo as the sun dipped steadily toward the horizon. Judging by its position, it would not set for at least another hour. Plenty of time to carry out what he needed to do.

It wouldn't be easy. Kate would be alert, probably still rattled by the altercation earlier that day. She thought King was someone he wasn't, and that would create fear. Fear would lend her crucial speed. King got in Billy's sedan and fired it up. It started with a familiar rattle. He checked the gas tank. Still more than half full. It wouldn't need refilling for a few days, and by then he planned to be miles away from Jameson.

He pulled out onto the main road, wary that his profile had been raised. He was almost certain that the bikers had high-tailed it out of the area, but if they had decided to stick around they would be looking for him. Determined to end him for causing them trouble. Sure, they were incapacitated, but a confrontation would cause quite the scene. Something he was striving to avoid.

On top of that, he would be priority number one on Kitchener and Dawes' to-do list. He hadn't deliberately shut them off, but he'd spent almost his entire career operating outside of anyone's jurisdiction.

He wasn't about to change that.

He pulled out of the parking lot and kept a reasonable pace as he drove out of town. Passers-by glanced at him intermittently. Perhaps wondering what a massive stranger was doing driving the post office guy's car around. It was irritating, but none seemed to let their gaze linger. None seemed to have ulterior motives.

Soon the buildings grew further apart and the woods wrapped around the road once again. It had taken him just over twenty minutes to walk from the post office to Kate's street earlier that day, which meant it only took a couple by car. He swung the wheel when he saw the gravel path branching off to the left. The sedan's suspension vibrated as it rolled over the new surface. The uneven ground distracted him for just a second.

He jolted when he looked up and saw Kate's car rolling toward his from the other end of the street.

'What the—'

He quickly realised it was a coincidence. She stared straight ahead from behind the wheel, not focused on anything other than the road. Even from a distance he noticed her vice-like hold on the wheel, knuckles white. Her face seemed paler than usual. There was something on her mind. It had lowered her spatial awareness. She didn't notice him.

He had to act.

They would pass each other by within seconds. For a moment he considered swerving into her path. Then he dismissed it. A head-on collision carried with it the likelihood of serious injury. He had no intention of bringing her any harm. He just wanted answers. Such a reckless manoeuvre was unnecessary.

What he wanted to do would take precision. King took a deep breath and focused. He waited until the old Subaru had almost passed him by, then spun the wheel. The nose of his sedan crushed into her rear bumper. A horrid grating sound emanated from the impact point. The noise of metal scraping against metal. His car came to a halt just behind the Subaru, which also screeched to a stop as Kate slammed on the brakes.

He knew she would be more frustrated than scared. From her perspective, some idiot had just accidentally run into her. King opened his door and darted out of the car, pulling the Beretta he'd acquired in the police station out of his belt. The safety was on.

She wouldn't know that.

'Oh my god, you fucking—,' Kate began as she fumbled out of the driver's seat. In the midst of her tirade, she locked eyes with King and noticed the pistol aimed in her direction. Recognition spread across her face. She shut up instantly.

'Hey, Kate,' King said.

'Shit.'

'Long time no see.'

'You escaped custody?'

'I was never in custody.'

'What do you want from me?'

'You won't believe me, but I'm not with whoever made you deliver the package.'

'Oh, I believe you. I worked that out after the cops took you away.'

'You did?'

'You were genuinely confused when I said you were working for them. So I take it you're not.'

'I'm not working with anyone.'

'Then why are you pointing a gun at me?'

'I need to make sure you won't run away.'

'Silence.'

'I'm also going to need you to get in my car.'

'No way.'

'It's for your own safety.'

'How exactly would that be beneficial to me?'

'I need answers. And I want to help. And you're the only person who knows anything about that package.'

'What happened to it?'

'It got picked up by two hitmen.'

She recoiled. 'Hitmen?'

‘I saw them kill two people. Construction workers, who I’d say were in the wrong place at the wrong time and saw something they shouldn’t have.’

She stared at the ground. ‘Fuck. I never should have got involved.’

‘I can help you get out of this. Are you going to trust me?’

‘No. I still have no idea who you are.’

‘And I still need you to get in the car. Sorry.’

After a beat of consideration she stepped away from her Subaru and crossed to the passenger side of his sedan. Although reluctant, it seemed she had come to the conclusion that there were few other options.

‘The neighbours are going to see my car, you know,’ she said. ‘Just sitting here. Empty. In the middle of the street. They’ll call the police.’

‘It doesn’t matter. I’m already wanted anyway. I broke out of the station to get here. But you really shouldn’t have told me that.’

‘Why?’ she said again.

‘What if I wanted to hurt you? You just reminded me to hide your car.’

She shrugged amicably. ‘You’re not going to hurt me.’

‘You’ve changed your mind on me very quickly.’

'I had some time to think. And I guess I overreacted. You're definitely not with them. You would have killed me otherwise. They don't fuck around.'

'Let's talk about this in the car.'

'Can I at least get my bag? It has my laptop and things. It'll get stolen if I just leave it here.'

He shrugged in return. 'Sure.'

She ducked into the Subaru and came out with a beige carry bag. She slung it over her shoulder and headed for Billy's sedan. King kept the gun on her, wary of any sudden movements. He couldn't let her get away. She was the only link between him and the people killing witnesses in Jameson.

She ducked into the passenger's seat seat. King followed suit, still aiming the gun in her direction.

She looked at him. 'You're really not one of them, are you?'

'That's only what I've been saying for the past three hours.'

'Then who are you?'

'Just a guy.'

'I'm sorry I got you arrested.'

'It's fine. In fact, it ended up helping.'

'Huh?'

'There's a police officer missing. Which means this is a lot more serious than I thought.'

'I think they've killed a lot of people,' Kate said, staring into the distance.

'How do you know?'

'I don't. I know as much as you do. They've kept me in the dark this whole time, I swear. I was paid three grand to deliver that package to the post office … I think to keep themselves off any cameras. All my instructions were delivered over the phone and I've never seen a single one of them. And now you're following me around, demanding answers. I'm fucking scared. I just want to get away from all of this.'

King lowered the pistol. She meant no harm, that much was clear. 'Where were you headed just then?'

'To get payment.'

He raised an eyebrow, surprised. 'From them?'

She nodded. 'They called me ten minutes ago. Said they had my money ready and waiting. Told me to drive to an old landfill site a few kilometres down the road. It overflowed years ago and the owners closed it down.'

'And you decided to go?'

'Well, yeah,' she said. 'I'm dead broke. Why do you think I did this in the first place?'

'Terrible idea.'

'Why?'

'Did you miss the part where I said they were killing off witnesses?'

'Oh…'

Kate fell silent, the situation dawning on her in a new light. She stared vacantly out the window, processing what might have occurred had her journey gone uninterrupted.

King reversed a dozen feet, then guided the sedan around her empty Subaru. The door lay wide open. Neighbours would know something was wrong with a single glance. It didn't matter. There were greater concerns than the worry of Jameson's residents.

'Are you sure they would have killed me?' she said. Her voice had grown timid. Scared.

'We'll find out soon enough,' King said.

'Wait, surely you're not going to…'

Kate trailed off as he pulled the car out onto the main road and sped away from Jameson, towards the site.

CHAPTER 16

'You're making a serious mistake,' Kate said.

King stared out the windscreen at the looming pine trees on either side of the road. They cast broad shadows, blocking much of the natural light apart from the stretch of sky directly overhead.

He sped up. Determined to catch whoever was waiting for Kate off-guard.

'It's the only lead I have,' he said.

'They'll kill you too.'

'I can handle myself.'

'And who are you, exactly?'

'Jason King.'

'You told me that earlier, when you knocked on my door.'

'Well, that's who I am.'

'What do you have to do with all of this?'

'Not much.'

'Have you always been this talkative?'

'I used to talk less.'

'I can't imagine that's possible.'

They rounded a bend and he noticed a gap in the trees ahead. Another road, twisting away into the woods. The rest of the view was obscured. No vantage point. No place to set up watch. Just a sharp corner and then another indiscriminate gravel road.

'Is that the place?' he said, pointing.

Kate nodded.

King slammed on the brakes and the sedan screeched to a halt in the middle of the road. It sat on the asphalt, idle, engine running. There was no passing traffic in either direction to worry about. They were in the middle of nowhere.

Kate stared at him. 'What are you doing?'

'Thinking. We're probably heading into a trap.'

'Isn't that what you just told me before?'

'I'm going ahead.'

'I figured that.'

'I've walked into worse situations before. You're welcome to get out here.'

'And just stand in the middle of the road and wait for someone to shoot me?'

'Kate, get out.'

She shook her head. 'I feel safer with you.'

'You thought I was going to kill you ten minutes ago.'

'Now I know you won't. And I'd rather stick with you than be alone.'

He shrugged. 'Suit yourself. I can't promise you anything though. I don't know what we'll find.'

'I'm not asking you to. But I want to see who put me through all this. If anyone's there.'

'Okay.'

He accelerated. By now he had grown accustomed to the change of surface. The sedan bounced and jolted across the gravel. This path seemed a little narrower than Kate's street. One way. It looped and twisted through the woods, lined with dead leaves and pine needles. King kept one hand on the wheel and the other wrapped around the Beretta. Ready to react to anything unusual. Kate stayed silent, chewing a thumbnail. Her nerves were palpable.

Suddenly the tree line expanded as the trail opened out into a small clearing, its ground just as uneven. King guessed it used to be a makeshift parking lot. Now it lay completely empty. Trees boxed in three sides. The fourth was home to a chain-link fence topped with barbed wire, running the length of the clearing. He looked through its steel mesh and saw the ground drop sharply away. The forest ahead dipped into a sea of green, stretching as far as the eye could see. A swathe of landfill covered the valley floor. He saw the mountains of junk stretching across the man-made region. Entire sections of forest had been chopped down to make way for the pit. Beyond the fence, a precarious path trailed down to the valley floor, just wide enough to fit a dump truck. He guessed the fence had been built when the place shut down, to prevent vehicular access.

Whatever the case, there was no-one here to meet Kate.

King reached over and placed a hand on her shoulder. Warning her. 'Stay here. Be ready.'

She nodded, eyes wide, gaze flicking around the empty clearing. King opened the door and got out. In the relative silence of the area, the creaking hinges sounded deafening. Like the action had drawn all the attention in the world.

A breeze blew across the valley, slotting through the fence and whispering through the clearing. King's clothes flapped. He felt a shiver run down his spine. It was too quiet. There would be no meeting here. That much he was sure of.

He turned his attention to the valley. After a lifetime of training to seek out threats, he'd become quite adept at it. There was little to see. Nothing but forest, and the sun steadily declining toward the opposite horizon. It sat behind a cluster of clouds, eliminating the glare.

That was what saved his life.

If King had been squinting, he wouldn't have seen what he saw. On the far side of the valley. Amidst the trees.

The unmistakeable sight of a muzzle flash.

It sent him back to a different time, when his whole existence had revolved around nothing but conflict. That period of his life had hammered such a sight into his subconscious. He found himself acting out of instinct. In the same moment that he saw the small burst of light he felt his legs give out, darting away from their purchase on the gravel automatically. He didn't even think about the action.

He just dropped.

Without a moment to spare.

The bullet passed a couple of inches over his hair. An impressively accurate shot, especially from that distance. If he'd kept his head in the same position for a millisecond longer the round would have taken the top half of his head off. He'd seen it done before. It wasn't a pretty sight. Then Kate would have frozen up, shellshocked from seeing King die in an explosion of brain matter. She'd be a sitting duck inside the sedan.

But that didn't happen, because King was faster than any man his enemies had seen before.

The noise of the rapport had yet to reach the clearing by the time he had scrambled to his feet. Judging his distance from the marksman, he guessed it would take close to two seconds for the sound to reach his eardrums. Right now it would be echoing across the valley. And whoever was behind the gun would be adjusting their aim.

'Kate, down!' King roared.

She still hadn't realised what had just happened. Then the *crack* of the discharge hit them, and she flinched involuntarily. She saw King running for the car, and she heard the sound, and she put two and two together. She ducked into the footwell.

Another round destroyed the windscreen of the sedan, punching a hole through the thick glass. The entire pane shattered. A cacophony of noise hit King at once. The breaking of glass, the almighty racket of the sniper rounds, Kate's panicked screaming.

He wrenched the door open, fearing the worst. She cowered in the footwell, visibly shaken but unhurt. He saw the passenger seat's headrest torn to shreds. The second bullet had smashed through the windscreen and buried itself inside the polyester. She'd avoided death by a hair.

King ducked into the driver's seat and dove out of the line of sight. The portion of seat above him rattled suddenly, accompanied by the sound of tearing cloth. He swore. The sniper had his aim locked on. He was hitting each target with remarkable precision. As King hesitated, a fourth shot struck the front of the sedan.

Once again, he shook his head in surprise. Now that the marksman knew both targets were out of sight, the engine had become a priority. The sniper was improvising as the altercation unfolded. It would only take one well-placed shot to immobilise the vehicle.

And then they were stranded.

King clicked the safety off the Beretta and fired three times out the open windscreen, keeping his head well below the dashboard. The shots were blind, but hopefully they would achieve their intended effect. He had no time to deduce whether they had paid off or not. He simply had to act, and hope the sniper had been rattled by the returning gunfire.

He had to hope he didn't catch a bullet in the brain.

He'd left the car running, so all it took to get moving was a quick change of gear and a vicious stamp on the accelerator. He felt the tyres spin. It took a second or two for them to find purchase. Then the sedan shot off the mark.

King kept his head low, turning the wheel in a sharp arc, aiming for the path they'd come through by memory alone. He felt the pressure in his stomach as they rocketed toward the other end of the clearing.

Convinced the sniper would have difficulty hitting a moving target with precision, he sat up and got his bearings.

Lucky he did.

They had drifted off-target. Their sedan wasn't on track to enter the path anymore. He panicked as he saw the bonnet rushing straight for one of the pine trees. Neither he or Kate were wearing seatbelts. The collision would throw them through the open windscreen, almost definitely killing them given the speed they had picked up. He swerved hard, throwing Kate against the passenger door. He heard the metal groan, but the door held. The sedan lost traction on the gravel and skidded. He held firm on the wheel, battling for control. In the middle of the manoeuvre, a fifth bullet shattered the rear window and sunk into the dashboard, sending a cloud of sparks flying.

Kate screamed.

Finally the wheels regained control and King gunned the car back up the path. The forest enveloped them once more. Now they would be harder to hit, but the first stretch of the trail was dead straight. Perhaps two hundred feet in length. There was still an opening for the enemy sniper. He waved at Kate to stay in the footwell and ducked again.

Twin jolts shook the chassis as another pair of bullets sunk into the sedan's rear, threatening to find their mark in one of the tyres at any time. If one of them burst, King knew they would be incapacitated. It would take little effort to ambush them at the top of the path.

He left it until he felt they would hit the trees on the far side of the bend at any moment. Then he gave the steering wheel a quick pump in either direction, swerving the car from left to right. Any aim the sniper had settled on would be rendered useless. Following the move, King righted himself in the driver's seat.

This time, he'd judged their position better. The car was just about to reach the turn. He heard the displacement of air as a final shot whisked past the driver's side door, but that was the last chance the marksman would have to hit them. King gripped the wheel with both hands and took the car round the corner at breakneck speed.

And just like that, the trees blocked them from view.

They'd survived.

CHAPTER 17

'You can get up now,' he said.

'Oh my god,' Kate muttered, crawling back into the passenger's seat. She looked at King for a long period of time.

He turned and met her eyes. 'What?'

'You … reacted so fast. I don't know what happened, I've never been in a situation like that before. I felt so weak. Like it was hard to move.'

'That's shock. Don't worry, I'm not inhuman. We all experience that.'

Her face had become pale and clammy. 'How are you so calm?'

'That kind of thing used to be my job.'

Kate didn't know what to say to that. She paused, looking at him. Deep in thought. 'Do you want to talk about it?'

'Not really.'

She nodded. 'Figured as much.'

They sat in silence as King drove back up the path, towards civilisation. The wind beat at their faces, howling in through the windscreen's frame. He let his heart rate slow. It was a trick he had practiced in the midst of combat many times in the past, when staying calm and level-headed was the only means of survival. Now he could recover from the adrenalin rush of a life-or-death situation at will.

Kate was not handling the sensation well. Her hands shook violently as she stared out the passenger window. King remembered back to the first time he'd been shot at, to the sheer terror he'd experienced. There was something otherworldly about the feeling, when your life lay in the hands of how accurate your enemy was. So he wasn't surprised by her reaction. Not at all. Coming close to death was a horrifying experience. Which perhaps made it worse that he had grown so accustomed to it.

On a whim, he reached over and took her hand. 'Hey.'

She looked at him. Tears in her eyes.

'I know what it feels like,' he said.

'Do you?'

'I felt that way once. Everyone does. I hope you never see enough of that stuff to find it normal. I wish I hadn't, but I have.'

'How can that be normal?'

He sighed. 'I'll tell you later. Now isn't the time.'

She shrugged through tears. 'I'll get over it.'

'It's not something to get over. It's natural. Trust me, I wish I could feel that scared again.'

'Why on earth would you want to feel like this?'

'Maybe I'd try harder to avoid these type of situations.'

'We're getting close to the road,' she said.

'I know. Get in the footwell. There could be more of them up here.'

Kate swallowed hard, her hands still trembling. She sunk below the dashboard, away from the line of sight of anyone aiming weapons at them. King didn't want to emphasise how close they had come to death back in the clearing. In fact, he found it hard to believe himself. But there was no time to dwell on the past.

The path opened ahead, spilling out onto the main road. There was little visibility in either direction. King wouldn't be surprised if there were ten men waiting on either side of the forest, weapons up, ready to fire at any moment.

He wouldn't let them hit their shots.

He pressed the accelerator into the floor and the sedan picked up speed. Travelling at close to sixty miles an hour, it rocketed off the gravel path and its wheels spun on the asphalt. King shot a quick glance in either direction, scouting for any sign of trouble.

Nothing.

No men.

No weapons.

Just empty road for as far as the eye could see.

He slowed to the speed limit and turned sharply, putting them on track to return to Jameson. Kate stayed in the footwell, eyes squeezed shut, knuckles clenched. He tapped her on the shoulder.

'All clear,' he said.

She scrambled back into the seat. 'No-one there?'

'No-one.'

'This doesn't feel right.'

'I agree,' King said. 'Maybe there's not as many of them as I thought.'

She returned to chewing her nails. 'So what the hell do we do now? We don't know anything. That didn't give us any answers. All I know is that they want to kill me.'

'They're eliminating any possible witnesses. I have a video of the two hitmen picking up the package you dropped off. Did you get a look at it?'

'It was just a box. They left it at my front door and I dropped it off. I didn't look. I just wanted it over and done with. I knew they were doing something shady.'

'Was it heavy?'

'Reasonably.'

'Kate, I'm going to need more than that.'

She turned to him. 'I don't know anything else. I don't know how we get out of this, and I don't know why we're being attacked. Do you have *any* reason that people might want to hurt you? Because I don't.'

He drummed his fingers on the wheel, deep in thought. 'No-one knows I'm here.'

'So what is this?'

'It doesn't have anything to do with us. We're pawns. Something bigger is going on here.'

'You're saying we can just leave? Forget about all this?'

'You can if you want.'

'I don't want to.'

He looked across. 'No?'

She didn't respond. Turned away. Looked out the window again, deep in thought. He stayed quiet and let the sounds of the forest take over. They passed her street once again. Her Subaru was still there, parked in the middle of the road.

'We can't go back to my place,' Kate said. 'They know where I live.'

'I know.'

He kept driving, heading for Jameson.

'I left England a year ago,' she said suddenly. 'My whole life I lived in this tiny flat in Brixton. My older brother fell in with he wrong crowd. Bunch of thugs, always coming in and out of home. Drugs, guns, you name it. It didn't take long for them to start harassing me. Threatening to rape me. And as soon as I got scared, I up and left. Bought a plane ticket and chose the smallest town in a country as far away as possible. Left my friends behind. Left my family behind. Just told them I was going.'

'I'm sorry to hear that,' King said. He reached across and gripped her hand.

'So I'm not just going to leave again,' she said. 'I really don't care what happens. I'm sick of getting rattled and just backing away.'

'This is different, Kate. You could die.'

'Whatever. I have no work experience, nothing to start a new life with. Everyone around here has come to know me. I can get by on odd jobs. If I leave here, I've got nothing. I'm staying.'

'I'll do my best to make sure it's safe for you to stay.'

The sedan trawled into the town centre just as the sun disappeared behind the trees. Old streetlights scattered along the main road flickered to life, casting a warm halogen glow over the footpath on either side.

'Where are we headed?' Kate said.

'I think I can get us a safe place for the night.'

He pulled Billy's sedan into the lot of the same motel he'd stayed at the night before. The same small light shone above reception, inviting them in. There were no other cars around them. A quiet night of business. He made sure to tuck the Beretta into his waistband before heading in. Best to keep the gun out of sight.

The same elderly lady manned the front desk. She gave a genuine beam as the pair stepped in through the front door, accompanied by the tinny jangle of a bell overhead.

'Mr. King!' she said. 'I wasn't sure if I'd see you again.'

'Hi, Yvonne,' he said. 'Nice to see you.'

'And who's this?' she said with the hint of a wry smile.

'This is Kate, one of the locals. Would we be able to stay the night again?'

'Of course. I fixed up your room earlier today. You can use the same one. If I'm not mistaken, you still have the key.'

King tapped the pocket of his windbreaker and smiled. 'I do too. Sorry about that. It's been a busy day to say the least.'

'That's quite alright,' Yvonne said. 'I knew you'd return it at some point.'

King reached into his other pocket and withdrew a pair of fifty-dollar notes from the stack tucked away. He slid them over the counter. 'The extra is for your generosity last night.'

Yvonne smiled. 'Thank you very much.'

King leant on the counter with both elbows. 'Yvonne, listen. I have a favour to ask.'

'Don't worry,' she said. 'I already know. I won't tell anyone.'

Silence. 'What?'

'I already had a couple of police officers pop in today. They were looking for you. I said I'd never heard of you.'

He was momentarily taken aback. At a loss for words, he cocked his head. 'Why did you do that? I could be anyone.'

'I've been on this earth a long time, son. I know a good man when I see one. You don't mean anyone harm. Whatever you're doing, you're trying to help.'

He smiled. 'Well, I'm not sure how you know that, Yvonne, but thank you.'

'You two lay low for as long as you need, dear.'

King nodded his thanks and led Kate out of reception and upstairs to the same room he'd stayed in the night before, the number '4' still scribbled on the door. He unlocked it and stepped inside. The room had been cleaned to perfection, the type of job that could only have been accomplished after years of experience. The bed had been made, the toiletries replaced, the curtains straightened, the floor vacuumed. He guessed Yvonne had been in the motel business for a very long time. Perhaps why she was able to work out his intentions so effortlessly.

'You stayed here last night?' Kate said, following him in.

He nodded. 'First night here.'

'What did you see on the way into town? What got you wrapped up in all of this?'

King sat down on the bed and pondered his next move. It would do no good to keep secrets from her. They had to combine what little information they had if there was any hope of working out what was happening behind closed doors in the town of Jameson. He wasn't sure if she would react well to what he had done. But after a long moment of consideration, he decided he wouldn't hold back.

So he told her everything.

Kate sat in the chair opposite the bed, listening to what had transpired the night before. She gave nothing away in her expression as King spoke. He told her of how he'd watched the construction workers die, and how he'd retaliated against the killers, eventually murdering them both. Still, she did not react. When he finally finished she sat completely still, mulling over what she had heard.

'You killed them?' she said.

'I've killed a lot of people, Kate.'

'Bad people?'

He ran a hand through his hair. 'I wish I could sit here and tell you that I'm some kind of hero, but if you add up everything I've done I can't be. I always try to do good things, but over my career I've killed far too many people for it to be acceptable. No matter how bad they are.'

'Were you a soldier?'

'A very specialised one. I operated off the books, outside the boundaries of the law. The division of the military that I worked for officially doesn't exist. And sometimes I found myself in situation where if I didn't succeed, the consequences would be enormous. So sometimes I went above what is right. To get the job done. And I don't know if I can stop.'

'You mean with what's happening here?'

'I think I might go too far. If something terrible is going on behind closed doors here, it might make me revert to my old ways. And I don't want you to think I'm some kind of monster.'

'You're not,' Kate said. 'Not at all.'

'You sure?'

'I'm sure. You saved my life.'

'That doesn't make me a good person.'

'Your intentions are pure. I've spent less than a day with you and I can already tell that.'

He smiled. 'Didn't you tell me to fuck off this morning?'

'I'm not telling you that now, am I?' she said.

He looked at her and saw a woman who had spent much of the last year in isolation, dealing with her issues, attempting to forge a new life out here in the woods. He saw much of himself in her. That had been the whole point of his journey to Australia. To escape the demons of his past. To try and find some kind of normality.

Perhaps they could find it together.

He leant in and pressed his lips against hers. Briefly, he thought he'd made the wrong move.

But he hadn't.

She kissed back with a passion King hadn't anticipated. Her lips were soft and as they fell back onto the bed he found himself wondering when he'd last enjoyed a moment as much as this. For as long as he could remember his life had been a whirlwind of pain and hostility. Now he let everything slip away and just focused on Kate, the way she moved against him, the way she touched him, caressed him. They locked eyes and King saw years worth of pent-up frustration in her green irises. He knew his probably showed the same, or worse.

As they tugged at each other's clothing he noticed she was lithe, fit from physical exercise. He reached back, eyes closed, still kissing her. He pulled the bedsheets free. They slipped underneath and let the tension of the day dissipate. Nothing in the outside world mattered at that moment, not the killers in the forest or the imposter at the police station or the ten years of carnage King had wreaked across the globe that came back to him in night tremors. All forgotten. They moved against each other, naked, gasping, finding relief in the madness.

When it was over they lay back, out of breath. Kate rested her head against his chest and draped a bare leg over him and closed her eyes, relishing the calm. King felt his eyes grow heavy. Then his stomach grumbled, reminding him to eat. He rolled over and looked at her.

'Dinner?'

She nodded. 'I know a place.'

They went down to the main strip together, hand-in-hand. King stayed wary for any signs of trouble, but it seemed whoever wanted them dead had called it a night. Kate led him into a deserted diner near the end of the strip, sporting a handful of two-person booths pressed against the dirty front windows. The tabletops were scratched and the checkered tile floor looked like it hadn't been washed in some time, but the owner was kind and the food was good. King ate and talked, and before he knew it the sky outside had fully darkened. When they finished they paid for the meal, scurried back to the motel and fell into bed.

It had been a monumental day. The bikers and the arrest and the breakout and the kidnapping and the assassination attempt shifted into a kaleidoscope of bad memories.

He slipped into a much-needed sleep, finding some semblance of relief amongst the chaos.

CHAPTER 18

They'd fallen asleep early — not long after ten in the evening — and as a result King found himself awake at just before six the next morning. He couldn't sleep in anymore. Not since the military. That constant feeling that he had to be awake and alert to prevent an ambush would never leave him. For years he'd trained to be wary at all times and now it affected every aspect of his daily life.

Kate lay beside him, her arm still across his chest, her naked breasts pressed against his shoulder. She looked peaceful in sleep. He shifted his position in the bed and she stirred. She opened her eyes. Looked at him.

'Hey.'

He smiled. 'Hey.'

'That was fun.'

'We were supposed to do investigative work last night,' he said.

'Well, that's a shame, isn't it?'

King kissed her again, relishing the feeling. 'We don't have much to go off. I've got a USB drive, with video footage of the two men I told you about picking up your package. That's it.'

'Worth a shot. We can watch it on my laptop.' She hesitated. 'What would you have done without me?'

'Huh?'

'You don't have a computer. No phone, nothing. You're a ghost.'

King stared at the ceiling, one arm around her. 'Getting off the grid was the whole point of coming here. When I up and left I knew there would be a lot of people wanting to follow my every move. I didn't want anyone to be able to contact me, or know where I am. It meant leaving everything behind.'

'No luggage?'

'I barely had any possessions in the first place.'

'What about clothes?'

'I've just been buying them along the way. I'll get a carry bag soon, and start fresh. But I wanted to sever all ties to my past. That meant nothing from America came with me.'

'That's efficient at least. Where were you planning to go from here?'

'Wherever. I've got all the time in the world now.'

They got dressed and Kate retrieved her laptop from the chair near the door. She slid a thin notebook out and turned it on.

'Got the stick?' she said.

He handed her the USB and she plugged it in, bringing up a folder containing a single file.

'That's it,' he said.

She smiled. 'I figured that. You're a little bit ancient, aren't you?'

'I'm not that old,' he said, smiling.

She turned. 'How old *are* you? You keep saying you retired.'

'Thirty-two. You retire young in my field.'

'Huh,' Kate said, mulling over the new information. 'I'm twenty-seven. We're not that far apart after all.'

'You're saying I look old?'

She laughed. 'No, not at all. But the way you talk doesn't line up with your age. At thirty-two you should be worrying about your mortgage, or complaining about your nine-to-five, or having a mid-life crisis.'

'I guess I've seen a lot.'

'I guess so.'

She double-clicked on the video file, bringing up grainy security footage inside the post office. The camera faced the row of PO boxes. For a long minute there was no movement. Then in the top corner of the screen the doors swung open and the pair of contract killers walked in. They moved quickly, both determined to draw as little attention as possible. They paused by one of the largest boxes. The man on the left produced a key and unlocked it with a twist of the wrist.

The package gave nothing away. It was square and wrapped in brown paper, indistinguishable from any other parcel. The man on the right — who King recognised as Buzzcut — withdrew it and they headed for the door.

'Fuck,' King whispered. A dead end. Now they were left clutching at straws.

And then in the final few seconds of the video Buzzcut ripped open the top of the package and extracted a slim black device. A smartphone. He opened his jacket and tucked the phone inside, into a pocket. The other man opened the door and the pair disappeared from sight.

'Well, that's something,' Kate said.

King stared long and hard at the image of the empty post office frozen on the screen. It definitely *was* something. Which was far more than he'd expected to see.

He strode over to the bed and snatched his windbreaker off the duvet. The Beretta went back in his waistband.

'Where are you going?' she said.

'I know where that phone is.'

'Oh, god,' she said. 'You're seriously not going to…'

'That's what this kind of life entails, Kate. Killing bad people. Searching dead bodies. Like I said, it would be healthier for you to have nothing to do with me.'

'You know that's not true.'

He couldn't help but smile. 'Stay here, okay? I'll be back in an hour.'

'And if you're not?'

He paused. 'Then get as far away from Jameson as possible, and forget all about what happened here. Exactly like you said.'

'I told you I'm not—'

King crossed the room and rested his hands on her shoulders. 'Look, I don't mean to sound arrogant, but hundreds of people have tried to kill me before. If I die today, then these people are trained professionals beyond anything I've ever seen. Which means that you will die if you stay here, no questions. It's not worth sticking to your refusal to leave if it means getting killed. Maybe even slowly.'

'I don't—'

'Promise me you'll leave if I don't come back.' He could see the tears brimming in the corner of her eyes.

'I don't want to,' she said. 'There's nowhere to go.'

'You can go anywhere. It's better than being dead.'

Reluctantly, she nodded. 'Okay.'

He kissed her. Unsure for how long. When they finally parted, Kate touched a hand to his face and looked him in the eyes. 'Will I see you again?'

He snatched Billy's car keys off the coffee table and opened the motel door. 'Of course. You think I'm going to let them do anything to me?'

She shook her head.

He knew it would do both of them no good to linger and contemplate what would happen if he didn't come back. So he closed the door behind him and made his way down to the carport without a shred of hesitation.

It was an icy morning, much like the last one. A thin layer of dew covered everything. The sun had only just risen and the temperature still hovered close to zero. Before he got in the car, he glanced down the main road, looking into town. There was little activity at this time of morning. He guessed the daily bustle didn't start until around seven. All around him, the ringing cacophony of bird calls added to the eerie feel of the woods.

He decided he didn't like the country all that much. Its stillness and tranquility had been ruined by the chaos of the last two days. Now the isolation only meant his death would go completely unnoticed. His body would rot in the woods. An unnerving thought, to say the least.

It took several attempts to get the car started, which he chalked up to leaving it outside as the night froze over. On the third try it coughed and spat to life, eventually settling into a rhythmic chugging. He reversed out of the parking space and set off along the mountain roads, which had become all too familiar. He knew the rough location of the metal work factory. He hoped there would be some way to access the clearing by vehicle.

It took five minutes to reach the area where he'd seen the two construction workers die, and in that time he did not pass a single vehicle on the roads. Once again, the emptiness of the landscape sent a shiver down his spine.

Zero witnesses. Zero help.

After trawling through a maze of deserted routes he came across yet another indiscriminate gravel path. It seemed there was one everywhere he looked. He pulled the sedan up to its entrance and stared down its length. It trailed away into the forest. He couldn't determine exactly where it ended, but it seemed to head toward the general vicinity of the factory. He would never know for sure unless he tried it. There was nothing to do but hope he wasn't heading into a trap, spin the wheel and guide the car down the rocky path.

As he drove, he grimly accepted that he would most likely be heading to another dead end. If the phone had a passcode, or simply didn't hold any useful information, then he was unsure of what to do next. He'd been moving forward this entire time, yet his barebones investigation would probably come to a screeching halt at the bottom of this path. Nevertheless, he forced the thought to the back of his mind and concentrated on what lay ahead. It was what he'd always done. He wasn't about to give up yet. Not until he was dead, or he'd found out who was trying to kill him.

The path opened out into the clearing, just as he'd thought. He pulled to a stop in the middle of the dead grass. The factory lay ahead. In the daytime it was far less imposing. Still large, the majority of its exterior had rusted from exposure to the cold and the wind. Metal awnings shadowed the surrounding ground, and a twisting array of brick and steel arced toward the sky. King spotted the open warehouse door on the ground floor. The construction workers' pickup truck still sat where he'd left it, battered into a wreck. Further inside, he saw the machine that housed the four bodies. A cylindrical cone. Some kind of industrial grinder.

What came next — searching the bodies — would not be a pleasant task. He got out of the sedan, hoping that the decomposition process had yet to begin. After only two days in often sub-zero temperatures, he didn't think it would have.

He strode into the warehouse and listened to the creaks of the empty factory around him. The pickup was parked close enough to the cone to act as a stepping stone. He leapt onto the bonnet, which groaned under his weight. He gripped the rim of the cone and scurried over the edge.

The entire ordeal turned out to be less disgusting than he had anticipated.

Overnight the bodies had frozen. They lay stiff and rigid, completely pale, lifeless. Far less of a problem than if they had been kept in heat for two nights. King had seen enough dead men in his time to remain unperturbed. He opened Buzzcut's jacket and peered at it in the gloom. Sure enough, there was an inside pocket at chest height which he'd missed on his first search, held shut by a single button. He prised it open and withdrew the iPhone that lay inside.

He pressed the home button, and to his surprise the screen fired up. The small battery symbol in the top right corner indicated it had less than four percent left. Which wasn't a problem, as either Kate would have a charger or the hardware store in town would.

He leapfrogged out of the cone, leaving the bodies behind. Hopefully they could be at peace and he would never have to look at them again. As he crossed the stretch of ground to the entrance, heading back the way he'd come, he decided to try the phone. He turned the screen on once again and flicked sideways.

It unlocked instantly.

The sheer stupidity of Buzzcut's actions surprised him. He peered down at the home screen, wondering just why a hitman would fail to secure his phone. Perhaps he'd been confident enough to throw caution to the wind, sure that he would not meet his match in a small country town like Jameson. King stepped out into the empty clearing, still staring down in disbelief. The lack of a passcode had thrown his awareness out the window.

Which meant he momentarily lost concentration on his surroundings.

When he looked up, he realised the clearing wasn't so empty after all.

His sedan was surrounded. But not by mysterious hitmen or assassins. Four men stood facing him, all brandishing state-of-the-art automatic weaponry. All sporting bruises and swollen faces and jagged cuts. All men he recognised.

The bikers.

CHAPTER 19

'Long time no see, pal!' the nearest man called.

It was Jed. No doubt hopped up on painkillers. His jaw had turned black and blue and there was a strip of duct tape covering the wound on the top of his head. Even from a distance away, he looked like shit. Skinny stood beside him. Behind them was Beefy, and behind him was the first man King had knocked out, who he had yet to ascribe a label to.

King couldn't believe that they had returned. He knew he'd made a mistake by keeping them alive, but he hadn't found it within himself to kill the four men back in the clubhouse, even after what they had done. They were just local thugs, after all. They had deserved a beating, but not death. And Beefy had looked at him as if he were the devil incarnate. Such fear couldn't be faked. King had been certain that the four of them would flee. *So why were they here?*

Then he noticed the weapons they held, and everything made sense.

King recognised the design all too well. There had been enough of them around during his time in the Special Forces. Colt M4 carbine assault rifles, issued to the US military. Brand new, shiny. As if they'd been taken right off the production room floor. Expensive, exclusive firearms that were entirely out of place in the hands of a ragtag group of small-town bikers.

These guys had probably been intercepted on their way out of town by those in the shadows of Jameson. Geared up with state-of-the-art weaponry and told to go headhunting for Jason King.

Big mistake.

'Hey there, Jed,' King said, heading for them.

Jed and Skinny raised their weapons like the amateurs they were. They held the massive rifles in trembling hands. King knew they had never used assault rifles before.

He had.

'Keep your hands up when you come over here,' Jed said.

'That's good, Jed,' King said. 'You sound stern. I like it. Much more imposing than sitting on the dirt and sobbing.'

'Shut the fuck up.'

'Didn't think you'd come back.'

'We did.'

'I can see that. How much did they pay you?'

'Huh?'

'How much were you offered to kill me?'

‘What are you talking about?’

‘Those guns you’re holding,’ King said. ‘Who gave you those?’

Skinny perked up. ‘They’re ours.’

King laughed. Spitefully. Sarcastically. ‘No they’re not. You’re a bunch of backwood thugs who haven’t seen a real fight in your life. I took care of all of you without breaking a sweat. Now you come back with an arsenal of guns, because you all know you won’t be able to do anything against me unless you get help from your sugar daddy. Am I right?’

King knew he didn’t stand a chance from twenty feet away. If the bikers desired, they could light him up at a moment’s notice. He’d die, without a doubt. His heart pounded against his chest wall, pumping his veins with adrenalin, but on the outside he made sure to exude cockiness. He kept his demeanour confident and arrogant and insulting. If he could antagonise the bikers to the point where they decided to get up close and personal, then he had a chance.

He was far from the one in control. But he made it seem like he was. He preyed on their desire to show him who was boss.

It worked swimmingly.

Jed and Skinny, guns up, made for him. They closed the gap until they were within touching distance. Another big mistake. Jed walked with a pronounced limp, no doubt still battered from the altercation the previous day. He prodded King with the barrel.

'Get on your knees,' he said.

As King dropped to the ground, he scrutinised their M4's up close. Once again he struggled to comprehend how such powerful arms had been transported to Jameson. Who were these people supplying them? What reach did they have? Whatever the case, it was more than clear that he was now a definite target, and not just someone in the way. His enemies had, instead of showing their faces, supplied a bunch of local bullies with enough weaponry to arm a special forces unit and sent them after him. And they would succeed in getting the job done unless he capitalised on the situation.

Jed saw the object in King's waistband and withdrew the Beretta. He tossed it away into the overgrown grass. Disarming him.

King began to laugh. At first, sniggering. Then that built to a crescendo, until he was cackling in glee. He made sure to make eye contact with Jed's weapon.

'What the fuck is so funny?' Jed said.

'You guys really are amateurs.'

'You say that, but you're the one on your knees.'

'You're not going to kill me.'

'Pretty sure I am, you dumb fuck.'

'Don't think so.'

'And why is that?'

'You've all got the safety on.'

King said it with such disdain that for a brief, panicked moment … they believed him.

Both Jed and Skinny's eyes darted to their weapons, searching for the safety near the trigger, wondering if they really had made such a colossal mistake.

It was a fraction of a second of hesitation.

All that a man like King needed.

He exploded off his knees. A single burst of energy, tapping into something deep within, some kind of primal rage. It lent him a strength and a speed that he knew no common civilian could match. A rush that he'd trained himself to unlock when a split second could mean the difference between life and death. He reached up and snatched Jed's gun with unrestrained power. The sudden movement shocked the man, causing an involuntary reaction. A flinch. His grip loosened.

That would do.

King ripped the gun away and spun it around and slotted his finger perfectly into the trigger guard and pulled down. All in a single swift movement. Streamlined, with the practiced flow of a trained professional. Something these men were very far from.

The weapon fired instantaneously. Safety off.

It had never been on, but the statement had made the bikers pause. Made them question their decisions. Made them hesitate for that minuscule amount of time that — in combat — meant death.

He unloaded the entirety of the thirty-round box magazine before the other three had time to aim. They all died in a blaze of gunfire, jerking like marionettes on strings, blood spurting from their torsos like a grotesque fireworks show. King saw all four collapse. Their limbs hung limp, signifying that they were all corpses. Their weapons cascaded away, eliminating any threat of danger.

He knew he had escaped catching a stray bullet by a hair. He also knew that a hair was all it took. King thrived in the milliseconds separating life and death. He'd been there too many times to count. That talent had kept alive all these years. Once again, it had yet to fail him.

Unloading a full M4 cartridge created a deafening rattle. He knew it would be heard for a mile in any direction, and he hoped this section of the forest was largely uninhabited. But it didn't matter either way. If anyone was drawn to investigate the noise, he would be long gone by the time they arrived.

He let the sudden energy fade away. By now, the steps had become a practiced ritual. He'd calmed himself after the incident with the sniper, and he would ensure he calmed himself now. The blood-pumping rush of a firefight was useful in the moment, but now he had to remain level-headed. Calm. Rational. Saner heads prevailed when the rush that came with killing had dissipated.

The four bikers had sprawled out over the grass, spread around Billy's sedan. He checked each body. All were stone dead. Blood blossomed across their torsos, soaking their filthy clothes. Each man had taken at least three bullets. Most in the chest. Some in the head. Whatever the case, they had all died fast, probably before they even realised what had happened. Even though all four were degenerate pieces of shit, King never wanted anyone to suffer more than was necessary. They'd tried to kill him, so it was within his right to try to kill them. That was his version of justice.

The law wouldn't see it that way.

Therefore, he had a job to do.

He stared past the dead bikers and saw the cylindrical machine sitting in the middle of the factory floor. Already home to four dead men.

Its occupancy rate was about to double.

CHAPTER 20

The job was messy, but King had dealt with far worse in the past. As he carried each man into the bowels of the factory and levered their bodies over the edge of the cone, he thought back to the Special Forces. The bikers' deaths had brought old memories to the surface, taking him back to times when killing was nothing more than second nature to him. When it was natural. Years spent working in the upper echelons of the military meant he had done a lot of good, but often that meant bypassing standard operating principles. It meant killing a lot of people. He liked to think that they had all been scum, but after all he had done, there was bound to be some innocents thrown into the mix. People who had been in the wrong place at the wrong time, recruited into third-world mercenary forces through lies and deceit.

There was a reason King's entire career was off the books.

When he was finished, eight men lay in the machine. Six he had killed himself. Once again, he told himself they had all deserved to die. But as he left the factory and slipped back into the driver's seat of Billy's sedan, a familiar thought began to niggle in the back of his mind.

You're a murderer.

It had come to him hundreds of times before. In his line of work, inner demons were unavoidable. You could only kill so many people before it became impossible to convince yourself that it was all for the greater good. No matter how pure your intentions were.

He accelerated out of the clearing with all four of the carbine rifles scattered across the back seat, and the Beretta returned safely to his waistband. If there was a federal investigation into what had happened, the thirty bullet casings would inevitably be discovered. By then, King would be in another country. Far from this hellhole.

Dust from the gravel path blew in through the shattered windscreen. He coughed and wiped sweat from his brow. He ignored the doubt nagging at him and forced it to the back of his mind. Likely an unhealthy thing to do. But an action that was necessary right now. He had a single lead, and little time to follow it. Self-reflection could come later.

When the path met the mountain trail, King slammed on the brakes and screeched to a stop by the side of the road. As usual, there was no traffic. He was alone.

He slid the phone from his pocket and unlocked it once again. The battery had almost entirely depleted. It would shut down at any second. He quickly checked the messages.

Empty.

He clicked back to the home screen and opened the call history.

Empty.

No contacts. No leads of any kind. Nothing. King wondered just why on earth Buzzcut and his friend had gone to so much trouble to get this phone. In one last desperate attempt, he began to open apps at random.

When the notes application flashed onto the screen, a single document sat in its folder.

A message. Two sentences, short and sharp:

Room 32 at the Discount Inn, Queensbridge. Already booked.

King let out a sigh of relief. He had a lead. It wasn't much, but it was better than moving on from Jameson, helpless to stop witnesses being murdered as he continued on his travels.

He reversed onto the asphalt, turned the wheel in the other direction and made for Queensbridge. The sedan coasted past the same looming pine trees which seemed to cover every inch of empty land in these parts. An inkling of claustrophobia crept in. He passed the stretch of road where his troubles had all began. Spotted the exact place he'd decided to sit and listen to the night. An exercise that had led to witnessing the death of David Lee and Miles Price. Ale House flashed by next. Three cars sat idly in its lot. A popular place, given its location.

Next came more of the same winding mountain road. King was glad he didn't get carsick. These parts would be hell for anyone who suffered from that kind of nausea. Never-ending bends, twisting their way through uninhabited woods.

He rounded a corner, travelling close to seventy miles an hour, and was instantly blinded by a bright flash. The light lasted for only a split second, crossing his vision from somewhere ahead. Any normal civilian would have no knowledge of what was to come, simply passing the flash off as an anomaly.

They would die.

King knew exactly what the flash meant. A few rifles he'd used in the past had come equipped with the same red laser mount that had just passed across his face. The device emitted a single powerful dot which let the triggerman know exactly where their aim lay. Someone had a powerful weapon locked onto the sedan. He had no idea who, and no idea where they were. But the brief flash was all too clear.

For the second time that day, instinctual, rapid reaction speed saved his life.

As soon as he felt his vision go a small section of his brain screamed danger and his limbs fired on all cylinders. He switched instantaneously to survival mode. Ducked to one side of the driver's seat, at the same time wrenching the wheel in a vicious arc, throwing the car off-course. The stomach drop as the wheels screeched on the asphalt almost overrode his senses, but he was still able to feel a volley of rounds dot the inside of the car, blasting in through the open windscreen frame. They were powerful shots. High caliber. He felt his seat vibrate as a couple thudded into the fabric of his seat. Inches above his head.

Being fired upon was always terrifying, no matter how many times King experienced it. His heart hammered in his chest as gunfire destroyed the interior of the sedan. If a shot hit him, it would be all over. His organs would rupture and the car would career into a tree at seventy miles an hour. But his evasive move at the last second had thrown the marksman's aim off just enough for him to escape a direct impact.

Now, though, he had created another lethal problem.

The sedan careered wildly, out of control.

It swerved and bucked across the road. King tried to turn in the opposite direction but he overcompensated. The car slid sideways, tyres screaming, heading straight for the forest on the far side. Time seemed to slow as he turned his head and saw the trunk of the nearest pine coming straight at him, about to crumple the chassis. His stomach fell further. Not from the rush of vertigo. From fear. He could outsmart a man trying to kill him. An uncontrollable vehicle was a different ball game.

He managed to twist the wheel one last time, straightening the car ever so slightly. It began to correct course. But by then it was too late. It came off the road and ploughed through a stretch of ground covered by leaves, built up from the end of autumn the month before. Then the right-hand side of the bonnet directly in front of King crumpled against a pine tree, metal on wood, shaking the whole car. A violent, savage impact. His brain rattled inside his skull and an explosion of sound surrounded everything. He felt his ass lift off the seat and before he knew it the directed force of the crash sent him flying out of the windscreen's frame.

He hadn't been wearing a seatbelt.

Which, in hindsight, probably saved his life.

If a strap of leather had kept him in place the sheer force of the car slowing so rapidly would have unquestionably knocked him unconscious. Which would have been fine, had someone not been trying to kill him. Instead, his vision devolved into madness as he spun like a rag doll out of the wreckage. Nothing but twisting, blurring colours. The sky. The ground. The forest.

He hit the leaves along the side of the road like a freight train. The collision shook him to his core. He attempted to roll with the landing but only managed a half-hearted attempt. He twisted once and smacked chest-first into the ground, finally coming to a halt. Nerve endings fired across his skin. Pain exploded in too many areas to count.

He lay amongst the leaves for what felt like an hour but in reality was nothing more than a couple of seconds. Quickly, he assessed the damage. There would be injuries. That was inevitable. But he wasn't paralysed. He could move. The adrenaline and the urgency of staying alive would allow him to push through until he was safe enough to tend to his aches and pains. The blanket of vegetation and eucalyptus leaves had created a slight crumple zone. It had removed most of the impact from the landing. If he'd landed onto the asphalt road instead, they would have had to scrape him off the pavement.

There was no time to recover. Not yet. He stumbled to his feet, ignoring the icy stabs of agony along his back and down his arms. He was up so quickly that shock barely had time to set in. His blood still flowed hot from the sudden altercation. Perhaps all the evasive action had been for nothing, and he was about to take a bullet to the skull.

He saw Billy's sedan in front of him, resting idly, nose buried in the trees, one side of the bonnet completely destroyed. Smoke sizzled from its bonnet. He spun and searched for the source of the gunfire. Right now, he stood in open territory. There was no cover nearby. If they wanted to kill him, he was helpless.

But he stayed alive.

He guessed the assailant had used up an entire magazine firing at his sedan. As he scanned the tree line on the opposite side of the road, he saw movement between two trees. A shadowed figure, disappearing into the forest. Retreating. Probably out of ammunition. Needing to reload.

He had no time to think. No time to retrieve one of the M4 carbines from the back seat of the wreckage. If he took the time to arm himself, his enemy would be long gone. He had to give chase now. The Beretta M9 had a few rounds left. That would have to do.

King broke into a sprint. He crossed the mountain road at a lightning pace and dove into the scrub on the other side.

Pursuing the man who had twice come close to ending his life.

CHAPTER 21

As King followed the man into the woods, he couldn't shake a feeling of deja vu. It brought back memories of Buzzcut's demise. That's how it all started. Chasing killers through the forest. A small part of him considered giving up. He'd just survived a devastating car crash. Statistically, the odds were already against him. He wasn't sure if he would survive what came next.

But by now he had committed to the chase, fuelled by some kind of animalistic motivation. He was determined to get answers. Determined to rid the planet of whoever wanted him dead.

The forest on this side of the road was perched on uneven ground, slowly descending into a valley below. The terrain was treacherous. Turning an ankle or breaking a leg would spell disaster. He would be helpless, wounded, incapacitated. He gritted his teeth and urged himself not to let such a precarious situation unfold.

Below, the fleeing man ducked underneath a low-hanging branch and disappeared from sight. King swore, knowing he needed to make up ground or risk losing the target. He drew the Beretta from his waistband and slipped a finger inside the trigger guard as he ran.

Then he heard rustling, close by. It startled him. He hadn't anticipated such a noise, especially from such close proximity. It came from the side, behind a cluster of trees, all shrouded by undergrowth. The sound of frantic movement.

King spun and raised the Beretta and squeezed off a single shot just as a pair of men came charging out of cover. Both were dressed in tactical gear, different to any others that he'd encountered so far. One look at them and King knew they were also amateurs. Their gear was cheap shit, probably purchased from a civilian store selling wannabe tactical clothing. They weren't real soldiers. It gave him a small surge of reassurance. They'd taken him by surprise, but he had the upper hand in skill, size, athleticism and experience.

His wild shot missed, and the man on the left swung a serrated combat knife at his outstretched arms. He fell back, dodging the blade by a hair. It swished through the air near his hands. The guy had put too much into it. He'd been hoping to take a limb off. He staggered forward, thrown off balance by exerting maximum effort and missing. King kicked him hard as he stumbled into range, just above the knee. His boot crushed into tendons. He heard a loud snap and the man went down screaming, twisting away from the source of pain.

By then, the second man was already on King. He swung an identical knife, both probably purchased together, both seemingly badass until they were put up to the task of attacking an ex-Special Forces soldier. This time, King's weight was resting heavy on his lead leg and he had no time to completely avoid the attack. The blade caught the back of his hand, slicing along the skin and drawing blood instantly. He winced and let go of the Beretta involuntarily. It clattered to the forest floor and as he retreated the second guy stepped over it, advancing toward King. The Beretta was impossible to access without going through the second guy. Perhaps King had underestimated them. One of them had just effectively disarmed him.

He squared up to the man, head pounding. The guy's friend was struggling to get to his feet behind him, sporting a freshly broken leg. For now, it was one on one.

King feinted a low kick. If the guy across from him had any kind of martial arts experience he would know not to over-react. He smiled inwardly as the man flinched as hard as he possibly could, bringing both hands down to protect his stomach against a non-existent kick. By the time he had covered himself up fully, King had bull-rushed him. He slammed into the guy, putting all his weight behind the impact, knocking him senseless. As their bodies clashed King seized the man's knife hand in a vice-like grip and shook it. A sharp, targeted move, full of violence. The guy's grip slipped and the knife cascaded away.

King caught it.

He reached down and plucked it out of the air by the handle before it hit the ground. Up close, King heard the guy's heavy breathing and panic as he realised that his enemy excelled in a messy, close-quarters fight. By now there was no time to separate the two.

King brought his arm up and sunk the blade into the man's gut, all ten inches of it, tearing through skin and opening his stomach. He slid the knife out with little resistance. The man stood in place, frozen in shock. King decided to end it quickly and shoved the blade up under his chin. The knife penetrated through his mouth and burrowed into his brain. He was dead before King pushed him away.

His limp body clattered to the forest floor and King stepped over him and snatched the Beretta off the ground. The guy with the broken leg raised a hand in desperation, as if to say *Wait!,* but King was beyond caring. These two men had tried to kill him. They'd intended to stab him to death, two on one, an unfair ambush. They had asked for it.

He fired twice, which was all that was necessary. Both 9mm rounds hit home, dotting the top of the guy's forehead. He jerked back and face-planted the dirt. Just as dead as his friend.

Mulling over what had occurred would come later. Right now, there was no time to think. These two were nothing more than hired goons. He checked his wounded hand. Bloody, but far from life-threatening. He wouldn't bleed out from the cut. He would worry about it later, just like everything else.

He turned back to where he had last seen the figure. The man who had shot at him from a vantage point. That was the man he wanted. Preferably alive, so that he could piece the mystery together. Without a shadow of remorse he set off on the same path, leaving the pair of corpses in the undergrowth. He would not come back for them. He would forget they had ever existed.

The forest grew thicker the further he headed into its depths. Brambles and foliage and trees pressed in on all sides, obstructing his attempts to move efficiently. He found himself zigzagging down the hill, eyes wide, searching desperately for any sign of the shooter. So far, nothing. He ducked under a cluster of branches, Beretta raised. Unsure of how many rounds left. The adrenalin rush had obscured his ability to keep track of the ammo count. He would simply keep firing until the gun clicked dry.

He'd reached the bottom of a small valley. A rocky hill ascended in front of him, home to clusters of boulders wrapped in moss and plants. At the base of the formation there was a gap between two of the boulders, the space in between spiralling away into shadow. A cave of sorts. As soon as King broke out into the open area, a shot whistled past him. The crack of the report came blasting out of the cave, accompanied by a sharp muzzle flare. King fired back, two or three rounds, straight down the entrance. He saw nothing but darkness. It was impossible to tell whether he had hit his target. He would never know unless he ventured inside. Which was a foolish thought in the first place, as his adversary would be able to see him much clearer than he could see back.

King crossed the space in front of the cave quickly, before the man inside had time to regroup and fire back. Hopefully, his warning shots had made the shooter recoil, abandon his aim. He made it safely to the lip of the cave and ducked behind one of the boulders, creating cover between them. He pressed himself against its wet stony surface and waited.

It made for a tense and difficult situation. The woods lapsed into silence, all wildlife scared off by the gunshots traded between the two men. King listened for any kind of noise from the cave, breathing heavy.

He thought he heard a noise. Footsteps on the rock, approaching fast. He stuck an arm around the boulder and pumped the trigger of the Beretta, once, twice, three times, firing blind. He continued to unload the clip. He lost count of the shots. He knew the Beretta M9 had a fifteen-round box magazine, but he had no idea when it would expire.

Finally, the gun clicked. King waited a moment, allowing the ringing in his ears to settle. Then he stuck his head around the corner, searching for any sign of a body near the lip of the cave.

Nothing visible.

A cacophony of heavy gunfire came back at him. He felt the displaced air all around his head and ducked back behind cover. The noise of the automatic rifle was deafening. The shooter had planned to overwhelm King with a swarm of bullets as soon as he stuck a limb out of cover. King heard the rounds continue to whizz past and knew aggression was taking over. The man was spraying and praying, hoping he had hit King.

Hoping it would all be over.

When King heard the unmistakeable *click* of another empty magazine ring out from the cave entrance, he didn't hesitate. Now was his chance. It may be the only one he got.

He raced around the corner and charged headlong into the cave. At first he saw nothing but darkness. Then his heart skipped a beat as a figure came rushing out of the shadows. He hadn't been expecting such a sudden response. He got one look at the man's outfit — expensive khakis, a brand new bulletproof vest, jet black gloves, a woollen balaclava covering his face. A professional version of the last two men. This guy had experience. He moved with the agility of someone who kept themselves in impeccable shape. King began to regret adopting such a foolhardy approach, but by then it was too late.

The pair collided and sprawled out across the rocky floor of the cave. They had met just inside the entrance, before King could sink into its dark recesses. Enough light spilled into the space to make their surroundings visible. King knew he had potentially met his match, and an urge to gain the advantage early overtook him. He scrambled to his feet and charged at the man, dropping his shoulder low, attempting to crash-tackle him into the opposite wall.

The guy reacted explosively, faster than King thought possible, and swung a knee hard and fast. It caught King on the forehead. He felt the sharp *crack* against his skull and his neck whipped back and he spun away, shocked by the impact. Not concussed, but close. He slammed into the rocky wall and blinked hard. Seeing stars.

The man sensed he was shaken and moved in for the kill. He came charging in and lashed out with a strong uppercut, putting everything into it, searching for King's chin. King sidestepped just in time and the punch whistled through the air near his head. Now they were too close to each other to rely on technique.

The fight quickly became a rabid brawl.

King swung with everything he had, loading up on all his punches, hunting for the knockout blow just as hard as the other man was. Pure, unbridled energy crackled in the air. The energy of two men trained in combat, knowing that it only took one shot to land to ensure they would live, knowing that one of them had to die. King felt something primal in him break through, lending him extra speed and strength. He simply *had* to land the blow.

It came in a flurry. He ripped a body shot into the man's stomach, below the vest, twisting his torso as he swung and driving his fist into the soft spot with everything he had. A powerful right hook grazed off the top of his head but did not faze him. He felt the guy begin to double over, all the breath knocked out of him, accompanied by a grunt of exertion. A single moment of much-needed recovery. Which, as always, was all King required. With his other arm he cracked the guy in the jaw. It gave off a grotesque sound, which he knew translated to a concussion. The man's brain rattled inside his skull, dazing him, rendering him useless.

King surged forward, gritting his teeth in anger, and wrapped his big hands around the back of the guy's neck. He pulled him down, using all the fire in his muscles, all the chaotic adrenaline of a life-or-death brawl. The guy's head dropped without resistance, still affected by the flash knockout seconds earlier. King guided his face on the correct trajectory and met it with a vicious knee straight to the nose. The sound of breaking bone rang off the mossy walls and the man's legs gave out and he collapsed to the floor of the cave, out cold.

As silence descended once again, King began to feel the effects of the fight. During such a brawl, one became almost superhuman, able to withstand any shot that didn't lead to unconsciousness. He'd been cracked across the chin and the neck several times. He knew they were blows from a trained fighter because they hurt like all hell. His head pounded, his eyes ached. He felt the warm sensation of blood on his lips and knew he'd been cut bad by a grazing punch. It might not have taken much more to finish him off.

If he hadn't landed the perfect combination, he had no doubts that the man lying unconscious in front of him would have out-struck him. Then beat him to death. He'd got a glimpse of the guy's eyes during the fight. They were much like his.

Cold. Emotionless.

He'd killed before.

King knew that much.

He also knew that concussions were nothing like the movies. The guy would be awake in seconds. Perhaps not fully aware, but awake nonetheless. If he stayed out for hours, like in films, it would mean permanent brain damage.

Sure enough, his limbs began to twitch and he came to with a groan. King made eye contact and knew he was helpless. Spaced out. Defenceless. King squatted, wrapped a hand around the top of the guy's balaclava and ripped it off. He wanted to get a look at the face of the man who had almost got the better of him.

At first, he didn't realise what he saw. Close-cropped hair, blue eyes, a steely expression, a scar on the left cheek, chapped lips. He stared at the features, and knew that he recognised them, but for some reason he failed to process the man in front of him. A wave of sheer disbelief crashed over him.

'You can't be serious,' he whispered, finally accepting what he was seeing. 'Cole?'

He knew this man.

Which changed the entire dynamic of the situation.

Somehow, some way, his past had followed him across the planet, to a small country town in the middle of isolated Australian woodland. An old friend from years ago had just tried to murder him violently. He had spent a full year with Cole Watkins in the Delta Force before being offered a more secretive, more specialised position.

This man had been his friend.

A wave of crippling nausea almost buckled him. He came to the realisation that he hadn't just stumbled upon a random conspiracy in the town of Jameson. This entire ordeal had something to do with him. He was no closer to the truth, but now he knew that whoever was behind this had intended his involvement from the beginning. None of this was random.

He was trapped in some kind of sick game, and it didn't matter whether he left Jameson behind, because this would follow him until he discovered how he was connected. Or died in the process.

'What the fuck are you doing here?' King said. 'What is this?'

Cole stared at him with blank, cloudy eyes. He wasn't sure if it was the effects of the concussion, or if the man was drugged, or if he simply did not care to answer the question. What came next certainly answered that.

Cole reached back with a shaky hand and ripped a combat knife out of his belt. He swung it low, aiming the tip at King's stomach. King reacted fast, outstretching both hands, searching for Cole's forearm, finding it, reversing the swing of the blade, slamming it home into his old friend's throat.

The man died spluttering in a pool of his own blood, and in that moment King knew his best chance at getting answers had died with him.

CHAPTER 22

The slow trek back to the main road passed in a haze.

King left Cole's body in the cave, too deep in thought to bother attempting to hide it. He continued up through the verdure. Stepped over the two men who had ambushed him on the way down. They remained as dead as ever. He left them there too. At that moment, nothing mattered but the revelation that he was being hunted by people he knew. He had no idea why, or how many of them there were. It had skewed his perspective on the last few days, to the point where he questioned every encounter he'd made since stepping foot in Jameson.

He approached Billy's sedan in a daze, uncaring as to whether it was still drivable. He opened the door and got in. Started the engine. Reversed out into the middle of the road, thinking how lucky he was not to be stranded miles from any town without a working vehicle. It seemed the crash had missed most of the important mechanics, but he wasn't sure the car would last much longer. The smoke creeping out of one side of the bonnet threatened to shut the engine down at any moment. King knew he had to get to Queensbridge, to the Discount Inn, but his mind was far from concentrated on the task at hand.

He covered the last few miles to Queensbridge in record time, keeping his foot all the way to the floor. The wind battered his face as he drove, but that's what he wanted. Anything to mask the anger and confusion. It didn't take long to see the familiar buildings on either side of him, signifying that he was approaching the town centre. He'd passed through Queensbridge two mornings before. It felt like an eternity ago. So much had happened in such a short space of time. And this fresh revelation had shaken him to his core.

He rolled the battered sedan into the parking lot of the Discount Inn and got out. The place lived up to its name. It was a two-storey building with paint flaking off the exterior walls and cheap plastic chairs littering the tiny spaces outside each room. Even from outside King heard a crying baby in a downstairs room and a couple arguing at the top of their lungs directly above. The whole place smelt of stale cigarette smoke. He spotted reception, which was all he needed.

By now the sun had almost fully risen. It shone over the horizon, blinding him, making his head ache more than it already was. In a terrible mood, he slammed the car door, drawing the attention of a pair of women jogging past. Early morning exercise. They took one look at him and gasped in shock. As they continued running, King swore that their pace quickened.

He wondered why.

It didn't take long to find out. As he approached reception, one of the tinted windows displayed his reflection. He studied the image, and even he felt like gasping. His nose had run rivulets of blood down the lower half of his face, caking his lips. A large gash at the top of his head had opened up, and that too was bleeding. One cheek was in the process of swelling. Judging by its rapid development, most of his face would be completely purple by tomorrow.

The absolute chaos of the morning had numbed his injuries. It had acted as a masking agent, hiding just how battered he truly was. He knew he had come close to unconsciousness in the fight with Cole. Now he realised just how dangerous of a position he'd been in. He looked down at his hands. One looked like it had been covered with red paint. The stab wound had bled heavily all up his forearm.

He was a mess.

But it was too late to turn around now. He pushed the reception door open and stepped inside.

The receptionist looked up from a stack of papers and visibly paled. He was a balding man with a rotund belly and wire bespectacled glasses. Probably in his mid-fifties. His face was full of warmth and kindness, but that began to dissipate when he saw a bloodied, beaten stranger heading for the desk.

'Uh, can I help you?' he said, stumbling on his words.

'I know how I look,' King said. 'And I'm sorry. I don't want to scare you. I just need your help.'

'What happened to you?'

'I can't really explain much.'

'You'd better, or I'm not going to help you at all.'

'A couple of guys stayed here last night,' he said. 'They probably seemed a bit off. A bit different to everyone else that comes through. Do you know who I'm talking about?'

The man nodded.

'Well, I need access to their room.'

'You know I can't do that.'

'Please.'

'I can't just go around handing out room keys to strangers. Especially those that look like you.'

'That's flattering.'

'Sorry. Nothing I can do.'

'Okay—' King glanced at the man's name badge, '—Ronald. Here's the thing. I have had a very, very bad morning. Those two men have done a lot of terrible shit that I unfortunately can't go into detail about. I'm not a cop, but you need to treat me like one. I need access to that room. It's for the right reasons, I promise you. And if you don't give me a key, I'm just going to kick the door of Room 32 off its hinges and find what I'm looking for anyway. And I don't want to do that, because you seem like a nice guy. Now you might call the police if I do that, but by the time they get here I'll be gone and you'll have a broken door that will probably cost you a hell of a lot of money to replace. And you won't sue me for it, because you'll never see me again. So either give me the key or pay for repairs.'

A pause. 'You're not giving me much of a choice.'

'No, I'm really not.'

'I'm calling the police the second I hand this over.'

'Go right ahead. I'm beyond caring.'

'I hope you're doing the right thing.'

'I am.'

'Is there anything I can do to avoid either one of those two situations you listed?'

'Not really.'

Ronald handed over a key. 'Fucking asshole.'

King nodded his thanks, then turned on his heel and left reception. He walked down a narrow corridor which opened out into a spacious courtyard with a small water fountain at its centre, surrounded on all sides by motel rooms.

He tried to ignore how much pain he was in and located Room 32 after a minute of searching. It was a small single room, the brick exterior painted white to match the other fifty rooms in the Discount Inn. All bland, monotonous, cheap, nondescript; the qualities of a standard motel room. King unlocked the door and stepped inside.

It was immaculate. By the look of the rest of the Discount Inn, he guessed it had not been cleaned by staff. They would not give each room this much attention. Which meant the killers were men of habit, who kept everything neat and orderly at all times. They were hitmen, after all. A field where organisation and routine were of the utmost importance.

A pair of black duffel bags lay side-by-side on the kitchen table. Their belongings. King crossed to them and spent the next five minutes scrutinising their contents for anything suspicious, anything that could possibly lead to the people at the top, to answers. By the time he'd rifled through each possession twice he had to conclude that the bags were clean. Nothing but clothes, toiletries and a pair of passports that were almost certainly not their real identities. Seasoned professionals. They didn't leave anything to track them to their employer.

King stopped.

Unless they didn't know who their employer was.

Suddenly everything clicked. If they'd known who was paying them, then the post office activities were entirely unnecessary. They would have simply been supplied with the information in some clearing in the middle of nowhere, away from prying eyes. Kate had served as the bridge between the two parties, to ensure the people in charge remained anonymous. She was the fall girl. On all the cameras. Vulnerable. She would have taken the blame after this was all over.

Whatever this was.

Then King had approached her at her home. A mysterious stranger, full of questions, right after their two contract killers had vanished off the face of the earth. They'd decided to eliminate both of them. Clear up loose ends. Hence the sniper at the landfill site, and the imposter at the police station.

It still didn't explain the package. There was something more to it than just a phone. On the security footage, Buzzcut had extracted the phone from the top of the box, but it contained something else. King was sure of it. Therefore, it was here somewhere.

He looked up at the ceiling. It was made of gypsum boards, all square and white and identical. He wondered if they were fixed into place. He climbed onto the bed and reached up, prodding at one. It gave way. He slid it to the side, revealing a dark space above the motel room. Empty space. A decent storage area for a package.

He glanced around the room. There was no better vantage point to reach the boards than from on the bed. Hopefully, the package would be where he thought it was. He stuck a hand into the space and patted the other side of the gypsum all around the hole. Nothing but dust. Then, at the very edge of his reach, his fingers brushed something. He clawed at the object until it rolled over and he was able to tug it down from the space.

A brown paper package, torn open at one end.

With a smile of relief he dropped it onto the kitchen table, alongside the hitmen's bags, and tore the remaining paper off. It was a briefcase, not locked, simply secured by a pair of clasps. King unlocked it and swung it open, revealing a customised foam interior. There were three outlines carved into the material. Two were in the shape of handguns, now empty. Weapons, supplied by the employer. Probably necessary after a quick flight to Australia. The final outline was small and square and still held its contents. A note. Folded immaculately. Old school. It read:

Targets are David Lee and Miles Price, from Rafael Constructions.

An address was listed under that. King guessed it led to the head office of Rafael Constructions, where the pair of construction workers had made a living. There was nothing else.

He swore and threw the briefcase across the room, at the same time making sure not to damage any of the walls. He'd caused Ronald enough distress already. It would do him no good to destroy his property. King scrunched the note up and shoved it in his pocket. He left the room as it was.

On the walk back to the sedan, the frustration of dead ends began to eat away at him. Coupled with a splitting headache and throbbing wounds, King felt anger rising inside his chest. No, not anger. Stifling rage. The leads had been worthless. He had the address of the construction company, which he probably could have located on a computer anyway. He doubted there were many competing near Jameson.

He passed reception only a few minutes after leaving it. On the way past, he stuck his head in the door and saw Ronald with a landline phone pressed to his ear, speaking animatedly. Probably still on the phone to the police. King waved, smiled, and tossed the key back over the desk. He registered the disbelief on Ronald's face, then slipped back into his car and drove the smoking, bullet-ridden wreck out of Queensbridge for the last time.

CHAPTER 23

The second he stepped into the motel room he saw Kate's face fall. He knew why. If she had even an inkling of concern for him she would be appalled by the injuries he'd sustained.

The drive back from Queensbridge had not been pleasant. As he came down from the high of combat, the pain had begun to seep into his face, his hand, his ribs. By the time he pulled up outside Yvonne's motel and stumbled up to room four, he was ready to pass out.

'Oh my god,' she whispered.

They hugged for a moment, then King tossed the phone onto the bed. 'That's what I found.'

'What was on it?'

'An address. For a motel in Queensbridge. I went there. There was nothing.'

'There had to be something. You're beat half to death.'

King sat down in the rickety chair by the door and sighed. 'Let's not get into it. What's done is done.'

She nodded. 'Did you see *anything?*'

'The package you delivered was there. But it was empty. It had a couple of guns in it and an address to Rafael Constructions.'

'I know the place. It's down the road.'

'Well, that's all I've got.'

'You think they have something to do with what's going on?'

'I don't know. It's where David Lee and Miles Price worked. Doesn't necessarily mean it's connected. Unless...'

'Unless what?'

King stared blankly out the window. Thinking hard. 'Do you have a phone?'

'Of course.'

He fished around in his back pocket, searching for something, unsure if it had remained in place throughout the commotion of the morning. His fingers closed around the business card Richard had given him the previous day. Bent out of shape, but still intact.

Kate fished a smartphone out of her bag and handed it across. He took it with a nod of thanks and punched in the number scrawled on the front of the card.

Richard answered on the second ring.

'Hello?'

'Richard. It's Jason King.'

He heard elation creep into the man's tone. 'King! My God, I didn't think I'd hear from you again. Do you have good news?'

He recalled Richard asking him to keep an eye out for potential employment opportunities.

'Far from it, my friend,' he said. 'But I'm wrapped up in a bit of a situation here, and I need some answers.'

'I see. Well, anything I can do to help.'

'We talked about how you were laid off?'

'We did.'

'Can I ask where you used to work?'

'Place called Rafael Constructions. Worked there about two years before it got bought out.'

'When we talked you mentioned overseas buyers. Do you know who?'

'None of us do. The whole thing was done so fast … next thing we knew we were told to leave.'

'Did you see them?'

'I saw one of them. I don't know how many there were. It might have only just been him. He looked similar to you. White, tall, in shape. He wore a suit. Didn't match his surroundings.'

'You sure he was from overseas?'

'Well, not certain. But it looked like he'd flown in. All I saw of him was when he walked into the factory floor and shook hands with the manager. They both headed into the office after that. But he looked important. Like he didn't belong in a town as small as this.'

'Did you see anything else?'

'Nope. They must have finalised the deal, because the next day most of us got informed we would be let go. I haven't been back there since.'

'Most?'

'They kept a couple of guys on. To help them with some temporary work, I think.'

'David Lee and Miles Price?'

'Uh, yeah … how the hell did you know that?'

'Richard, I have to go. But thank you. You've been a huge help.'

King hung up and tossed the phone back to Kate. 'Rafael Constructions is now priority number one.'

'What was all that about?' she said, tucking the device into her bag.

'I met a guy yesterday who'd been laid off his job. Turns out someone bought Rafael Constructions and got rid of all the old workers. What could they possibly want with a construction company?'

'What about those two workers who you saw get shot?'

'They kept them on to help out with something. The pair of them must have seen too much.'

'So they're definitely eliminating witnesses?'

King nodded. 'They're covering something up.'

'We should visit their head office,' Kate said. 'I know where it is.'

He nodded again. 'I need to rest first. I'll pass out if we go now.'

She rose up onto her tip-toes and planted a kiss on his bloody lips. 'Let's get you fixed up.'

Kate left to visit the chemist down the road. He was wary of letting her go alone, especially given the nature of recent revelations. But he knew he was in no state to accompany her.

Besides, she could handle herself.

He stumbled into the bathroom and let the shower run cold. He needed the soothing relief. The water trickled over his wounds, washing away the blood caked over his body, cleaning him, reinvigorating him.

He stood under the stream for what felt like an hour but in reality couldn't have been more than ten minutes. He dried himself tentatively, taking care not to disturb the wounds already throbbing over his body. Now that he had time to stop and breathe, he could assess the damage.

Cole had landed several hard body shots, but no ribs were broken. Nevertheless, his sternum ached and three large welts had surfaced across his abdomen. His cheek continued to swell, beginning to obscure his vision in one eye. His nose was battered, but not broken. He knew the difference from past experience. Still, swathes of pain drilled into his skull underneath his eyes. His lips had been cut in multiple places, either from elbows or punches. The stab wound on his hand had finally stopped bleeding, but it was a nasty injury, throbbing incessantly. Overall, he had taken a serious beating.

He estimated his body would take over a week to completely heal.

He didn't have a week.

Still naked, he heard the door unlock and stuck his head around the corner to see Kate, breathless, wielding a pair of shopping bags packed with medical supplies.

'You okay?' he asked.

'Yeah.' She smiled at him. 'Just didn't want to be seen by the police, or … whoever. I got you new clothes too.'

She patched him up as best she could, rubbing antiseptic into the cuts, bandaging his hand, holding an ice pack to his face.

'Who did this to you?' she finally asked, digging blood out of his nose with a Q-tip. 'You can't keep me in the dark like this.'

'Somebody I wasn't expecting,' he said, staring into space.

She paused. Took his head in her hands. Made eye contact. 'Jason, what's going on?'

‘I don’t know,’ he said, struggling to control his emotions. ‘I honestly have no fucking idea. A man I used to work with showed up here. I hadn’t seen him in five years, and he’s here. Ten thousand miles from where he’s supposed to be. He tried to kill me.’

She went pale. The news hit her, too. The understanding that all the killings, all the violence, all the death … revolved around him.

‘You told me you were just passing through,’ she said, stunned.

King looked at her, tears welling in his eyes. ‘I am. That’s why I’m so scared now. I quit my position a couple of months ago. Travelled here, to get away from it all. No phone, no computer. I fell off the grid. And all this chaos still followed me.’

‘But…’

‘You should leave, Kate.’

She sat on his bare thigh and wrapped her arms around his shoulders. He held her tight. Thinking it might be the last time he ever would.

‘I’m not just abandoning you,’ she whispered.

‘This is on me. I’m being targeted. You need to get yourself as far away from me as possible. I knew I never should have let you get close.’

'They tried to kill me, too. You're not the only person being targeted.'

'I remember thinking the shooter at the landfill site had to be an awfully well-trained marksman to be so accurate. Now I know that he was. Because I trained with him.'

'Where is he now?'

'Dead.'

No need to elaborate.

She bowed her head. 'So you didn't find out anything else? All we have is Rafael Constructions?'

He nodded. 'That's it.'

'Then we go check it out,' she said. 'I'm not just running away from Jameson because it's somehow connected to you. You've saved my life at least twice now.'

'I'm not someone you want to be around, Kate.'

'I think you are.'

There was a brief pause as neither of them spoke. They looked at each other for a long time. Wondering just how they'd got each other into this mess. Wondering if it would end. Kate kissed him. Her hair spilled over his shoulders and they stayed that way for what felt like forever, moving slowly against each other, feeding off each other's energy. King stood up, carrying her, and they fell onto the bed. They moved gently. Carefully. Kate slid her pants off, revealing the same toned physique, and together they crept under the covers once again.

King felt the elation and the joy and the release of the experience and in that time he believed that there was a way out of this horrendous situation. They would find answers, they would leave Jameson behind, they would move on. He would finally rid himself of the demons of his past, and they could just disappear together.

The morning melted into a blur of pulsating colours, of motion and energy and connection. When they finally finished King drifted into a half-sleep, staring up at the ceiling until it faded away, one hand around Kate's slight shoulders, breathing in her smell. He put the tension and the stress and the pain on hold. Just for a few short hours.

When he came to around mid-morning, he heard the rare sound of a passing vehicle. Its engine grumbled by. Then, all of a sudden, the noise came to a halt. Right in front of the motel. There was a car stopped outside. He was sure of it. He stayed completely still in bed, but his senses perked up. He listened for any type of uncommon noise. In all likelihood it would be nothing more than a local, stopped for any of the million reasons why people stop their cars.

But maybe, just maybe…

Then the window shattered.

In the calm silence of the mid-afternoon the sound exploded through the motel room like a gun. King threw the covers away and leapt out of bed the moment he heard it. He shut off the nerve endings screaming at him to slow down. He wouldn't listen to them, because he had just seen the object that had launched through the window. A small round ball, heavy. It thudded into the carpeted floor and rolled toward the bed.

He couldn't believe his eyes.

A military-issue M67 hand grenade.

Pin missing.

Acting with the urgency of a man who knew exactly how much danger he was in, King scooped up the grenade with one hand and took an enormous bounding step toward the broken window. Before Kate had even propped herself up in bed he threw it like a baseball, knowing it would detonate at any moment. He'd thrown it blind, hurling it back from where it came from before he even had a chance to scout the area.

He made it to the window before the detonation. Got one look at the scene before him. A police car, from the Jameson Police Department, resting idly in the middle of the road. A single man standing by the driver's side door, staring up at the motel. King saw the slick hair, the white skin, the large eyes.

It was Brandt's imposter. He must have escaped from the station, stealing one of their vehicles in the process. Then he'd tracked King down and hurled a live grenade into his motel room.

And he certainly hadn't anticipated the same weapon hurtling back at him barely a couple of seconds later.

He didn't stand a chance.

The grenade bounced once on the asphalt, skidding along the road until it shot under the police car. The imposter could do nothing but stare. His reaction speed was not quick enough. From the time King threw the grenade, the man had perhaps a second to act. He didn't take the opportunity.

A vicious explosion tore the police car in half. There was no fireball, no theatrics like in the movies. Just an immense blast that sent loose parts flying in all directions. The imposter became a bloody, shredded corpse. At the same time the blast shattered every window in Yvonne's motel simultaneously. The noise almost destroyed King's eardrums. He ducked below the windowsill to escape the shockwave. The room's foundations shook around him. M67 detonations were close to the most terrifying experience on the battlefield, especially within such close proximity.

In a small country town, they caused pandemonium.

CHAPTER 24

The surrounding area erupted into bedlam. Screams of shock sounded from all levels of the motel complex as the entire building vibrated on its foundations.

Kate scrambled out of bed and threw her clothes on, her motions jerky and panicked. King followed suit, diving into the outfit she had bought him earlier that morning. A pair of jeans and a long-sleeved cotton shirt. Both tight fits. They gathered their things, speechless, reeling from how close they had come to getting blown to pieces. He sensed that she was unsure as to what exactly had happened.

'What's going on?' she said finally, scooping up her bag, ready to leave.

'Someone just threw a grenade through our window.'

Her eyes boggled. 'Was that what it was?'

He nodded. 'Let's go. Right now.'

They threw the door open and headed out into the street. On the way to Billy's sedan they passed Yvonne. The old woman had staggered out of reception, tears in her eyes, staring vacantly at the widespread destruction across her motel. Repairs would be expensive. King took one look at her, then reached into the windbreaker he carried in one arm and took out the remaining stack of bills from the biker's clubhouse. At least ten grand, maybe more. He peeled off a couple to get them through the next few days, then handed the rest over to Yvonne.

She met his gaze. 'What's this for? Did you do this?'

'No. But there's people who want to hurt me, and I stayed here knowing they might target me. So it's on me. You use this money to fix it all up. I'm sorry, Yvonne.'

'It's not your fault.'

'Everyone's telling me that, but I'm starting to think it is.'

They left her and took Billy's sedan out onto thc main road. Kate averted her eyes from the grisly remains of Brandt's imposter, lying in pieces next to the smouldering police car wreckage. A surreal sight when contrasted with the peaceful country town around it. King stared at the scene as they passed, knowing every police officer for miles in any direction would be on their position in no time. They had to get out of Jameson, at least for the time being.

'To Rafael Constructions?' Kate said. Her voice shook, probably from the shock of seeing such a grisly death up close and personal.

King nodded. 'There'd better be something significant there.'

They passed the chemist, and the post office, and the convenience store, and the cafe, and a swathe of other buildings. Already shopkeepers and customers alike were out on the street, their eyes searching for the source of the almighty racket they'd heard before. King kept his gaze fixed on the road ahead and in no time they were out of town, heading north.

Kate turned to him, as if to say something. She stopped. Decided against it.

'What are you thinking?' he said, aware there was something on her mind.

'It's about time you told me what you used to do. Specifically.'

'Why now all of a sudden?'

'Because that was insanity. I heard the window smash, and I paused for what couldn't have been more than a second … I think just to register the noise. And in that time you jumped out of bed, picked it up and threw it back. Before I even realised what was happening. No-one is that fast. I've never seen anyone react the way you do. You're an anomaly.'

King sighed. 'I made it to the Delta Force at twenty-two. That's where I met Cole. He was one of the only people I got along with. He and another man named Dirk. Everyone else hated me. I was at least five years younger than any of them. They accelerated me through the ranks quicker than most.'

'Was that all?'

King shook his head. 'I only spent a couple of years there. In training drills I was noticed by a few higher-ups. They watched me. Ran some tests. Turns out I have close to the fastest reaction speed on earth.'

'Jesus.'

'And these men were right at the top of the food chain. Four-star generals, that sort of thing. They were already in the planning stages of an unofficial operation. They called it Black Force. I was their first recruit. And there's zero evidence that anything I did ever happened. They sent me into the worst hellholes on earth. Often alone. I was their freak science project. I saved a lot of good people, killed a lot of bad people. I was Black Force's main operative for eight years. I don't know how many others there were. No-one told me anything. I was a ghost, a secret independent contractor. They paid me enormous sums of money to do the things that never would have ordinarily been sanctioned.'

'When did you retire?'

'Two months ago. Everything was beginning to catch up to me, and I couldn't take much more of it.'

'All the killing?'

'Not so much that. Partially, but not all. It was how close I kept coming to death, over and over and over again. I knew it wasn't sustainable. Sooner or later, I'd be too slow. I'd get caught from behind. I'd find myself in open ground, with no cover. Something like that. It ate away at me until I finally mustered up the nerve to call it quits.'

'How did the higher-ups react?'

'They knew I meant it. They had enough goodwill to let me go.'

'Maybe not.'

King turned to her. 'What do you mean?'

'Maybe that's what this is. They want you out of the picture. They don't want someone so dangerous roaming around. Maybe they think there'll be peace of mind if you're eliminated.'

He shook his head. 'I already considered that. But this is something else. If they wanted me dead, they could have done it as soon as I gave my notice. No-one would have ever known. They didn't need to follow me here. Construction workers and police officers and civilians didn't have to die. This is something I've stumbled upon. I'm connected in some way. I don't know how. But it's bigger than just me.'

He stared at the trees passing by, rustling in the mountain wind. The cold sliced in and beat at their faces, chilling them to the bone.

'It's up here,' Kate said, motioning to the forest on the right-hand side of the road. 'The head office. We're close.'

As they drove further out of town, a section of the forest cleared up ahead. They began to pass large industrial sites; factories, warehouses, farmland. Dirt trails branched off in many directions, inter-connecting the facilities. She beckoned to a path slicing between two enormous metal warehouses and King swung the sedan over its rocky surface.

They pulled up to a long low building made from polished timber planks. An old home that had been converted into an office. A wooden deck ran round its entire perimeter, much similar to Kate's house. Behind the building he could see a sprawling industrial complex home to a concrete plant and an array of mixing trucks, lined up in orderly fashion. Beside Rafael Constructions' land, an abandoned factory sprawled into the sky. A lot of potential vantage points. Many places to hide a marksman.

King got out of the sedan, wondering if he would make it to the head office without catching a bullet in the brain.

As his feet touched the gravel surface, the door to the office opened and a small rotund man dressed smartly in a pair of slacks and an oversized dress shirt hobbled out onto the patio. His name badge read *Bernie.*

'What brings you two all the way out here?' he said, an overly false smile plastered across his face.

CHAPTER 25

Bernie led them through the main reception area. A pretty receptionist sat behind the desk, but apart from that the building was entirely devoid of people. The rest of the room consisted of a few waiting chairs, with various magazines strewn across a coffee table. Nothing out of the ordinary. Bernie strode into a small interview room and beckoned them through. This room was smaller, furnished with a conference table and a handful of rickety chairs.

King shivered involuntarily. The whole place made him feel uneasy. Everything was too clean, too unimposing. He looked at Bernie's greasy comb over and awkward gait and soulless black eyes and couldn't help but find the man suspicious. Nevertheless, he and Kate sat down without a fuss. On the front porch, he'd simply explained to Bernie that he wanted to ask a few questions about the company. Bernie had ushered them into this room. Now, he sat down on the opposite side of the conference table and clasped his hands together.

'What can I do for you?' he asked with the same over-the-top smile.

'My name's Jason.'

'American?'

King nodded. 'On vacation.'

'Ah! Of course.'

'I'm just passing through and I thought I'd drop in here to visit an old friend.'

'Is that so? Let's see if I can go find him for you.'

'His name's David Lee.'

A split second of hesitation. Unnoticeable to the average civilian, but in that moment King knew that Bernie was a lying piece of shit. The man cocked his head to pass off his surprise and said, 'Well, Jason, I'm sorry to inform you that David actually stopped working for us a few weeks ago.'

'Oh.'

'Yes, very unfortunate.'

'May I ask why?'

'He was just a contractor. Came into town looking for some temporary work. Nothing more.'

'So he's out of town?'

Bernie nodded. 'He left almost straight away, I'm sorry to say. Did he tell you he'd be here?'

'He said he'd be around.'

'Well, I haven't seen him for weeks.'

‘What about Miles Price?’

‘I’m sorry?’

‘Miles Price. He’s another friend of mine. Did he conveniently happen to leave a few weeks ago as well?’

Bernie coughed and laughed sardonically, a bad attempt to dissipate the tension in the room. ‘Give me a moment to just check my files. I’m not up to speed with everyone who works for this company.’

‘That’s a shame. You should be.’

Bernie shot him a glance, then pulled out his phone and flicked at the screen. He used over-the-top gestures, to make it look like he was scrolling through notes. Another poor performance. King had seen a lot better in his time. Sweat broke out across the man’s brow. A thin droplet ran down his forehead.

‘Ah yes, here we are,’ Bernie said. ‘Miles Price! He only worked here for a couple of days. Even less than David. That was weeks ago also. I’m afraid you’ve missed both of them. Are you able to contact them?’

‘No.’

‘You don’t have their numbers?’

‘I have their numbers.’

Bernie cocked his head.

‘I think you know why I’m not able to contact them, Bernie,’ King said.

'I'm sorry, sir, but I can't say I follow.'

'I think you know they're dead.'

He feigned surprise. 'I'm sorry?'

'I think you're in on this whole thing.'

'What whole thing?'

'You know exactly what's going on. You've done a shit job of covering it up, too. So you're going to tell me the truth; you're going to tell me everything you know about why Miles and David are dead, and who bought this place a month ago, and why people are trying to kill me, and what exactly is going on behind closed doors.'

Bernie shook his head. 'I'm afraid you're awfully mistaken, Jason. You must think I'm someone I'm not.'

'Oh, I don't think you're behind this. You're sweating and shaking. You're shitting your pants. This isn't your gig. But someone is paying you to keep quiet, or use your facility. You need to let me help you, or you're just going to end up the same way everyone in this town is ending up at the moment.'

'I beg your pardon,' Bernie said. 'Was that a threat on my life?'

'Not from me. But I can pretend you talked.'

Kate said, 'We know enough already.'

King said, 'They'll kill you slowly if they think you divulged important information.'

Bernie scoffed and rose out of his chair. 'I think we're done here. You seem delusional, Jason. And as for you—' he turned to Kate, '—I don't know why you're hanging around with this lunatic. Surely you have better things to do.'

King got up slowly and took a step toward the door. Putting his bulk in between Bernie's means of escape. Making sure he couldn't take off running. 'I'm just about done with all this stalling.'

'I'm just about done with your ludicrous accusations,' Bernie said.

Movement behind them. From the reception area. Hurried footsteps, urgent. King's reflexes kicked in and he spun rapidly, ready to explode, primed for combat.

He didn't expect to see another pair of familiar faces. Guns up. In uniform.

Kitchener and Dawes.

The trio recognised each other simultaneously. Dawes nodded a greeting, despite the tense circumstances.

'Been a while, King,' he said.

'What the hell's going on?' King said. 'Are you two in on this?'

They both looked confused.

'In on what?' Kitchener said. 'Someone just called us reporting an aggressive visitor. Guess that's you.'

'I told my receptionist to call,' Bernie said.

'We've only been here minutes,' King said. 'You must have done that before you came out to greet us. So you know who I am.'

'Enough with your assumptions!' Bernie said, raising his voice now that figures of authority were present. Now that the risk of violence had dissipated. He stepped in front of King and approached the two police officers. 'This man is insane. He's accusing me and my co-workers of some kind of conspiracy. Please get him out of here.'

Suddenly Kate perked up, talking to Kitchener. 'You need to listen to us. It's—'

The female officer raised a hand, cutting her off. 'Right now, it's best if we just take you both to the station. We'll sort everything out there.'

'But—'

King made eye contact with Kate. He knew it would do no good to cause a scene here. 'At the station, Kate. We don't have a choice.'

Dawes grabbed him by the arm and led him back through reception to the parking lot. He saw their police sedan parked next to Billy's. He was forced into the back seat, and Kate ducked in beside him. The doors slammed on either side of them. King watched the pair of officers approach Bernie and speak to him, their mannerisms calm. Bernie nodded along, playing the victim. Tears appeared in his eyes.

‘Piece of shit,’ King muttered under his breath.

‘Surely those two know something’s afoot,’ Kate said. ‘Didn’t you break out of their station yesterday?’

‘They know. But they’re not going to discuss it in front of him. At least, I hope that’s what’s happening.’

The pair walked back to the car. They opened the front seat doors. They got in. Kitchener turned in her seat and faced King. ‘You’d better have some answers.’

He started to speak, but she held up a hand to stop him. ‘Save it for the station. We’ve had a lot of shit to deal with lately. Let’s just have some quiet for a while.’

Dawes drove them out of the industrial zone, beginning the short trip back to Jameson. It seemed that whatever he did, wherever he went, King was unable to escape the pull of such a small town. He feared he’d never leave it alive.

CHAPTER 26

As they trawled back through the town, King noticed much of the road in front of Yvonne's motel cordoned off. A forensic team scoured the crime scene. They'd hid the imposter's mangled body from view, obscuring it with a tarpaulin sheet. It seemed like half of Jameson had come down to check out the scene. He guessed it would be the talk of the town for months, if not years, to come.

'I'm guessing this was you,' Kitchener said, pointing a finger in the direction of the commotion.

King shook his head. 'No idea what you're talking about.'

'Oh, I'm sure.'

They carried on. As King stared out the window, he decided he'd seen enough trees for one lifetime. When he got out of here — *if* he got out of here — he would make a change of scenery as soon as humanly possible. Another forest would drive him insane.

They pulled into the Jameson Police Department. He and Kate were led through into a different room than the one he'd last been held in, this one much larger, much more open. A floor-to-ceiling window faced out onto the front yard. King noticed Dawes and Kitchener's relaxed attitudes. There were no handcuffs. No hostility.

They sat down opposite him, and Dawes took a deep breath, as if releasing all the tension of the past twenty-four hours.

'Let's start from where we left off,' he said.

'I broke out,' King said.

'We know.'

'I'm sorry.'

'We know that also. It seems like you're doing the right thing, at least.'

Kitchener pointed at Kate. 'How'd you get her wrapped up in all this?'

'After the whole debacle with Brandt, I figured that she would be the one to have answers. So I decided I needed to kidnap her. And you two wouldn't approve of that, obviously. So I left.'

'And?'

'Dead end. She doesn't know anything.'

'I was paid to deliver a package to the post office,' Kate said. 'I don't know who by, and I don't know why. I swear.'

Dawes leaned forward. 'Brandt's imposter escaped.'

'Wow, that's news,' King said.

Kitchener shook her head. 'No it's not. Because you would have been staying in that motel. He would have come after you. He stole one of our vehicles.'

'How exactly did he manage to do that?' King said.

'We're still trying to work that out. We found him dazed in the hallway. He refused to speak. Didn't say a word. We put him in a cell and made the necessary calls. He must have slipped a key, or picked the lock, or something. That's still unclear. But now he's dead. That's very clear.'

'Do you have anything else on him?' King said.

'We ran him through the system. He flew in from America the day before last. Fake passport. We don't know his real name. Now we never will.'

'How did he get his hands on a grenade in the time it took to get to the motel?'

'How do you know it was a grenade?'

'I know what the remnants of a grenade blast look like. I was in the Special Forces.'

'We know that also,' Dawes said.

'You do?'

Kitchener pointed at him. 'I did some digging, King. After you escaped. Made some calls. You weren't just a soldier. You were part of something called Black Force. What are the chances that a government mercenary just happens to come wandering through Jameson at the same time that all this shit goes down?'

King cocked his head inquisitively at Kitchener's speech. Then he answered. 'Very slim. Which is why I'm thinking it has something to do with me.'

'I'm starting to suspect that too,' Kitchener said.

'You think I'm the one in charge?'

'I don't know what to think. This is a clusterfuck.'

'Why would they send an imposter into the police station to try and kill me if I was the one in charge? See how little sense that makes?'

Silence.

'See my face?' King said. 'You think I'd do that to myself?'

'Like I said, I don't know what to think.'

'Well, use basic reasoning. I'm trying to help you stop this. And it has something to do with Rafael Constructions, I am one hundred percent certain.'

Dawes detached the radio from his belt and held down one of the buttons. 'Helen, you there?'

Another voice crackled out of the speaker. 'Here.'

'Still at the motel?'

'Yep. Forensics had to come down from Hurst. Twenty minute drive. They'll be here a while.'

'Can you run an errand for me?'

'Sure.'

'Head down to Rafael Constructions. Their head office. Just check it out quickly. Make sure everything looks okay.'

'Will do.'

The conversation ended sharply. Dawes slotted the radio back into its place and leant on the conference table on his elbows, running a hand through his hair.

'I've barely slept,' he said. 'We went to check out Brandt's place yesterday afternoon. No sign of him. He's likely dead. There's something bigger going on…'

'That's what I was trying to work out,' King said. 'Before you two crashed my party. That Bernie guy is a slimy fuck. He knows something we don't.'

'Helen will give the place a look-over.'

'Who's Helen?'

'Another officer.'

'Can she protect herself?'

'Of course.'

'I'd say we should all head back there right now,' King said. 'Because that place gives me the creeps. And after all the shit I've seen in my life, anything that gives me the creeps is definitely worth checking out.'

'We'll let Helen handle it,' Kitchener said. 'Until then, we're going to need a statement of everything you've done from the time you left yesterday to the time we picked you up today.'

King sat back in his chair and stared at them, allowing the silence to grow to an uncomfortable length. 'You know I'm not going to be able to do that.'

'Why is that?'

'Well I could lie. It wouldn't take much effort to make up a bunch of bullshit. But I don't want to waste your time. I want to get to the bottom of this.'

'Then tell us what you saw.'

'Nothing I saw has done anything to develop the investigation. I was close to developing it, but you two interrupted. Now we're here.'

Then the radio crackled to life. A short, sharp burst of static. A moment of silence. Then a voice. Helen's.

'Uh … Dawes?'

Dawes picked up the radio, his hand twitching, his face reddening. 'Helen, all clear?'

'Kind of.'

'What do you see?'

'There's no-one here.'

'What?'

'Everyone's gone. The place is empty. A whole bunch of paper has been shredded. Looks like they left in a hurry.'

Rage flooded King and he slammed a fist on the desk, causing everyone in the room to startle. For once in the last three days he had come close to the truth. Close to getting the edge over Bernie and finding out exactly what the new owners of Rafael Constructions were doing with its resources. Now he was sitting in a police station, answering useless questions, letting the people behind this slip away without reprimand.

'Get me there,' he told them, ice in his voice. 'Right now. I'll sort this out.'

It didn't take long for them to make up their mind. They glanced at each other, mulling over what decision to make next, wondering just how legal any of these processes were. But common sense eventually gained the upper hand.

They knew he was something else. Some kind of force they couldn't contain.

Kitchener looked at him. 'Back in the car.'

CHAPTER 27

Dawes broke the speed limit for the entire duration of the trip. They made it back to the head office in less than five minutes. King and Kate in the back, the two officers up front. What they were doing was completely against the law. Punishable by serious jail time. But in this situation, the smartest play. They'd recognised that King was a trained killer, and that they needed his help.

There was greater danger than King in the forest.

It was clear that Rafael Constructions had been deserted on a moment's notice. The front door to the building lay ajar. Three vehicles that had previously been in the parking lot were now gone. There were no cars left except for Billy's abandoned sedan, almost crumpled beyond recognition. A woman in police uniform stood on the front deck, beckoning them over. King guessed she was Helen. She looked to be at least six-feet tall, slim, in her late forties. A stern, no-nonsense woman. That much was clear.

The four of them got out of the police car and approached the office with an air of apprehension. Dawes and Kitchener withdrew jet-black pistols from the leather holsters at their waist and aimed them at the building. King recognised their make. Smith and Wesson M&P40's. Standard issue for Victoria Police. Semi-automatic. Reliable. They'd do the job.

'Fun morning, huh, Dawes?' Helen said as they stepped onto the deck.

'To say the least,' Dawes said. 'You been inside?'

'Briefly. There's no-one around, I can tell you that.'

'Helen, this is Jason King.'

'Who is he?'

'He was passing through. He used to be a soldier. He can help us.'

King nodded a greeting at Helen, but he wasn't focused on pleasantries. He scanned the office's exterior, looking for anything out of place.

A loud shattering noise sounded inside the building.

A window breaking.

Someone was still here.

'Gun,' King said to Dawes. 'Now.'

The officer took one look at his steely expression and did not protest.

'This is so illegal,' he muttered as he handed across his firearm.

King took it and advanced through the front door, gun up, eyes flicking left and right, searching for any sign of danger. There was nothing in the reception. It was exactly how he remembered it, save for an overturned chair in one corner.

He kicked the door to the interview room open, but it was just as bare as it had been an hour earlier.

A couple of hallways branched away from reception, leading to an array of offices. King didn't know where to start.

Then he heard a noise. Some kind of rustling, at the end of the back hallway. A chair scraping against the floor. He let the familiar rush come back to him, juicing up his limbs, targeting his central nervous system, hyping him up. He took off down the hallway, heading for the source of the sound. As he got closer he pinpointed it. One of the rear offices, facing the lot out back. The door lay slightly ajar. A tiny sliver of the room inside was visible.

King didn't slow down.

He launched himself at the door, slamming a boot into its centre. It shot open, revealing a small nondescript office. A large wooden desk sat in the centre, covered in shredded documents. A man stood behind the desk, rustling through one of the drawers, papers in his hands. He stood slumped, unconfident, worried. Before King could charge headlong into the room he produced a pistol and fired twice.

King spun out of trouble. He slammed into the adjacent wall. Taking cover from the gunfire.

It seemed they had left without something important. This man had been sent back to retrieve it. King fired his M&P blind into the office. The space was small enough to give him a solid chance of hitting the worker. But there came no cry of agony, or the sound of a body hitting the ground.

Just silence.

Then a window shattering. Struck by some kind of blunt object.

The worker fled. Fast, too, spurred on by the fight-or-flight mechanism hardwired into the human brain. Motivated to get away from danger as quickly as possible.

As soon as he heard him leaving, King spun on his heel and powered into the room. The guy was halfway out the window on the other side of the desk. His legs scrambled over the broken glass, kicking hard, a second away from dropping to the ground outside. King vaulted the desk and snatched at his legs. Too late. The guy disappeared from sight, successfully out of the building.

King felt an icy determination coursing through his veins. He would not let the worker get away. He took a deep breath, still in motion, and dove. He aimed for the centre of the window to avoid the shards of glass dotting the sill. His head passed through first, and he followed through by tucking his chin to his chest and turning his legs over. He hit the dusty earth outside shoulder-first and rolled with the landing, springing to his feet not a moment later.

Now he had all the time in the world.

The worker fled through an enormous gravel area packed with construction machinery; flatbed trailers, cranes, rusted forklifts. But he was nowhere near cover. King had a clear shot. He would take care not to miss.

He dropped to one knee and lined up the sight, pinpointing the fleeing worker's back. Then he lowered his aim. It would do no use to accidentally kill the man. He'd killed too many leads already. He exhaled, breathing deep, tapping into that old feeling of being out in the field, of having to hit his mark or facing certain death.

He pulled the trigger.

The guy went down.

Bingo.

King stood up and walked toward him, boots crunching on the gravel. He passed through rows of machinery. The guy dragged himself feebly across the ground. Bleeding heavily from his left leg. King had shot him in the calf. A crippling injury that all but eliminated movement for the foreseeable future.

He dropped to one knee and wrapped a hand around the timid man's shirt.

'What's your name?'

The guy panted. He had thin, dishevelled hair and pronounced cheekbones. 'Jonas.'

'You work here, Jonas?'

He nodded, gulping at the same time. In too much pain and shock to speak.

'Why'd everyone leave?'

'I can't tell you.'

'I'll shoot you if you don't.'

'Please, man.'

'You can either tell me, and I'll let you live, and then you might have a chance of getting away from whoever you work for. Or you don't tell me, and you die, without question. Pretty easy.'

'The boss told me to come back. I forgot one of the files. He said he'd kill me if I left if there.'

'What document? Who's the boss?'

'I really can't tell you, man. Please.'

King slammed a fist into the guy's stomach. He moaned and doubled over, clutching his ribs.

'You can play the victim all you want, but there's innocent people dying here,' King said. 'You're willingly working for the ones responsible. So your pity party isn't getting through to me.'

'Alright, alright,' he said, coughing. 'There's a concrete—'

Harsh static erupted through the lot, cutting Jonas off. It seemed to come from everywhere at once, blaring across the terrain. It fizzled and cracked and died out. King noticed the wooden poles dotted around the construction site, megaphones mounted on top. The loudspeaker system, designed to communicate with workers operating the machinery.

Someone was using it.

A voice came to life, low and booming, resonating all around them.

'You always had a big fucking mouth, Jonas.'

King looked down at the worker. He was petrified. His face had turned to a mask of sweat. His eyes grew wide. The two of them made eye contact for a single moment.

Then the man's head exploded in a gruesome spray of brain matter.

Hit by a fifty calibre bullet, long range.

King watched the faceless corpse of his only lead flop to the gravel, dead before the sound of the discharge echoed through the empty lot.

CHAPTER 28

For the second time in two days, King found himself under sniper fire.

He'd seen Jonas' head pop from the left, meaning the round had come from the neighbouring factory. There was a sniper buried somewhere in that maze, using one of the hundreds of vantage points that King knew would be a good setup. He darted behind one of the forklifts nearby. Putting something large and metal between him and a bullet.

But no further shots came. Just the lone round that had killed Jonas. Palpable tension rose from the silence.

The back door of the head office burst open and Dawes came sprinting out, gun raised, reacting to the report that had echoed through the site seconds before.

'No!' King screamed. '*Back inside!*'

Too late.

He watched in horror as Dawes jerked sideways, taking a bullet to the temple with equally graphic results. There was little doubt that the officer was dead. He slapped against the gravel with the looseness of a corpse, half his head blown apart.

Kitchener was in the process of following Dawes outside. She had been halfway out the door when she saw him career off to the side. She screamed and fell back into the office, colliding with Kate in the process. The pair disappeared from sight.

Despite Dawes' brutal demise, King managed to breath a sigh of relief. They would live if they stayed inside the building. He, on the other hand, faced a significant problem. The forklift against his back provided a rudimentary, temporary shelter. But sooner or later he would have to make a move. He didn't know how much of a professional the enemy sniper was. First he'd assumed the talent of long distance shots had died with Cole, but it appeared there was more where he came from. He wondered how many more…

A round struck the ground a few feet in front of him, slotted precisely through the empty space in the forklift's cabin. He ducked. They wanted him dead, that much was certain. And they would succeed if he stayed put.

He had a single M&P handgun. They had an unknown number of forces, and enough ammunition to bother supplying a group of local bikers with military-grade assault rifles.

As he lay there on the gravel, scrunched up into as little space as possible, pressing the back of his head against the cold steel, he came to the conclusion that he would not bother fleeing. These people had some kind of connection to him, unless he was facing the most unbelievable of coincidences. Which he knew he wasn't.

He knew the distance to the factory would not be impossible to close. There was little cover in between save for a handful of industrial vehicles and a few mounds of scrap. He knew the closer he got, the more trouble it would be to hit him. Sniper fire relied on long range, on stationary targets. Yet he had no knowledge of how talented his adversary was.

There was only one way to find out.

He waited until the next shot came. He knew it would. It was only a matter of time. When the report blasted in his ears and the ground nearby kicked up a handful of gravel he turned and got his feet underneath him and powered out from behind the forklift, running wildly, zigzagging, jerking his head off-centre, doing anything possible to throw off the marksman's aim.

He had little time to get a grip on his surroundings. A single moment of opportunity came to take a glance at the nearby factory. He saw a blurry mound of steel and metal twisting above the trees. Too many open spaces. Too many vantage points. Nowhere near enough time to pinpoint the sniper.

He dove behind a rusting flatbed trailer on the very edge of the property. Another round slammed into it, shaking it on its wheels. A near miss. Luckily, the space between each neighbouring property had no obstructions. No chain link fences, no barbed wire, no barriers of any kind. Which gave King a slight advantage. He could make one more burst across open ground and then the awnings of the factory would shield him from view. He'd be swallowed up by the enormous building. Once he was inside, he knew the playing field would turn ever so slightly in his favour. He thrived off confusion. Tight spaces, wild close-quarters combat, no strategy or tactics or anything of the sort. It brought all encounters down to speed, power and timing.

Three things he excelled at.

There came a break in the gunfire. Silence descended over the site, but none of the familiar sounds of the forest returned. All the wildlife had been scared away. Now the only audible noises came from the groans of long-dormant machinery, spurred on by a cool breeze. The sudden quiet was eerie. King zoned in and slowly looked over the top of the flatbed.

Nothing. No gunshot. If there was, he would never know anyway. He would be dead before the sight or sound registered. But he stayed alive, because the sniper had run out of ammunition. King knew he would be reloading.

Now.

He vaulted off the dusty earth and slid across the width of the trailer, moving with the efficiency and energy of a man running for his life. He saw nothing from the factory ahead. No muzzle flashes, no sudden movements. There was only time for a rudimentary glimpse, though. When he touched down on the other side of the trailer he surged toward the ground floor of the factory like a man possessed.

He heard the sound of another gunshot — and ducked reflexively — but felt nothing. It had missed. He wasn't sure where the bullet had impacted, how close it had come to ending his life, but in the end it didn't matter.

Whether it missed by a hair or a mile, he'd made it to the building in one piece.

He ran underneath an open roller door into a large space that had long ago been the factory floor of a slaughterhouse. The space was filled with rusted hydraulic equipment, conveyor belts, chains, hoists; anything that could be useful in the killing of animals. A row of broken industrial-scale refrigerators ran the length of the far wall. It was dark and musty and putrid, like the workers had abandoned the place without caring to salvage any of the machinery. Which gave anyone trying to sneak up on him plenty of cover to do so.

The roof far above creaked and the wind battered the outside of the structure and somewhere far away came the sound of dripping water. But otherwise, no hostile sounds.

Then a sharp crack filled his ears and his vision exploded and he dropped to his knees, the action involuntary. He'd been struck from behind. Whoever had crept up on him had done so with impeccable precision. Usually he was able to sense most attacks, yet this one caught him completely off-guard. He fell to the dusty floor, on the verge of retching. He careered forward. Crashed into the ground. Knocked senseless.

Another impact to the back of his head, from something long and hard and metal. This strike put him dangerously close to unconsciousness. He saw nothing except darkness. He heard nothing except a roaring in his ears. He felt his senses depleting, slipping away.

Then a male voice, close by, in his ear:

'Jason King. Just who I expected to see.'

He used all the effort in his system to turn his head and attempt to get a glimpse at the assailant. In his peripheral vision he saw a blurry outline, dressed all in black, before another blow crashed against the side of his skull and he collapsed to the floor. Agony flared across one half of his face. The weapon had struck his already swollen cheek.

Everything shrunk to a pinpoint and disappeared.

CHAPTER 29

It was one of the worst concussions King had ever suffered.

Over the course of his time in the military he'd been battered, shot, cut, tortured, knocked out multiple times. The sensation of losing consciousness was impossible to get used to. His memory became sporadic. The next stage of his life passed in nothing but flashing, distorted images.

Someone helped him to his feet.

Dropped him into a car.

Still disoriented, he slurred his words. Unclear as to which way was up, which way was down, where he was headed, who he was with.

The trees flew by. They were driving on twisting mountain roads. The journey blurred into a single incomprehensible rollercoaster. His head throbbed and his eyes watered and he battled to control his senses. If he could just urge his limbs to act, then he could deduce whether he would survive the rest of the day. Was he being driven to a grisly death? Where was Kitchener? Where was Kate?

Then there were no more trees.

A building appeared in front of him.

Someone helped him inside.

He was in a small room with a double bed and flaky white walls and a cheap kitchen and a circular table. He lay on the bed and someone pressed a cool towel against his forehead. Time shrank and expanded and then suddenly, all at once, he could think clearly. He could still felt the concussion's devastating effects. The pressure in his skull was immense. He felt like he would pass out again at any moment. But at least he had control of his bodily functions.

A woman sat on the bed next to him. Resting a hand on his chest. Her face was freckled. Her long brown hair fell over one shoulder. She sported a look of concern and worry and anger all wrapped up into one emotion.

Kate.

'Are you okay?' she said.

King shook his head, and immediately regretted the decision. His head pounded like nothing else. 'I've been badly concussed.'

'I know.'

'Which means I'll feel like this for weeks.'

She gasped. 'That bad?'

'Trust me. It's happened before.'

'What the hell happened, Jason?'

'Where did you find me?'

'In the factory. Alone. You were just coming to when I made it to you.'

'You followed me in?'

'I wasn't going to just stay in the office. We were sitting ducks in there. The lady was a mess after seeing her partner get shot. She was no use. I saw you go into the factory and figured I would help you out. However I could. I waited a few minutes then came in after you.'

'And you didn't see anyone else?'

She shook her head. 'Not a soul. Who did this to you?'

'I don't know,' King said, pressing a pair of fingers hard against his temple. He struggled to suppress a bubbling cocktail of emotions. 'I'm being played with, Kate. We're all being toyed with. All I remember is being hit from behind. I remember being completely helpless. I could have been killed right there. Easily. But I wasn't.' He looked around. 'Where are we?'

'Hurst. It's a small town. Ten minute drive from Jameson.'

'How did you get here?'

'I...' She trailed off.

King touched a hand to her face. 'Kate.'

She wiped her eyes, drying fresh tears. 'I put you in Billy's car and just drove. I was so scared. I had no idea what was happening.'

'You just left Kitchener there?'

'I'm sorry!' she yelled. 'I'm not used to this shit. I'm just a normal person who does normal things like make mistakes when they get shot at. I'm not some kind of warrior like you. I don't just waltz into gunfights and danger and ... whatever. I just panicked and drove.'

'We need to go back and check on her.'

'You can't in this state.'

'I know. Give me a moment. I just need ... some water or something...'

'You need more than a moment.'

He dropped his head onto her shoulder and took a deep, long breath. The physical effects of recent altercations were catching up to him. Everything hurt. He wasn't sure where to start with addressing his injuries. It had all moulded into an intricate web of pain. He thought back to that night where he'd first wandered up the road to Jameson, expecting a relaxing visit to an unassuming little town in the middle of nowhere. What he'd encountered was something brutal, something visceral, something he still couldn't quite put his finger on.

'Why did you leave?' Kate said finally, breaking the silence.

He turned and looked at her. 'What do you mean?'

'Black Force. Why did you really leave? I don't believe what you told me before. Something made you quit, just like that, and come all the way out here. Looking for peace and quiet. What was it?'

'How can you tell?'

'Something's eating away at you,' she said. 'You're a shell that I still can't seem to crack. You're so quiet, but I don't think you're usually this reserved. I think you're trying to suppress something.'

He didn't respond for a full minute. He lay back on the bed and wrapped his arm around Kate and stared at the roof overhead, listening to the forest sounds outside.

'I fucked up a mission,' he said. 'My last mission.'

She rolled over, draping a leg over him so she could look him in the eyes. 'You haven't failed one before?'

'I have. Many times. But this one was devastating.'

'Where?'

'Kuwait. Two months ago.'

'What happened?'

'They sent me in to infiltrate an anthrax weapon production facility. It was operating under the guise of a civilian biotechnology lab. The stakes were huge. They'd been producing hordes of the stuff for months, undetected. They had an enormous stockpile, just sitting there, officially labelled as government research. Intel said they had the means and the motivation to use it.'

'On what?'

'I don't know. Now I never will.'

'What did you do wrong?'

'Almost everything. I rushed my preparation. I was discovered early. They managed to cart the anthrax out of there while I was pinned down, and then I never saw it again. Half of them got away. It was a complete and utter failure. And I told everyone in charge that I could pull off without a hitch.'

'That's not your fault, Jason.'

'It is. The higher-ups wanted to send in a full team of Delta Force soldiers. Storm the compound from all sides, big gunfight. Make sure none of the product made it out of that facility, no matter what the consequences. They were willing to let a few soldiers die to stop a full-scale bioterrorism attack. I convinced them otherwise. I told them — no, promised them — that if they sent me in there it would be over quicker and quieter, with the same results. They let me. And now I have to live with the fact that my inadequacy left an entire facility worth of anthrax spores in the hands of a group of radicals.'

'I'd call you a hero for even offering to do such a thing.'

She kissed him for what felt like forever. Her hair spilled over his face and he let the sensation calm him. They parted.

'That's why I don't have a phone, or a laptop, or anything,' he said. 'I left that all behind. I don't want to look at the news one day and see how many people my failure has killed. I don't want to know how much pain I've caused.'

'You can't be sure that the others would have been successful,' she said. 'You blame yourself for everything that goes wrong, and you can't help getting yourself involved. That's why you're still hanging around this piece-of-shit town while everyone's trying to kill you.'

'I came here to get away from everything. I left the jobs I used to do to faster, stronger, younger men. I wanted to finally be free of all the responsibility that's been eating away at me for years. And now look what's happened. I feel like I need to succeed here, or I'll just cause more death.'

'If you never got involved there would be a lot more innocent people dead. You're a good man for staying. No matter what happens.'

'I don't know about that. What if I've caused more trouble by staying?'

'What do you mean?'

'If my old friends are showing up, and this all has something to do with me … then what am I still doing here?'

'Trying to help us.'

'But what if I'm just keeping them here?'

'I don't think you are. I think this is something bigger. You can see that too.'

King nodded.

'Well,' Kate said, 'at least we have this.'

She climbed off him and crossed the room to the table in the far corner. King watched her as she walked, admiring her. A thin manila folder sat on the surface. She picked it up and threw it to him.

'What's this?' he said, catching it.

'I don't know,' she said. 'But it's important.'

'How so?'

'It's the folder that the worker came back for. He dropped it on the way out of the office. I found it on the porch, before I came for you. Figured it might help.'

King clenched the folder in his hands, spinning it over and over. Slowly, a smile spread across his face.

'Kate, you're an absolute gem,' he said.

He opened it, and began to read.

CHAPTER 30

The folder contained a swathe of documents, all bundled together, all very official looking. King buried his head into the papers and tried to decipher their contents. Kate stayed by the dining table, chewing a thumbnail restlessly.

The first dozen pages had been written with only professional eyes in mind. They contained a plethora of complicated scientific terms, with no consideration for layman explanations. He read through the description of three stages of some kind of bacteria; incubation, prodromal and fulminant. Then an endless list of chemicals, prepared and organised to perfection. All scientific jargon. Information that certainly shouldn't be in the hands of a countryside construction company. He flicked through to the next section.

This part made a little more sense. It laid out the blueprints to some kind of facility, measured and drawn in exquisite detail. A report on the building stated that it had closed down a few months ago for private use. There was a comprehensive analysis of its usefulness for an unnamed client, including the fact that it was miles away from prying eyes, which apparently made it perfect for their needs. Needs which were seemingly undisclosed in the report.

'Kate,' he said, beckoning her over. He held out the papers. 'Do you know what this is?'

She studied the blueprint for a moment, then nodded. 'It's a concrete plant. Belongs to Rafael Constructions. I've delivered letters to some of the workers there a few times, back when I had a short stint at Jameson Post as a courier. Haven't been there in over a year. It's in the middle of nowhere.'

'Do you know how to get there?'

She nodded again. 'I think so.'

'Something's going on there. I can't work it out. Take a look at this.'

He handed over the first cluster of notes. Kate flicked the pages over, eyes narrowed, concentrating hard. When she reached the end she let out an exasperated sigh and passed them back.

'Absolutely no idea,' she said. 'But it looks dangerous.'

'You know what I'm about to say.'

'King, you're in no shape to just barge in there.'

He rose off the bed and shook the pages in her face. 'Did you read what I just did? This is big. I have a feeling a lot of people are going to die if I don't try to do something about it.'

'And did you hear what we just talked about?' Kate said, raising her voice. 'How long are you going to keep putting your life on the line? You quit the Force to get away from all this shit. How much more are you going to take? They already could have killed you, you said it yourself.. I don't think this is something we can just waltz in and stop.'

King fetched the keys to Billy's sedan off the table, his head pounding, his brow sweaty. 'I have to try.'

'Jason!'

'You want me to leave? After I've found out that an old friend is in on this?'

'I want *us* to leave.'

'I'm sorry, Kate,' he said. 'Not happening. I've had plenty of chances to walk away. Now I can't.'

'You can. You're the only one stopping yourself.'

'Not after what I've learnt.'

They stood facing each other for what felt like an hour, when in reality it could not have been more than a minute.

'Well, what am I supposed to do?' she said.

'Get as far away from me as possible. Like I've been telling you this whole time.'

'I'm coming with you.'

He paused. 'That is the complete opposite of what I just said.'

'If you're not going to leave, then I'm not. I'll see it out.'

‘It’s your choice, Kate. I won’t stop you, but I can’t promise that you’ll be fine either. I don’t even know if I’ll be alive at the end of the day.’

She shrugged. ‘That makes two of us, I guess.’

King gripped her hand as they made their way back to the car. He unlocked it and they climbed in. A strange smell permeated the vehicle. The combination of lead and smoke and blood and destroyed mechanics. He started it up. The battered engine took a moment, but it chugged to life soon enough and settled into a steady rhythm.

‘Possibly the most reliable car in human history,’ he muttered. He pressed three fingers against his temple, wincing through a particularly vicious wave of nausea. The concussion, rearing its ugly head. Then he sucked it up and touched his foot to the accelerator.

They drove through the empty streets of Hurst, which turned out to be very similar to all the other small towns King had seen during his travels through Australia. They left a crowded main road that acted as the bustling heart of the area, complete with an array of local businesses. As the buildings grew distant and the trees wrapped around them once again, the feeling of seclusion crept back in. It seemed no-one spent time on the roads between towns.

The drive to the concrete plant took longer than expected. Winding roads cut through the forest like a knife through butter, making the scenery identical no matter which way they travelled. They headed in the direction of Jameson. Kate peered out the window, strangely silent.

'You okay?' he asked her.

'I've never thought about dying this much before. I don't know how to feel.'

'It's a strange feeling. And nothing I say will help you suppress it. Trust me, I've been feeling that emotion for years.'

'You haven't become numb to it?'

'You can't. But I've dealt with it so much that it feels normal. Which isn't healthy.'

Kate flicked her eyes ahead, then pointed to the left where it branched off to a dusty side road. 'Down there.'

This rutted track took them through farmland, where great swathes of the forest had been carved out to make way for pastures. Long, low farmhouses dotted the landscape, surrounded by paddocks of mixed grasses and endless rows of fence posts. A few were topped with barbed wire, which had rusted from the elements long ago. Sheep, cows and horses covered many of the paddocks.

'I lived with a family here when I first flew over,' Kate said. 'I helped them out around the farm, all day every day, until I could get on my feet. They were lovely people.'

‘Sometimes I wish I’d gone down a route like this,’ King said. ‘Open skies, long days of labour, full meals. I wouldn’t have had to fear for my life every single day.’

‘But a lot of innocent people would have died. You wouldn’t have been there to save them. You’ve lived a good life, even if it wasn’t pleasant.’

‘Have I?’

In the distance they heard the rumble of a tractor sweeping over its paddock. King took a moment to let the serenity of the setting wash over him. Down the track, the top of the concrete plant rose out of the forest.

They were close.

When the pastures ended the trees swallowed them up once more. This section seemed to be a little more remote than the others. The trunks were clustered closer together. The moss winding around the trunks grew thicker. The weeds covering the forest floor stood higher. It felt like no-one had set foot in these parts for years.

‘Long to go?’ he asked Kate, slightly unnerved by the change of setting.

’Not far now,’ she said. ‘I told you it was in the middle of nowhere.’

Finally the track led into another clearing, indistinguishable from all the others King had seen during his time in Australian woodland. This one had been set on a slope which descended ever so slightly in the opposite direction. The majority of the space was taken up by the concrete plant, broken up into two sections. The main facility was an enormous warehouse, constructed of steel. Behind it lay the concrete plant itself. Six massive cement bins towered over the warehouse, clustered close together. They were all connected to a belt conveyor that descended into the main building, bringing all the structures together into an amalgamation of industrial prowess.

Already, the effects of neglect were beginning to set into the plant. It seemed the freezing weather had started taking a toll on the outer surfaces of the plant. Machinery left out in the open had been worn down by the elements, the dormant cement bins had rusted and the whole place had a feel of dilapidation about it.

They got out of the car and crossed the open stretch of ground. No sounds of activity came from the plant. It appeared deserted. King took the lead as they approached a small door at the front of the warehouse. He made sure to be cautious. Aware of all his surroundings. Ready for an ambush. No-one would sneak up on him this time.

He reached out and twisted the handle.

Unlocked.

The door swung open to reveal a massive interior space with a dirty concrete floor, packed with all sorts of machinery. This equipment, however, had a different feel to the rest of the plant. They were out of place, seemingly brand new. As if they had been produced recently, specifically for a certain project. Not the regular gear that usually fills a concrete plant. These machines had a different purpose.

King cocked his head as he looked around. There wasn't a soul in sight. The shiny new contraptions lay in the open, unmanned, untouched. The place gave off a similar feeling to Rafael Constructions' head office. Like the entire area had been deserted in a hurry.

He stepped inside and crossed to the nearest machine. His footsteps echoed off the walls, the only noise inside the cavernous space. The contraption was a large metal box, bolted shut, with two exhaust pipes trailing out of the top. A small glass window had been installed on one side. He squatted and peered in, squinting in the dim gloom of the unlit warehouse.

The box was filled with a white powdery substance, still coarse. King took one look at it and recognised it instantly. His throat dried and his stomach fell and his hands grew cold and clammy even before he stood up and read the label plastered to the side of the container.

Bacillus anthracis.

'Kate,' he whispered, his voice hoarse.

She sensed the panic immediately, and quickly came to his side. 'What is it?'

He rested a shaking hand on top of the box and took a deep gulp of air. 'This is the anthrax. From Kuwait.'

'That's impossible.'

What the fuck is it doing here? he asked himself. *Why Jameson?*

'I know what they're doing now,' he said, now speaking quietly. Demoralised. In over his head. 'I know what this whole thing is about. If these spores get weaponised into an aerosol, it's enough anthrax to wipe out an entire city.'

'They're weaponising it?' she said. 'Here?'

'That's what all these machines are for,' King said. 'I read hundreds of files before heading into Kuwait.'

'I didn't think anthrax could do that.'

'Enough of it can. It took 9/11 for people began to realise the power of a biological attack.'

'9/11?' she said.

'A week after the planes, letters containing concentrated anthrax spores were mailed to news offices and government officials. They killed five people, and the shitstorm that followed was unprecedented. It opened up a whole new side of terrorism.'

'That's what this is? Terrorism?'

'I'm certain. But why here? Why me?'

'Maybe it's a huge coincidence.'

He turned to her, and registered the shock on her face as she saw how pale he had turned. 'It's not. My last mission in

Black Force fails, and somehow the result of that failure ends up in the exact place I decide to travel, halfway across the globe?'

'You still think it has something to do with you?'

'Of course it does.'

'Who's doing this?'

'I don't know. Not the terrorists from Kuwait. Someone else…'

Noises, outside. The sound of heavy footsteps.

'Let's go,' he said.

'What?

'This is far worse than I thought, Kate. It's a national security crisis. I need to make some calls. We have to go, right now.'

They hurried for the door they'd come through. King hoped it wasn't too late. He drew the M&P and stepped outside, barrel up, ready for confrontation.

He need not have bothered.

The warehouse was surrounded on all sides. More than ten men had emerged from the forest, forming a rough semi-circle around their position. They all possessed similar qualities. Tall, well-built. Hard expressionless features. Seasoned combatants. Each man held an M4 carbine, identical to the weapons brandished by the bikers back at the metal work factory. But these men knew how to use them. If King took a single step further he and Kate would die in a storm of gunfire. He knew that much.

Without command from any of them, he threw his pistol onto the wet grass. Kate let out a noise, a resigned sigh, accepting that they had been defeated. King felt a cold tingle creep up his spine. Perhaps this was it. He would die without answers, never knowing how everything fell into place.

Then a voice, from behind.

The same voice he'd heard in his ear just a few hours earlier.

'Smart move, buddy.'

He turned and saw a man standing just inside the warehouse. He had short, close-cropped hair and small beady eyes that hung over a tight-lipped mouth. His features were soft from lack of exposure to the elements. He'd obviously spent much of his life indoors, probably behind a desk.

King knew which desk.

He knew which building the desk sat in.

He knew the man standing across from him like he was part of his family.

Since its inception, Black Force had been run by a single man. This man held more power than the Joint Chiefs of Staff, yet officially he did not exist. Lars Crawford held no government title, but for over ten years he had organised and commandeered some of the most dangerous missions in United

States military history. For ten years, he'd told King what to do, and where to go, and who to kill, and who to save.

Now he stood across from him. In the middle of a forest. In the last place King had ever expected to find him. When he'd walked out of the same man's office two months ago, he thought he would never see Lars again.

How wrong he was.

CHAPTER 31

'What the fuck are you doing here?' King said.

He couldn't think of anything else to say. His senses were reeling, half from the injuries he'd sustained and half from the massive revelation that a man he'd trusted with his life for almost a decade had engineered this entire situation.

'Officially, I'm on leave,' Lars said, sneering. 'Visiting family.'

'Your aunt…'

'What?'

'I met some of your family. In Jameson. I told your aunt that I'd never heard of you. I couldn't say a word.'

Lars scowled. 'Bunch of abusive fucks, the lot of them. I'm never laying eyes on them again. Convenient excuse, though. The higher-ups lapped it up.'

'So what are you really doing here?'

He motioned to the warehouse in a broad, sweeping gesture. 'Preparing for a show. Have been for months. Your presence is a bonus. Thought I'd show you the price of walking away.'

The ten soldiers behind King didn't make a sound, but he knew they were still there. Kate stood by his side, dead silent, not moving a muscle. He knew she was scared out of her mind. He was too.

'That's the anthrax from Kuwait,' he said. 'What those corrupt bastards escaped with.'

'Bingo,' Lars said. 'Want to know why I have it?'

King said nothing.

'You see, sitting around in the bowels of the Pentagon just wasn't cutting it for me anymore. You and Slater and a handful of other operatives made a fortune. The four-stars revered you. And me? Well, I was given a slightly larger office. No-one gave a fuck about me. No-one cares about the brains behind the operation. I'd had enough.'

King still did not respond. He looked at the man across from him with utter contempt. Shocked as to how a seemingly good person had stooped so low.

'You know, King,' Lars said. 'I never knew how you did it.'

'Did what?'

'Managed to stay sane while you were treated like dog shit.'

'I was treated fine.'

'None of us were. We were thrown around like slaves. It's about time I did something for myself. Wouldn't you agree?'

'Not really.'

'The only people who are remembered are those who do great things, and those who do terrible things. We did great things, King. The pair of us. And no-one gave a shit. No-one cared. What we achieved ... it should go down in history.'

'You're a sick fuck.'

'You see, the benefit of doing terrible things is that you can get rich in the process.'

'You got in touch with the lab employees after they escaped with the anthrax? You thought that was a rational thing to do?'

Lars laughed, a cruel harsh noise. 'Who gives a shit what's rational? I knew enough anthrax spores to decimate a city had just left the premises. I knew they wanted to weaponise them. I knew they didn't have the resources to do it. But I did. I'd spent enough time in the Pentagon to have private knowledge of the worldwide power structure. So I knew exactly who was willing to pay billions of dollars to carry out a bioterrorism attack on a major city. All the pieces fell together. It was too good to pass up.'

'You knew where the anthrax was?' King said, fists clenched, knuckles white. 'Even after it left the facility?You could have tracked them down and ended it just like that.'

'What's the point of stopping them?' Lars said, now smiling. 'To do what? Go back to a shitty job. Retire with a shitty paycheque. Waste away a shitty retirement. I don't think so. I thought, you know what, let's shake up the world a little. And as it turns out, a few of my underlings like money a whole lot. Including Cole Watkins. I take it you two had a meeting, because I haven't seen him since yesterday.'

'I've met a few of your friends.'

'I can tell. You've looked better.'

'Who's funding this?'

Lars laughed again. 'A couple of royals in Dubai. What do you care? There's always a certain few extremists with more oil money than they know what to do with. And I'll happily take the payday. Sure beats what Uncle Sam was paying.'

'Why me? Why here?'

'You were our best operative. By far. And what did you do with it, King? You broke. You caved in. You walked away when the going got tough. You left me to run a division of men who were ten levels under you.'

'I couldn't do it anymore.'

'Neither could I. We chose to move on in different ways.'

'That doesn't explain how this facility ended up here. In the same town I happened to be passing through.'

Lars cocked his head. 'You still haven't realised?'

'Realised what?'

'Remember when you came into my office and told me you wanted out?'

King nodded. 'Like it was yesterday.'

'Obviously not well enough. What happened after all the shouting died down?'

'You asked what I'd do. I said I'd travel.'

'And who suggested you see the backwoods of Australia? Who made up a lie saying that they'd taken a holiday down in Victoria a few years ago, and that they'd loved it?'

King's stomach fell.

How had he been so stupid? He remembered the conversation vividly. Lars must have known he was in a bad place, battling inner demons. King had been easily influenced by the subtle recommendation. He hadn't even given it a second thought. Lars had manoeuvred him like a chess-piece so that he ended up in the exact location he wanted him.

'You were plotting this attack before I told you I would retire?' King said.

'Of course I was,' Lars said. 'This facility was under construction well before you walked into my office. While you went off and disappeared for a month after Kuwait, I was left to clean up your failure. This has nothing to do with you. But then you showed up one day, high and mighty as always, telling me you'd had enough. So I thought I'd teach you a lesson. Show you who's the real superior. There's no rules out here. There's no bureaucrats sniffing around, no official structure, no paperwork. You can have all the success you want over your career, but it doesn't mean shit when I manage to pull off the largest bioterrorism attack in the history of man right under your nose. What good are you?'

King did not know how to respond. It was true, Lars had outsmarted him. But he was taken aback by the horrid bitterness that had been crumbling the man's insides for so long, that he'd failed to detect until now. Lars had done well to hide it over the years. King had known him as quiet and reserved, but he'd never anticipated that timidness festering into resentment. It was undeniable that Lars was a genius, responsible for planning some of the most tactically sound and effective operations in military history. King never guessed that those skills would be used to create something so devastating.

'How did you set this up out here?' King said.

'It's simple enough,' Lars said. 'You have no idea the influence I hold. The contacts I have access to. Anything I want. It's as easy as picking up a phone and dialling.'

'But surely this type of equipment would warrant an investigation.'

Lars smiled knowingly. 'Have you heard of Project Bacchus?'

Silence.

'I'll take that as a no. I was involved in it, right when I was first starting out. 1999, I believe. I was just a lowly worker at the DTRA. We tested whether a bioterrorism facility could be constructed with regular everyday materials, and kept secret.

Our team was able to produce almost a kilogram of bacteria — much like anthrax — without detection. So when I got wind of the Kuwait payload, I knew I could get away with it.'

'Who are these people?' King said, motioning to the men surrounding them, weapons raised. 'More Delta Force? Black Force boys?'

Lars shook his head. 'You underestimate those two factions. Cole was the only one from Delta who I knew would take the bribe, so he was the only one I offered it to. The rest are all hired guns.'

'Amateurs.'

'Amateurs compared to you. But they're trained mercenaries. And look where you are now. All that speed won't help you here, will it?'

King reluctantly admitted to himself that it wouldn't. There was no way out of this situation. No magical solution to ten fully-automatic assault rifles aimed in his direction. He hoped Kate didn't think that he was superhuman. There were some situations that were impossible to resolve, no matter how much talent one possessed.

'I'd kill you now, but I really want you to watch me leave this place with everything I've made. So you know you failed completely. All those injuries, all that fighting, all that hard work, for nothing.'

'You're done here?'

‘The spores are ready. Took us a while. A few people chanced upon the site. Couple of construction workers, and a police officer. Think his name was Brandt. I killed that guy myself. Got some hired guns to kill the other two.’

‘I know. You won’t be seeing those hired guns again.’

Lars shrugged. ‘Figured it was you. Who cares? I win. You lose. I don’t give a shit about anything else, and neither should you. Because it all doesn’t matter, does it? Here we are.’

He signalled to his troops. Before King had time to react, a pair of men grabbed an arm each and escorted him inside the warehouse. Another pair shoved Kate in after him. They were manhandled toward a machine with steel poles on either side. One of the men pushed King’s back up against the pole and looped a thick rope around his midsection. He ran the rope across his arms, effectively pinning him against the pole, then tied it off behind him. King couldn’t budge. The same was done to Kate and then the men retreated. Lars slammed a button on the side of the warehouse door and a large set of roller doors began to groan toward the ceiling.

CHAPTER 32

King was helpless to do anything but watch as a pair of military-style trucks rolled into the clearing. He recognised them as Hawkei PMVs. Australian Defence Force vehicles. Big, brutish, fast. Designed for the battlefield. Probably purchased by Lars unofficially, through back-door systems, for a hefty fee. Clearly, they had been waiting for the call to enter. This entire event had been a set-up from the beginning. With grim realisation he figured Lars had kept him alive towards the end just to demonstrate that his plan would succeed.

It didn't take long to load the steel crates of anthrax spores into the back of the Hawkeis. With both drivers, Lars' forces numbered fourteen in total. They were a mixed bunch. Some black, some white, all stern and silent. They were paid to follow commands, and that was what they did without question. Lars ordered them around until every last piece of anthrax was inside the vehicles. Then he crossed to King and patted his face demeaningly.

'Guess I won't see you again, champ,' he said, his tone sardonic. 'Good catching up.'

'How much have you made from this?'

'Close to two billion dollars.'

'I still don't understand why you stooped this low.'

'Because you're going to die in here, and no-one will ever know who you were or what you did. I'll retire on a beach somewhere and sip piña colada's for the rest of my life. And they say crime doesn't pay…'

'You're batshit crazy.'

'Guess we'll have to agree to disagree. Have fun with dying.'

He turned on his heel and strode out of the warehouse. Kate let out a whimper, unsure of what was to come. King wanted to reassure her everything would be okay.

But he knew it wouldn't.

On the way out, Lars signalled to two of the mercenaries who King guessed were the most obedient. The pair who would be more than happy to carry out his wishes. He spoke within earshot of King and Kate, so they heard every word.

'You two want to stay back and finish them off?'

'Pleasure, boss,' one of them said. He was a bald man in his late forties with acne scars and a permanent scowl. The other guy was older, probably closer to sixty. King could tell they were both military vets. They carried themselves with the gruff demeanour of men who had seen a lot.

Lars got into one of the Hawkeis, followed by the other twelve men, who split themselves evenly between the two vehicles. Just like that they were off, carting an unknown quantity of one of the deadliest biological agents on the planet.

King bowed his head and knew there was no escape. He couldn't break free. The rope was too thick, too tight. The two men left staring at them would do what they wanted, and then they would die. There was nothing else to be done.

'Ex-army?' King said as the pair strode into the warehouse.

The older guy cocked his head and let out a harsh laugh.

'Look at this guy,' he said to his friend. 'Trying to be all friendly.'

'American bastard,' the bald guy said. 'And his little slut.'

'Bossman won't stop talking about you,' the older guy said. 'Said you used to be some kind of assassin. Most dangerous man on the planet, apparently.'

'Flattering,' King said.

'I don't believe him. Look at you. You're fucking useless.'

'How are you going to kill us?'

Baldie looked around. 'Well, there's no-one else here, is there? So, anyway I want.'

'Always wanted to do something like this,' the older one said. 'Never gutted anyone before.'

Baldie turned to him and raised an eyebrow. 'The girl?'

A sneer spread across the old guy's face. 'Why not? Let's make him watch!'

King felt his blood run cold. Rage flooded his system. He strained against the rope with everything he had, but even his immense strength could do nothing to budge the bindings. The mercenaries noticed. They started laughing in unison.

'All your macho toughness isn't working, is it?' the bald guy said. 'Untie the bitch.'

The old guy walked up to Kate and kissed her on the forehead. He began to work out the knots in the rope around her, taking his time, moving slowly. Tears ran down her face, but she made no sound. King could see she was fighting to remain calm, even in the face of such horror.

When the bindings fell away she attempted to make a break for it. She got off to a running start, but the old guy snatched her arm and threw her viciously onto the floor. Her head smacked on the concrete and she whimpered in pain. The pair of them moved in.

Baldie pulled at her thin shirt, trying to tear it off. Kate let out a scream, a primal yell of fear and terror and disgust.

King had never felt such anger in his life.

He bucked and writhed like a madman, veins pumping, teeth bared, trying to do anything possible to stop what was about to happen. The older guy turned and made eye contact with him, and let out another cruel laugh. He relished the rage he had caused.

King closed his eyes and forced the tears back into their ducts.

He felt nothing but unbridled fury.

Then there came a loud *bang* from somewhere outside. He recoiled at the sudden noise and opened his eyes. It took him a second to realise what had happened. The older guy flew off his feet and slapped the floor like a rag doll, landing in a rapidly-growing patch of crimson. King looked down and saw the man's leg fountaining blood. The liquid spurted out at an alarming rate. He knew the guy's femoral artery had been severed. He would bleed to death, that much was certain.

As the man screamed, another bullet sent Baldie's head snapping back, punching him square in the forehead. He splayed back across the ground, next to his friend. Dead from a single shot.

The old guy had left his gun on the table, which meant he could only watch as a woman in police uniform strode in through the open roller doors.

'Kitchener,' King said.

She took one look at the scene and wordlessly raised her gun, pointing the barrel at the older guy's face. His features were bunched up in agony.

'Don't,' King said, stopping her in her tracks.

She looked at him.

'Untie me,' he said with ice in his voice.

The old guy went pale and started dragging himself across the ground, moving with the fervour of a man who realised his predicament had turned dire. He hurried away from King. His leg poured blood as he crawled.

Kitchener moved behind King and worked at the bindings for a few seconds. She hadn't spoken throughout the ordeal. She knew what he was about to do.

No words were necessary.

As soon as the rope came loose King felt a wave of relief flood through his system. He was free to do as he pleased. Claustrophobia rarely affected him, but in that instance he'd felt like imploding from sheer frustration. He didn't wish to think about what might have happened had Kitchener not shown up.

He followed the trail of blood across the warehouse floor. The old guy hadn't made it far. He scrambled feebly for purchase on the dusty ground, dragging his useless leg behind him. King stood over him and wrapped two hands around his shirt.

'What was all that you were saying before?' he said.

'P-please…' the old guy spluttered.

'Oh, now you're sorry.'

He thundered a fist into the guy's mouth, breaking off several teeth in a spray of blood. Then he dropped his entire bodyweight behind an elbow which smashed the guy's nose into a million pieces. The pain knocked him out.

And that was that. King turned to Kitchener and raised a hand, signalling that it was time to finish it. She tossed him her M&P40. He caught it one-handed, spun and put a final bullet in the guy's brain.

He wouldn't hurt anyone else.

King's first priority was Kate. He crossed to where she lay curdled in a ball on the floor, sobbing softly. He lifted her to her feet and wrapped both arms around her, holding her close, kissing her hair, letting her know everything was going to be alright.

'I'm so sorry you had to experience that,' he whispered.

When they separated, Kate walked to the old guy's lifeless body and kicked him harder than King thought possible. In the stomach, in the face, in the throat. She let out all the rage and fear until there was nothing left, then came back and hugged King again, burying her face in his chest.

Kitchener watched patiently while they embraced.

'How did you find us?' King said.

'I've been driving around aimlessly for the past hour. I was stopped by the side of the road and saw your sedan go past.'

'Driving aimlessly?' he said. 'What happened at Rafael Constructions?'

She looked at him, and he saw something in her eyes. He sensed that nothing would be the same for her again.

'Helen went outside first and they shot her down like it was nothing,' she said. 'I don't know if they realised I was still alive. Everyone disappeared. Gone, just like that. I went back to the station … and the two officers there were both dead. Gunned down at their desks. I'm…'

She trailed off.

'You're…?' King said.

She looked up at him, terrified. 'I'm the only police officer left in Jameson.'

'It's my old handler from Black Force doing all this,' he said. 'He told me to come here when I retired. I took his bait. That's why everything has been revolving around me.'

'What is this place?' Kitchener said, staring in awe at her surroundings.

'It's an anthrax production facility.'

'Anthrax … like the—?'

'Yes, like the virus. Lars has manufactured a shitload of it.'

'That's precise.'

'I don't know how much exactly. I just know he plans to use it. And he left with the supply ten minutes ago.'

'I saw them. Two big military trucks, right?'

He nodded. 'Do you know which way they were headed?'

She shook her head. 'I waited for them to pass then continued on. Walked here all the way through the forest. Left my car in one of the pastures, because I knew I'd be spotted otherwise. I think they were heading for the main road.'

'I can't thank you enough for helping us out.'

She shrugged. 'You've been helping us out for the last three days and none of us realised.'

'We can't go back into town,' Kate said. 'They'll kill us.'

Kitchener nodded. 'I agree. We need a place to hole up for the night. It's getting dark. I was thinking the motel, but it's the centre of attention right now. An entire crew came in to install new windows.'

'What about the one in Hurst?' Kate said.

'No,' King said. 'Too far. I know a place.'

'You do?'

He nodded. 'You just have to promise not to look in one of the machines.'

CHAPTER 33

The metal work factory stood out against the darkening sky as Kitchener pulled up to its bulk. King sat in the back, one arm around Kate's shoulder, holding her close. Their bellies were full. On the way through Jameson, Kitchener had stopped at the convenience store and loaded up on supplies. They hadn't eaten all day. The hot pies and protein bars made him sleepy, and he'd almost drifted off, but the sudden stop jolted him awake. Kate stirred and touched his cheek. The one that wasn't swollen.

'You okay?' she whispered.

He nodded, and kissed her forehead.

They got out of the old Nissan and Kitchener went to the boot. She lifted it up and brought out two large flashlights, high-power, designed for camping. She gave one to King. Kate gathered the two M4 carbine rifles from the back seat that they'd taken off the dead mercenaries, and the three of them left the car behind.

They headed into the factory floor. It was just as decrepit and abandoned as seemingly every building around here was. King glanced at the machine in the far corner — home to eight dead bodies — and led them away from it, into a hallway branching off from the main area. It ran into the depths of the building, leading to a number of empty rooms. They were all sparsely furnished with various discarded chairs and desks. He guessed they used to be offices. He found one that was warm enough to hold back the shivers, surrounded by the thousands of tons of steel all around them. They settled on the dusty floor and propped the flashlights in the corner, leaving them on for added comfort.

For a long while, no-one spoke. All three of them had a lot to process. There had been little time for reflection over the past few days, and King took the time to rest his head against the plywood wall and attempt to deal with the waves of discomfort coursing through him.

I need a holiday.

A real holiday.

'What's going to happen?' Kate said, breaking the silence. He noticed her tone quivered. Her voice was laced with worry. 'What could that much anthrax do?'

King closed his eyes and grimaced. He'd been trying to keep his mind off that problem.

'A hell of a lot,' he answered honestly. 'I did a lot of research on it before Kuwait. If they manage to weaponise the entire lot in aerosol form … it could be devastating.'

'How bad are we talking?' Kitchener said.

'The worst part is that no-one will know they're infected until it's too late,' he said. 'If they release it over a populated city, hundreds of thousands of people would be incubated.'

'Incubated?'

'They'll inhale it, and become infected, but show no symptoms. It'll all start to kick in at once. Fever, vomiting, coughing, that first. But an attack of that size … any responses that the government has prepared aren't going to work. All the serious problems will start at the same time. Headaches, seizures, deaths. Across an entire city. It'll be total fucking chaos if Lars has the amount I think he has.'

'So what do we do?' Kate said.

'I don't think they're leaving the area just yet. We go searching in the morning.'

'What makes you say that?'

'Instinct. Past experience.'

'What made you get into the military?' Kitchener asked out of nowhere. The question took King by surprise.

'What?'

'Why did you join up?'

'That's an odd question.'

'I'm just curious.'

'Sorry, Kitchener, but I've talked enough about my past lately,' he said, glancing at Kate. 'I'd rather not get into it. In fact I'd be happy to never address it again.'

'I'm just thinking about why I signed up to be an officer in the first place.'

'Why did you?'

'I don't know,' she said, staring vacantly at the wall. 'Because it was stable, I guess. A good means of employment in these parts. I was dirt poor.'

'And now?'

'I'm still dirt poor, and I'm also holed up in an abandoned factory hoping I don't get murdered overnight.'

'You from around here?'

She nodded. 'I was born a couple of towns over. In Waterford. Haven't seen the world. Haven't seen anything.'

King reached over and gripped her shoulder. 'Is that what this is? You think you won't have an opportunity to in the future?'

'What future?' she said. 'We're sitting here while they run rampart around the countryside, doing who-knows-what. They'll kill us if we try to stop them.'

'You know we can't do anything while it's dark,' King said. 'We'll get killed trying.'

'We'll get killed no matter what.'

'Don't be so sure. I've managed to avoid it for ten years.'

She bowed her head. 'I just don't know if I was prepared for something like this.'

'No-one's prepared for this kind of thing.'

'It seems you are.'

'You don't want to be me. I'm ready for anything because I've seen enough shit in my life to give a psychologist nightmares.'

'That doesn't sound like it's good for you.'

'It's not.'

King leant out the door and glanced at the far end of the hallway. The daylight creeping into the factory floor had all but disappeared. Soon it would be night. He got his legs underneath him and clambered to his feet.

'What are you doing?' Kitchener said.

'Heading into town for a bit.'

She looked puzzled. 'What do you mean?'

'How else do you want me to put it?'

'I get it. But why?'

'I'm not going to sit here and twiddle my thumbs. I'm just going to have a look around. Plus, I operate better alone.'

She also got to her feet. 'Then I'm coming with you.'

'No you're not.'

She cocked her head. 'Why not?'

'I literally just explained.'

'You operate better alone?'

'That's right.'

'I don't think that's rational.'

'Clearly you didn't look hard enough into my file.'

He walked over to Kate and stuck his hand out, motioning for one of the assault rifles. She heaved one off the ground and handed it over. He slung it over his shoulder by the strap, kissed her on the lips, whispered that he would be back soon and turned to leave.

Kitchener stood blocking the doorway.

'That's not a good idea,' he said.

'I don't like this, King,' she said. 'I saved both your lives, and now you're just running off with one of our guns. What if you die out there?'

'I won't.'

'How do you know?'

'Because no-one will see me.'

'That's bullshit.'

'That's your opinion. Did you spend ten years in the Special Forces?'

'No.'

'Then move.'

He brushed past her, fed up with the stalling. Reluctantly, Kitchener moved to let him through.

'You don't have a phone,' she said. 'We have no way of knowing if you're alright.'

'I'll be alright.'

He paused in the corridor, looking back. He made eye contact with Kate. She nodded her understanding. He smiled. Then he turned and walked out of the metal work factory, albeit much slower than he had the first night in Jameson. He hadn't found himself on the end of multiple beatdowns back then.

Those were the days.

He let the cool night air wash over him, embracing the solitude. It was indescribable how much better it felt with no-one around. It was how he'd spent thousands of hours in combat. It felt natural. Like he was at home. Which he knew he should not relish in. He'd moved thousands of miles away from his past to start afresh, to clear his mind of all the horrors he'd seen. Now he found himself back in the same situation. Alone, armed. Heading into an area he knew was populated by men trying to kill him.

Old times were calling.

But he would not get into a firefight tonight. He had a single goal, which he hadn't cared to disclose to either Kitchener or Kate. There was something he had to do, and no-one could be around to see it. He had a hunch, and over the years he'd learnt to never underestimate a hunch. He would take precautionary measures tonight, to ensure that he had the upper hand in whatever lay ahead.

That was how he'd stayed alive for years.

That was how he was here today.

He ducked into the forest and began the slow trawl back up to the main road. He would head into Jameson.

There was a man he needed to see.

CHAPTER 34

He returned exactly three hours later, in the dead of night. The moon was tucked away behind clouds, obscuring its soft glow. As a result the metal work factory was almost invisible in the darkness. He trudged across the dewy grass, breath steaming in front of his face.

A dozen feet out from the factory's entrance, he heard the distinctive click of a safety catch flicking off. He froze, even though he knew who it was. Such a sound had been drilled into his head to signify imminent combat.

This time, it did not.

He calmed himself and said, 'It's me.'

Kitchener let out a sigh of relief from inside. She emerged from the black, M4 pointed at the ground.

'I've never used anything like this before,' she said. 'I was worried I would have to.'

'It's pretty simple. Just point and hold the trigger. Anything in front of you won't stand a chance.'

She stopped in her tracks. 'What did you find?'

'Nothing.'

'Nothing at all?'

'I told you. I was just doing some scouting. Nine times out of ten that turns up zip. I just wanted to see what's going on in Jameson.'

'What *is* going on in Jameson?'

'Well, there's a lot of people up, especially at this time of night. The ones I saw looked scared. The grenade at the motel definitely caused a scene. I'm not sure if people know about all the other dead people yet. That'll all start coming out soon. When people don't come home to their families.'

'This is fucked,' Kitchener whispered, more to herself than King. 'My entire station…'

'It must hurt.'

'I don't feel anything right now,' she said. 'I think I'm still in shock.'

'Try and get some sleep.'

'Where do we go from here? Even if we win.'

'I don't know about you, but I'm never setting foot in Jameson again.'

'We might have something in common there.'

They headed inside. Kate came out to greet him while Kitchener ducked into the room. They hugged tight. He whispered something in her ear, and she nodded. Then they parted.

'What's the plan tomorrow?' she said.

'I don't know. I'm still trying to work that out. I still feel like we're at square one. We just know who the bad guys are now.'

'That's useful, at least.'

'It might not be,' he said. 'They could be a hundred miles from here by now.'

'I think it was for show,' Kate said. 'I don't think he's done here. We should go back to the plant.'

'I should.'

'Jason…'

He couldn't help but smile. 'Ah, this talk again.'

'You know I want to stay with you.'

'And I'm glad you do. But let's get some sleep. I'm about to pass out.'

The office floor was far from comfortable, especially pressing into the dozens of bruises and cuts littering his skin. But he shifted his weight around until he found a position that felt somewhat bearable. Kate's head lay on his chest, her cheek warm, calming him. Kitchener curled into a ball on the other side of the room. He took a deep breath and let all the worry and the anger and the repressed memories of years past wash away. The coming rest would be vital.

He had a gut feeling that he'd need it the next day.

CHAPTER 35

The night passed restlessly.

Despite his attempts, he barely managed more than a couple of hours of sleep. Kate dozed softly on his chest, utterly exhausted from the madness. He wasn't sure how Kitchener slept. The room was too dark, and she stayed silent in the corner.

When faint daylight crept into the hallway he made his way out to the clearing and stared at the sun rising over the treetops. The trees were covered in frost. A thin fog had settled over everything, obscuring the sky. He heard the familiar morning calls of various birds and the creaking and groaning of the trunks as they swayed in the morning breeze.

Kitchener crept up behind him. She looked ahead, not interested in disturbing the silence.

'Did you sleep?' King said.

'Barely,' she said. 'I keep replaying everything. Over and over again.'

'That's natural.'

'Where do we go from here?'

'I think we should—'

Kitchener's phone buzzed in her pocket. She withdrew it and checked the screen.

'Huh, that's weird.'

He looked over. 'What is?'

'An old friend's calling…' she said. 'Give me a moment.'

She swiped at the screen, returning a missed call. She pressed the phone to her ear and began to pace back and forth in front of him, speaking intermittently, nodding along, listening closely. She talked for a couple more minutes, then hung up and dropped the phone back into the pocket of her uniform.

'We may have something here,' she said.

'An old friend?'

'Paul Robinson.'

'And he is?'

'He owns a skydiving dropzone not far from here. Twenty-minute drive, tops. I did my solo course there a few years back. Needed something to shake up the normal routine. Have you ever jumped?'

King scoffed. 'Thousands of times. Usually into hostile territory.'

She paused. 'Ah. I keep forgetting you're a different breed.'

'Continue.'

'A plane of his was stolen overnight. It's a PAC P-750 XSTOL.'

'Never heard of it.'

'They're built out of New Zealand. Perfect for skydiving. Large exit door, that sort of thing. Which also means you can load crates of anthrax in fairly easily.'

'How long ago was it taken?'

'Paul arrived at the hangar half an hour ago and found it empty. He called me straight away.'

'You think it's connected?'

'It's got to be.'

'We don't have much else to go off,' she said. 'What were you going to suggest before?'

He shook his head. 'This trumps anything I had planned. Let's go.'

He went back to the room and explained the new development to Kate. She nodded, yet her expression seemed dazed. Like the events unfolding were just another part of an unbelievable, improbable rollercoaster.

He drew her in, wrapping an arm around her.

'It'll be over soon,' he said. 'I promise. We're close.'

'I hope so.'

They packed up the rifles and the flashlights and the few supplies Kitchener had brought in from her car and the three of them slipped back into the vehicle. King looked back at the metal work factory as they peeled away from it and shuddered up the same gravel path. He knew he would never see it again. Whether his life depended on it or not, he was never coming back to this place. Too many bad memories. He'd spent too long in the same place.

He couldn't shake a feeling that the endgame was approaching.

They had to pass through Jameson on the way to the dropzone. Kitchener drove, guiding them from memory. For added caution, King lay down across the back seat as they passed through the main strip. It would do no good to attract unwanted attention. He got Kate to do the same. When civilisation dropped behind them once again, they resumed their positions.

'What are you going to do when this is all over?' he said to Kitchener.

'Leave. Find another job.'

'No longer a fan of police work?'

'I've seen enough lately to turn me off that career path.'

'And you?' he said to Kate.

'Still trying to work that out.'

He nodded his understanding.

'What about you?' Kitchener said. 'Where will you go?'

'Haven't quite figured that out yet either,' he said.

They passed through Hurst, and King eyed the motel Kate had brought him to. A supermarket, a stretch of cafes, a hardware store and a bank all flashed past. He saw regular civilians going about their lives. Carefree. Unaware that their world could be brought to a crashing halt at any moment.

The world's a strange place, he thought.

In seven days every man, woman and child within a fifty mile radius could succumb to violent, painful deaths, all dependent on the choices of a single individual.

Unless King managed to stop him.

Ten minutes later they arrived at the dropzone. It was a huge tract of land, mostly grass, with a stretch of runway in the centre of the property. A sunbaked single-lane road led onto the tarmac. Down by the far end King saw the hangar. They accelerated toward it, picking up speed. The building had nothing on the industrial sites he'd recently encountered. There was just enough room to fit a small plane. The hangar doors lay open, revealing nothing inside but gear and maintenance tools. It was conspicuously empty. Connected to the hangar was a long concrete structure, a single room that King guessed was for fitting harnesses and parachutes. Then alongside both these buildings lay a ranch-style clubhouse with a wide covered deck. A pair of big four-wheel-drives rested out the front of the hangar, both at least ten years old. Useful for picking up the day's jumpers.

King had enough skydiving experience to be knowledgeable about the craft. He appreciated the setup. Surprisingly, he found himself envying the owner, much the way he had appreciated the serenity of the bartender during his travels into Jameson. These men had set up a business for themselves, doing what they loved, and they made enough to live a comfortable and peaceful life. He wondered if it was too late to do something similar.

He was pulled from his thoughts when the door to the clubhouse opened and a short, stocky man with long flowing hair made his way across the runway. They climbed out of the car. Kitchener waved to the man, and he waved back.

'Long time no see, Paul,' she said.

He seemed like he would ordinarily be a happy, laid-back man. Now his face had creased with worry.

'Hey, Lisa,' he said. 'Nice to meet you guys. I'm Paul.'

He shook King's hand, then Kate's. As they went through the motions of rudimentary greetings, King noted his use of the name Lisa. He never had asked Kitchener's first name.

It suited her.

'Who are these guys?' Paul said.

'Just a couple of friends,' Kitchener said. 'We're … understaffed at the moment. So what can you tell us?'

'Actually, quite a lot,' he said. 'But I wanted you here to see it, of course. Don't wanna be snooping around behind your back, hey? Police need to know about this shit.'

'What shit?'

'GPS in the plane, mate. I know where it is. The buggers who stole it aren't that smart, are they?'

All three of their eyes widened simultaneously, but not for the reasons that Paul thought.

'You have its exact location?' King said. 'Right now?'

Paul nodded. 'I do. Wanna take a look?'

He ushered them into the clubhouse. The interior was fully furnished. Sports paraphernalia dotted the walls, ranging from posters to jerseys to footballs, many signed. A beer fridge lay in one corner, full to the brim with cans of lager. An entire wall had been taken up by a shoddily constructed bar. There wasn't a large variety of alcohol save for Jack Daniels and Malibu. Sprawling couches took up the majority of space, all surrounding a large television. There were several stands packed with flyers on skydiver safety and upcoming events.

Paul crossed to a laptop open on the countertop of the bar. He brought up a program which was nothing more than a large satellite map of the countryside. A small green dot shone in the upper left-hand corner. He zoomed in and pointed at it.

'The fuckers aren't moving,' he said. 'They've landed somewhere, but I'm not familiar with that area. It's back up near Jameson.'

King scrutinised the map. The green dot hovered in an area clear of trees. A long black strip cut through the forest all around it.

Another runway.

He studied the surrounding area. He saw a road that cut through pastures and a small grey cluster that looked very similar to a concrete plant.

'Is that…?'

'They're behind their facility,' Kate said. 'There's a runway buried in the forest back there. But it doesn't look like there's any way to access it on land. There's no roads leading in.'

'There has to be,' King said. 'They need to get the anthrax on the plane. That's why they landed there.'

Paul perked up, registering what King had said. 'The what?'

'This isn't what you think it is,' King said. 'They're not hooligans or petty thieves. A lot of people are in danger.'

'Did you say anthrax?'

'Yes.'

'Fuck me.' He ran a hand across his sweating scalp. 'How do you know that?'

'Can we make it there in time?' Kitchener said, ignoring Paul.

'Only option,' King said, heading for the door. 'They'll be loading the plane as we speak. They won't be expecting us.'

'Hey…' Paul said, following them out of the clubhouse.

He began to say something else, but King didn't hear him.

The blood rushing to his ears cut off all sound.

His heart skipped a beat.

He looked out across the runway to see a pair of vehicles in the distance, kicking up hordes of dust, roaring down the road toward the cluster of buildings. The two Hawkeis, barrelling at full speed. All loaded with men dressed in military-style khakis. The same men who had tied him up the previous evening.

Kate let out a gasp of surprise. 'How did they…?'

'Fuck,' King said. 'Into the hangar!'

He ducked in through the open rear door of Kitchener's car and grabbed both the M4 rifles off the back seat. He spun both weapons until they faced the right way, then racked the safety off each gun.

He knew if they were to make it out of the dropzone alive, a monumental firefight would be necessary.

'I'll talk to them,' Paul said. 'Pretend no-one's here.'

King looked at him, stunned. 'No you fucking won't. They'll kill you.'

'It's all good! I've got it.'

King moved to grab Paul, but he was just out of range. By then it was too late. The Hawkeis shot out onto the runway, closing the distance quicker than he had anticipated. Any longer out in the open and he would risk being spotted. Cursing Paul's idiocy, he retreated to the hangar and ducked inside.

CHAPTER 36

The hangar smelt of fuel and old machinery. It had a cracked concrete floor and barely any decent cover. The space previously occupied by Paul's plane now lay empty. Wooden shelving ran across the far wall, customised to fit the dimensions of the hangar. A door at the rear of the hangar led through to the concrete structure King had spotted previously. The door had a glass window at head height. He looked through and saw a long low room packed with skydiving gear. A handful of harnesses hung from the roof.

He instructed the two women to press themselves against the closest hangar wall. Then he did the same. He heard the squealing tyres of the Hawkeis pulling up outside and knew he had put himself in one of the most vulnerable positions of his life. All it would take was one man to round the corner and raise the alarm. He gripped the M4 in his hands, sweat running onto the metal.

Heavily outnumbered. A severe lack of cover. Vision still wavering from the effects of the concussion.

He knew he was in a bad spot.

The three of them crouched low, not daring to make a sound. Round the corner doors slammed and footsteps clattered across the tarmac. King kept his barrel aimed at the open entrance to the hangar. He let his pulse quicken and the familiar feeling of pre-imminent combat flooded his system. There was nothing quite like it. The heightened senses and increase of adrenalin proved a potent combination. After ten years of channelling such a feeling it had become second nature. He could control it. The nerves no longer affected him. He simply used them to react faster.

Beside him, Kitchener breathed heavy, her weapon up just like his. She would be experiencing the same rush, yet hers would be a little harder to control. She hadn't shared the same past as King. Police officer or not, she would not be mentally ready for the situation that was more than likely about to unfold.

His line of sight revealed nothing but a pretty landscape, with the runway ending a hundred feet away. The usual breeze rustling through the air had ceased. There were no natural sounds out here, just the odd groan from the hangar walls. It made the conversation outside clearly audible. He could hear every snippet of dialogue.

From somewhere nearby Paul said, 'Can I help you gentlemen?'

'Whose car is this?' a gruff voice demanded.

'That's my friend's. He's staying with me for a few days.'

'Where is he?'

'In one of the caravans out back. He's asleep.'

'Wake him up.'

'I'm sorry, but…'

'I said wake him up.'

'Mind telling me who you are? And what's with all the guns?'

No response.

The silence went on a beat too long. Long enough for King to realise that Paul was in serious danger. These men obviously knew that he was here somewhere. Which meant they knew Paul was simply stalling.

It appeared their patience had grown thin.

The din of rifle fire made the three of them flinch. It ripped across the empty dropzone, carrying with it the undeniable conclusion that Paul had been killed. King tried to count the shots, but they were too rapid. He guessed that two separate guns had been used to execute the man. There was no visual proof to back up such an idea, but there were little other options. Who else could they have been shooting at?

The following chatter confirmed King's worst fears.

One man said, 'That was a bit excessive.'

Another said, 'Fuck him. He was trying to hide them. Lars knows they're here.'

A third said, 'Spread out?'

The second man replied, 'Yeah. Sweep the property. They won't escape without us seeing. It's too open around here.'

Then there was movement, scuffling and rustling, heading straight for the hangar. He heard Kitchener inhale sharply behind him. Kate stayed quiet, but she would be terrified. King clutched his M4. He made his hands stop shaking. He calmed his breathing. It was an odd sensation when one knew that combat was inevitable. He could hear a cluster of men moving toward the hangar's open entrance. He raised his gun.

They would round the corner any moment…

When he saw the first flash of a limb, he didn't pull the trigger. Sure, he would kill one man, but the others would fall back behind cover, and then every mercenary in their general vicinity would know their location. They would be flushed out and overwhelmed.

So he waited for the first man to step into view, then the second and third followed a moment later, all three of them searching the hangar for signs of life, scanning it from right to left, taking just a fraction of a second too long to notice King crouched on one side.

A fourth man came into his line of fire just as he unloaded the M4's magazine.

They didn't stand a chance.

His aim had been locked on, and when he had time to zone in, he rarely faltered. Especially at this proximity. The carbine rifle coughed and spat as thirty bullets unloaded out of the barrel. The four mercenaries started to instinctively raise their weapons, reacting to the sudden noise. Not fast enough. Their torsos shook as they were dotted with lead. They stayed standing for a split second. Kitchener added a few shots of her own, squeezing off the M&P a few times in rapid succession. Unnecessary, but it made sure none of them would get up.

The four of them buckled and fell to the tarmac outside the hangar, dropping their guns, either groaning in agony or dead.

'Through there,' King said, motioning to the door set into the far wall. 'Now.'

The barrage of automatic weapon fire would attract every last man on the property to their location. He thought he'd counted ten men when he'd first seen the convoy approaching. Which left six, all fully armed, all ready for combat, all dangerous.

They ran for the door, fear lending them speed. King discarded the empty M4 in his right hand and gripped the second fully-loaded rifle double-handed. Thirty bullets left. No spare magazines. He reached the door first, praying it wasn't locked. He thundered a boot into its centre and it swung open, clattering on its hinges. He breathed a sigh of relief and ducked through into the gear-fitting room. The two women followed. He slammed the door shut and took a quick glance through the plexiglass.

Men dressed in khakis and brandishing all types of automatic weapons began to surge into the hangar, stepping over their dead comrades. King saw this and fell away from the door. A trio of shots destroyed the glass a moment later, several more thudding into the wood, some tearing through.

They couldn't stay here.

Under a heavy barrage of gunfire he grabbed Kitchener and Kate from their crouched positions and hurried them toward the door on the other side of the room. The pair had instinctively covered their ears and ducked their heads, hoping to avoid getting struck by a bullet. Often King felt the same urge, but he knew their best shot at survival was getting as far away as possible, even if it meant risking a bullet in the spine. They passed harnesses and unpacked parachutes and a rack of different-sized jumpsuits and then smashed open the double doors that led somewhere outside.

He found himself in a narrow gravel alleyway between the hangar and the clubhouse. The trail arced down past the two buildings, opening out onto a cluster of caravans that normally housed fun jumpers and solo course students. He gripped the two women by the shoulders, getting their attention, and pointed down the path.

'Take cover down there,' he said. 'Shoot anyone who comes near you.'

'What about you?' Kate said.

King looked at the clubhouse and said, 'I'm going in there.'

Kitchener said, 'You'll be trapped.'

'I know. But there's nowhere else to go. And I've made it out of worse situations before.'

'I don't doubt that, but that doesn't mean you'll make it through this.'

From within the hangar came the sound of a door crashing open. The mercenaries were through to the gear room.

King gave Kate a quick hug. They made brief eye contact, and he could see the fear in her eyes. Not so much for her own life, but for the fact that she might see King die in front of her. He nodded reassuringly, smiling, as if to show that everything would be okay. She nodded back, unsure. Then Kitchener dragged her away. The pair took off running down the road.

King spun, raised the M4's sights to his eye and fired a volley into the double doors. It would make the remaining mercenaries hesitate. They would take a moment to regroup, form a strategy, so that they didn't come running out to their own deaths. Which gave Kate and Kitchener precious time to find cover amongst the caravans.

King looked up at the clubhouse. Perhaps he would do better to make a break for it. If he ran for his life there was a chance he would live. But then what? He would be without a vehicle, without a proper arsenal, ten miles from where he needed to be as Lars loaded a plane full of weaponised anthrax spores. Then the six men left here would tear the property apart searching for Kate and Kitchener. He needed to kill these men, or he would never make it to the other runway in time.

And he worked best in close quarters. Messy fighting, just how he liked it.

He vaulted onto the clubhouse's porch and aimed the barrel of his M4 skyward. He fired a few shots into the air, drawing attention to his location. He stepped through one of the open doors, heading inside.

CHAPTER 37

The rounds of unsuppressed rifle fire had temporarily stunned his hearing, meaning the inside of the clubhouse felt like a mausoleum. He looked over the familiar sights. The main area branched off in two separate directions, the left-hand side leading to a set of offices where clerical work occurred, and the other leading to a communal kitchen. At one end of the kitchen, a narrow tiled hallway led to a shared bathroom. King took all this in, knowing it would be valuable information in the event that all hell broke loose.

He jogged to the centre of the room and ducked behind one of the couches. It was a disadvantageous position to wait for combat. The clubhouse sported a few large windows, some floor-to-ceiling, all positioned at random intervals around its perimeter. Plenty of vantage points if they decided to surround the building.

Which they did.

King saw movement on the far side. Nothing prominent, just a flash of limbs and the glint of a weapon. He skirted around, positioning himself between two couches. M4 up, searching for targets.

They were taking their time. Which meant they had their forces under control. They weren't bull-rushing in, like King had expected them to. With a sinking gut, he realised he had put himself in serious danger.

One of the windows shattered. Somewhere behind him, out of his line of sight. He spun, weapon raised. No sign of an enemy, nothing to shoot at. He searched for the source of the breakage, and found nothing. Then a second later he saw the small black cylinder skid to a halt on the linoleum, not far in front of him.

A flashbang.

He had no time to shield himself. The grenade went off just as he noticed its presence, an all-encompassing explosion of bright light, accompanied by an ear-splitting din. The combination ravaged his senses simultaneously, blinding him, deafening him. He knew he was ducking for cover but he couldn't see or hear anything. He loosened his grip on the rifle in his hands and it scattered away to parts unknown. He knew he wouldn't find it again.

He moved instinctively, crab-crawling across the floor, navigating by touch alone. His head spun. He felt the scratchy surface of a countertop. Somehow he'd made it to the kitchen. The bathroom should be somewhere behind him. He would be trapped, but he needed cover. Even if that meant cornering himself. Losing all senses was a terrifying sensation, especially in the heat of combat.

He felt shards of something brush across his skin. Fragments of plaster or ceramic. They were tearing the place apart. He couldn't see or hear the bullets flying all around him, but he knew they were there.

The bathroom was his only available option.

He crawled and scratched his way down the hallway, at the same time shaking his head vigorously side to side, desperate to regain some kind of sight. Even a blurry haze would do. Anything was better than total darkness, coupled with a pounding headache and ruined eardrums. He felt weak like this. Vulnerable. Exposed. Slowly his hearing began to return, and he heard the muffled thumping of automatic rounds ripping the walls of the clubhouse to shreds.

Movement, close by. He felt the displacement of air and a distant, tinny sound at the edge of his hearing. Like grunting. Someone had come charging into the bathroom. A large shape, directly in front of him. He shot forward, wrapping an arm around the man's midsection, still blind, acting merely on touch alone. He used his momentum to throw the guy off-balance and they both crashed to the floor amidst a tangle of limbs. He heard metal against linoleum, off to the side. A weapon hitting the floor. King's crash-tackle had sent the rifle spinning away.

It seemed they would have to brawl.

He swung wildly, scrambling on top of the guy. His vision was nothing but a pulsating, blurry mess. He landed a couple of shots, then the guy bucked him off and slammed a fist into his throat. He fell back against the bathroom wall. Disorientation and dizziness and a shortage of breath all combined together. Panic rose in his chest. He could see colours now, but his surroundings remained muddled. He saw the mercenary in front of him, scrambling to his feet.

He began to rise. His knee brushed against something long and metal.

He bent down and scooped up the dropped weapon, relying on reflexes alone. The man across from him was too close to get off a shot in time but he brought the butt of the rifle around in a scything arc. It cracked the guy's jaw, audible even with King's impaired hearing, sending him crashing to the bathroom floor in a heap, clutching his face.

King began to make out more features. He saw tiled walls, painted stark blue. There was a row of toilet cubicles on the other side of the room, and a row of showers on this side. The guy on the floor was white, middle-aged, fit. He kept his hair short. He was dressed in military-style khakis, but some kind of cheap knock-off, not the real thing. King's senses would not return to one hundred percent for hours, but this rudimentary form would do for now.

He reversed his grip on the weapon — which he noted was a Ceska Scorpion sub-machine gun with detachable stock — and put a few bullets into the dazed mercenary's skull. Blood arced from the man's temple. He was dead.

Five left.

King knew that he could not slow down. If he paused even to breathe, the remaining forces would come charging in through the hallway and outnumber him effortlessly. He would die in a blaze of gunfire. So he reached down and gripped the corpse underneath him one-handed. Using previously untapped primal strength, he heaved the dead man out into the hallway.

Bullets dotted the walls and the floor as the remaining mercenaries reacted to the sudden movement. They'd been ready to fire on King the second he left the bathroom. Distracted by their dead friend, they would now be caught off-guard. Just for a split second. The time it took them to shake off the sight of a deceased comrade and return to laser-focus.

But King thrived off capitalising on confusion.

He peeked down the hallway at the same moment as the gunfire ceased. Two mercenaries outside had been stupid enough to break their cover in an attempt to unload everything they had at the moving target. King raised the Ceska to his shoulder and picked them off effortlessly, drawing on the thousands of hours he'd spent on target practice over his life.

Two bullets each, a double-tap straight to the head.

Pop-pop. Pop-pop.

They jerked back like marionettes, dead on impact, blood fountaining from the wounds in their foreheads. Both of them collapsed out of sight.

Three left.

King decided it was time to wait. Three-on-one had a much different feel to it than ten-on-one. Especially when the one had taken out seven. The last mercenaries would prove much more cautious than their dead friends. He was sure of it. Reality would sink in. They would grow nervous. Their hands would shake. So he stayed poised in the bathroom. He shrank away from the corridor and ducked into one of the toilet cubicles.

The after-effects of the flashbang began to take hold. Between his ears his temple throbbed like crazy. His ears rang with the high-pitched whining of temporary hearing loss. His mouth was dry. His nose ran with blood. But he wasn't dead. And that was all that mattered.

He let the chaos settle, until a minute had passed without a gunshot. Directly following the previous barrage, it made for an uncomfortable silence. Not for him. He relished these moments. The times when the enemy was unsure of themselves. Combat tended to follow a predictable pattern. Countless hours of waiting, watching, preparing. Then an all-out blitzkrieg of action and adrenaline and pent-up energy that didn't cease until a single individual remained.

Not this time.

He heard shuffling in the clubhouse. Panicked whispering. Had they hit him? Was he dead? He knew their veins were pumping. They were desperate to finish the job.

It took them two full minutes to come storming in. Two minutes in which King had ample time to plan a course of action, to calm himself, to let the stoic focus return.

He got into position. He waited.

The hallway was barely wide enough to fit two men, so when they bull-rushed into the bathroom with their guns blazing it was in a clumsy, predictable manner. The racket was deafening but King barely heard it. His hearing had taken enough damage to muffle all sounds. The trio must have unloaded fifty bullets between them as they stormed into the cramped space. Tiles all over the walls shattered, fragments cascading to the floor.

But King remained unhurt.

He sat perched on top of one of the cubicle stalls, wedged into the short space. His back against the ceiling. It would not protect him from gunfire. In fact, he was completely exposed. But it meant that he stayed out of the typical level of engagement that most men decided to fire at when running into a room blind. For the single second in which they had the advantage they moved their aim in a horizontal arc, panning the room from left to right, brutalising their surroundings.

But they didn't think to aim up.

No-one thinks to aim up.

King waited until all three were inside the bathroom before he emptied what was left in the Ceska's magazine. It turned out to be sparse. No more than ten bullets. Enough to get the job done though. He lit up the chests of the two men in front, dotting them with rounds. Before he could bring his aim over to the third, the guy fell back into the hallway, reacting impressively fast. King's gun clicked empty, a bad sign.

He dropped down from the cubicle and snatched up one of the rifles discarded from the two men he'd just killed. Before he had a chance to ascertain the make of the weapon, he saw the last mercenary fleeing down the hallway, heading for the other end of the clubhouse.

Attempting to escape.

King couldn't let that happen.

It would only take one phone call and Lars would leave the Australian countryside behind, flying on to who knows where. Perhaps that had already happened. Perhaps all of King's efforts were futile.

But in the time he had left, he had to try.

He broke into a sprint, chasing the man through the destroyed clubhouse.

CHAPTER 38

He followed the last mercenary through the main room, passing the shredded couches and the bar covered in alcohol and shattered glass. Out the same door he'd come in, legs pumping, trying to gain ground. From the back, he noticed the man was roughly the same size as him. Muscular, too. If he had any kind of fighting talent he might be able to gain the upper hand on King, who was reeling from numerous injuries and beatdowns. He didn't know what his reaction speed would be like. It would almost certainly be impaired. If that affected him enough to struggle against a man his size, he would soon find out.

They crossed the same gravel path. The mercenary headed into the hangar, slamming the doors apart, running fast. Seeing his co-workers decimated by a single man must have shattered his morale. King had seen it on the faces of many of his past enemies. The sheer incomprehension. How could one man cause so much chaos and destruction?

The double doors leading to the gear room swung closed just before King burst into them, knocking them back apart. It disorientated him for a split second, as the doors were solid. They obscured his view into the next room.

Enough for the mercenary to capitalise.

King ran straight into a fist, cracking him low and hard across the face. He recoiled and involuntarily let go of the rifle in his hands. His boots skidded on the concrete floor. Pain flared up inside his head, just before his neck whiplashed against the ground. The gun clattered away, useless.

He spun and righted himself, knowing that one wrong move would lead to unconsciousness, followed quickly by death. The man in front of him moved with desperation. His actions were fuelled with a rabid intensity that only came in a life-or-death situation.

At least King felt the same animalistic sensation.

He studied the guy. He looked to be roughly the same age as King, with the hardened expression of a man experienced in combat. An ex-soldier also.

'Do you know what you're doing?' King said, facing off with him across the gear room. He spat blood in the space between them.

'Making a living,' the guy said.

'You'd kill hundreds of thousands of people for money?'

'That's not up to me. I'm getting paid enough to live well for the rest of my life. Just to protect the boss.'

'So you don't care?'

'Not at all.'

'Well,' King said, 'at least I'll feel better about this.'

He charged in, knowing a punch or two would land, bracing for them. A right hook glanced off the side of his head as he closed the distance but he rolled with it. Let his head move with the blow, knocking much of the power away. That way he wasn't disoriented for the next step. He wrapped an arm around the mercenary's neck, looping it over his shoulder, getting a tight grip, powering through his guard. He dropped his hips low and threw the guy head-first over his body. The guy landed with all King's weight on top of him. A pathetic wheeze escaped his lips.

He was winded.

King slammed an elbow into his head, feeling his skull bounce off the concrete floor. He dropped another one, then a third. Then he paused. Not many people could take three direct blows from him. At least, not that he had experienced.

Obviously this guy was different.

The mercenary used the hesitation to buck violently, throwing King's weight off his chest, escaping out from underneath. He clambered to his feet and staggered across the room, toward the hangar.

King felt a pang of shock.

The four dead mercenaries at the hangar entrance would be surrounded by their weapons, all fully loaded. If this man got his hands on one of them, he would be as good as dead.

He scrambled off the ground, stumbling slightly. Disorientation almost swept his feet out from underneath. He gulped and tried to ignore the ramifications of so much physical violence in such a short space of time. He would address the consequences later.

The clock was ticking.

A loud *thump* echoed through the gear room as the door to the hangar slammed shut behind the mercenary. He disappeared from sight. The glass window revealed a small patch of the hangar within. It showed nothing. King would be running in with no spatial awareness, no knowledge of where the man was.

But the longer he left it, the higher the chance he would be facing an automatic weapon on the other side.

So he sucked up his courage and threw caution to the wind and wrenched the door open and ran through into the hangar, flicking his gaze side to side as rapidly as possible, searching for any sign of the man.

He looked right. Nothing.

He looked left, and caught the sight of a wrench swinging at his face in his peripheral vision.

Instinct.

He spun away, feeling the end of the heavy tool brush past his nose, indescribably close. It sent a shiver of fear down his spine. The guy had put everything into the swing and as a result he overcompensated. His arm carried through, causing him to stumble. He stepped out of position.

King needed no other opportunity. He lunged in with a powerful stride, placing his body in just the right position so that a punch would create a perfect symmetrical diagram, transferring power from the balls of his feet, up through his legs, through his glutes, up his back muscles, through the shoulder, down the elbow, released through his knuckles. He threw all his bodyweight into the blow. Aware that if he missed the attempt would throw him wildly off-balance, leaving him exposed and vulnerable to another swing of the wrench. One connection from the heavy tool and he would go down. There was little left in his gas tank. He was already fighting on wobbly legs.

But the blow landed.

It crashed off the mercenary's chin in just the right spot, breaking bone. The guy sprawled to the ground. At the same time he released the wrench. It skittered away, out of reach. His legs had given out under the impact of the punch. King felt pain shoot up his wrist, and he knew damage had been done.

Yet it didn't matter. The mercenary's head would be a lot worse off than his hand.

Just like that the fight was over. No prolonged battle or heroic comeback from the brink of defeat. In a fight between two men of their size, it only took one shot with just the right timing and placement to send the other to a dark place.

A place where quick recovery was impossible.

King knew a devastating concussion when he saw one. For a moment he considered mercy. He questioned the potential ramifications of leaving the man to recover from the beatdown. But it would do no good to spare his life. He would wind up killing someone else, that much was certain.

Men who were swayed so easily by dollar signs had no clear path to moral redemption.

So after assessing the state of the guy and deducing that he would not be getting up anytime soon, King crossed to the other side of the hangar and fished a bloodied assault rifle out of the cluster of dead mercenaries. Another M4 carbine. Safety off. Whoever supplied them must have delivered a bulk discount.

He turned back to the dazed mercenary.

His face fell.

The man had produced a small satellite radio from somewhere, probably one of the pockets in his khakis. Before King could react, he thumbed a button on the side and spoke two sentences into the device. They were disjointed, and he stumbled over his words, but the message was clear enough.

'They're coming. Take off now.'

He tossed the radio away and stared at King. Smiling. The expression was full of contempt and jest and sick satisfaction.

Now Lars knew he had to hurry.

He would be gone by the time they got there.

The anthrax spores would leave Jameson, and King would spend countless days eating himself alive with worry, wondering when he would switch on the news to see the effects of the most devastating terrorist attack in history.

He shot four times, wiping the smile off the man's face, but what had been done would not be so easily repairable.

Silence descended over the dropzone, and with it came a tension so thick and overbearing that King felt the sudden urge to vomit.

He had failed.

CHAPTER 39

'*Kate*! *Kitchener!*' King roared at the top of his lungs. '*All clear!*'

It echoed out of the hangar and through the empty cluster of buildings, which were now populated by a wave of dead men. He strode into the sunshine, passing the bullet-ridden corpses of the first four mercenaries he'd killed. The runway stretched off in either direction, showing no sign of life. Adjacent to the hangar, the pair of Hawkeis now lay empty, engines still running.

He jogged to the nearest one, tossed the M4 carbine in the back and leapt into the driver's seat.

The two women rounded the corner a moment later, coming from the rear of the hangar. They passed the clubhouse, now torn apart by bullets, all the windows shattered and the deck splintered and the insides churned to shreds. They saw the dead bodies scattered across the runway, dressed in the same olive-colour khakis, most now stained red.

Kitchener couldn't hide the shock from her face. In her police uniform she seemed out of place, suddenly timid, taken aback by such a concentrated level of death. Her dirty blond hair had come mostly loose from the ponytail she'd put it in earlier that day. Locks stained with sweat and dirt hung over her forehead, adding to the disbelief plastered across her face. King studied Kate, and saw nothing but numbness in her gaze. As she looked over the death and destruction she did nothing but stare blankly, almost vacantly. As if she wasn't entirely there. He didn't blame her. It had been the most unbelievable three days of her life.

The pair of them recognised his urgency and piled into the back seat of the Hawkei. Without a word, he slammed the accelerator as soon as they were inside the chassis and the armoured vehicle peeled off the mark, tyres squealing.

'How did you do that?' Kitchener yelled above the wind pouring in through the open windows.

'Do what?' King said.

'They're all dead. It was ten-on-one and you killed them all.'

'I'm not sure if you looked hard enough into my file,' he said. 'That's what I used to do for a living.'

'Are we heading for Lars?'

He nodded. 'The last man managed to get in contact with him before I could kill him. He knows we're coming. We might be too late.'

On the other side of the back seat, King noticed Kate grip the Hawkei's frame and close her eyes. He saw her breathing increase rapidly. He knew panic had begun to set in.

'Kate,' he said, looking at her.

She met his gaze. 'You keep throwing yourself towards danger. Doesn't it go against your instincts? How aren't you scared out of your mind?'

'I'd rather die trying to stop him than sit back and watch him kill hundreds of thousands of people. That's just how I'm wired.'

She looked away, silent.

'I can go on alone if that's what you two want. It's what I've been doing my whole life.'

'No,' Kitchener said, firm and matter-of-fact. 'You need all the help you can get.'

Kate still did not reply, but she looked at him and nodded reassuringly.

That was all he needed.

The runway ended abruptly and then they were back on the main road, this time with no regard for the speed limit. King mashed the pedal to the footwell's floor until the trees on either side of them blurred into one stream of woodland. Thankfully, no traffic passed them by. He knew a collision at this speed would prove disastrous. The Hawkei was a speeding battering ram. An innocent passerby wouldn't stand a chance.

The wind howled as Kate guided him with short, sharp gestures through the forest, heading back to the concrete plant and — presumably — the hidden runway buried somewhere behind.

'What if it's too late?' she said. 'What do we do?'

'I don't know,' King said. 'I haven't thought that far ahead. We'll need to contact some powerful people. This is a shit-storm.'

'What will they be able to do?'

'Not much,' he admitted. 'If the plane is gone when we get there, then Lars wins.'

They blazed back through the town of Hurst, attracting the attention of every pedestrian in sight. Now, it didn't matter. Secrecy had been thrown out the window. He had a single goal of utmost importance, and if they failed to achieve it every moment of the last three days would be for nothing.

It took another five minutes to find the same gravel trail that cut through pastures and farmland, leading to the concrete plant at the very end. Every second that ticked away drew another bead of sweat from King's forehead. He felt suffocated by the tension, like every breath took a gargantuan effort. At that moment he did not care for his own safety whatsoever. The urgency flooding his system overpowered all other emotions.

He simply *had* to succeed.

The Hawkei's chassis rattled violently when they hit the gravel, shaking him to his core. Out of the corner of his eye he saw a farmer driving a tractor in one of the pastures. The man stopped what he was doing and stared in awe at the sight before him. In the middle of nowhere, a powerful armoured vehicle shot past his farm at close to eighty miles an hour, kicking up swathes of dust in its wake.

King battled to control the wheel against the bucking suspension. He kept his foot pressed firmly against the accelerator. There was no time to slow down. Then they were through into the forest. He saw the path leading to the concrete plant, branching off. He aimed the Hawkei for it.

'Wait!' Kate cried. 'You won't access it from there. Keep heading straight. I'm sure of it.'

'If you're wrong…' King said, not daring to think of the consequences if they hit a dead end. Intercepting Lars would come down to a matter of seconds, even if they timed it perfectly.

He blitzed past the trail to the concrete plant and roared further into the forest, narrowly avoiding the pine trees pressing in on either side. He couldn't see far ahead. The trail twisted and curved, showing nothing but thick forest in all directions.

'From the layout of the map…' Kate said, then she trailed off. Thinking hard.

'Are you sure?' Kitchener said to her.

'No. Are any of us?'

Kitchener made to reply but the Hawkei slid sideways across the trail, dropping her stomach, making her hesitate. King grit his teeth as he turned the corner, faster than he should have. For a second he thought they would continue sideways, crushing the vehicle into one of the sturdy trunks lining the road.

Then it corrected course and they continued down the trail, narrowly avoiding harm.

'Oh, shit — here!'

He heard Kate's startled exclamation and looked ahead to where the path branched off two separate ways. One continued deep into the forest, trailing away out of sight. The other led down to a metal chain-link property gate, roughly the height of a man. Beyond it, the trees dissipated into some kind of open area. It had to be the runway.

He spun the wheel and the Hawkei shot down the right-hand path, gaining momentum. The speedometer began to climb.

'King!' Kate screamed.

'Hold on to something,' he said, eyes locked on the road ahead in concentration.

Stopping the vehicle to open the gate would kill precious time they did not have. There was no guarantee it would even open for them. He studied the flimsy, rusting supports and the hinges that looked like they hadn't been oiled since their creation. He figured a fifteen-thousand pound armoured vehicle would win in a head-on collision ten times out of ten.

At least, he hoped.

Kate and Kitchener scrambled for hand-holds, panicked and urgent. He gripped the wheel with both hands and touched the accelerator a little more, giving the Hawkei a final surge. By now it was too late to slow down. They would collide with the gate no matter what.

With a groan of tearing metal and a heavy jolt of impact the Hawkei's bonnet struck the middle of the gate at close to seventy miles an hour. King shot forward viciously, but the seatbelt dug into his shoulder, slowing him. He felt Kitchener's hair whip the back of his neck as her head whiplashed forward. Then the gate was under them. Then behind them. They burst out onto open road, losing little speed in the process. The violence of the impact abruptly ceased. Kate let out a gasp of exertion.

They were okay.

The gate had buckled under the pressure and they had shot through into the property.

The Hawkei roared out onto another runway, this one more cramped than Paul's dropzone. The tree line ran right to the edges of the tarmac, demonstrating that the area had been carved out of the forest before the runway was constructed. Its surface was nowhere near as smooth as the dropzone's. King got the sense that grand plans had been made for this runway while under construction, then hastily abandoned. Perhaps its location was too secluded. Whatever the case, he presumed it had not been used for commercial purposes in years. Much like seemingly every building in these parts.

'There!' Kitchener said, pointing to one end of the runway. 'See that?'

Sure enough, he noticed activity far in the distance, perhaps half a mile away. A grey low-wing monoplane rested idly in the centre of the runway. Blurred shapes moved in and out of its fuselage. With relief flooding his veins, he aimed for it and accelerated to maximum speed.

'They're still there,' Kate said, her voice shaky.

'They're going to try to kill us,' King said. 'You two need to be prepared for that. Kate, stay down when we get close. Kitchener, give me your pistol. I need accuracy.'

She handed her M&P over the centre console, the butt of the gun facing him. He took it and quickly checked the safety was off, heart pounding.

'You have the M4?' he asked her.

'Yes.'

'You know how to use it?'

'Yes.'

Matter of fact. Straight to the point. In the heat of imminent combat, he liked nothing better. Best to keep all conversation short and sharp when the blood was flowing.

'If they don't put up a fight, don't kill them in cold blood.'

'Why not?'

'They deserve a long and tortured stay in some underground hellhole. I'll make sure that happens.'

'That will be a lot more difficult.'

'I know. But don't get me wrong. If you see any kind of weapon, don't hesitate to shoot.'

As they grew closer, the scene became more clear. A military truck with a canvas storage area attached to the rear was parked near the P-750 aircraft. The rear flap lay open. From what King could see, the boot was empty. Which meant the plane was fully loaded, and they'd made it with little time to spare. Just as he expected.

Lars stood in between the vehicles, watching them approach. A mercenary flanked him on either side.

His last two hired guns.

So I really did wipe out most of his forces back at the dropzone, King thought.

One mercenary held some kind of automatic weapon in his hands. Unclear from this distance, but King guessed an M4. It seemed to be the same shape and colour. Whatever the case, the man raised it as they came within range and began sprinting across the tarmac, charging directly at them.

King saw the unmistakeable muzzle flash and knew the mercenary had unloaded his magazine. Yet he did not duck. Kate and Kitchener dove into the rear footwell, shocked by the gunfire. But the bullets pinged harmlessly off the front windscreen. Its glass was bulletproof. King kept his speed up, refusing to slow down even under a barrage of gunfire.

Which clearly unnerved the mercenary, as he kept firing until his gun clicked dry, spurred on by the urgency of a vehicle heading for him at eighty miles an hour.

King waited for the sound of discharging rounds to stop. He knew it would. Typically when under fire drivers panicked and slowed, or swerved, or changed course even slightly. He refused to do any of those things, continuing on his course without fault.

It was then that the mercenary realised his mistake.

Realised how heavily he had been counting on King to panic.

Realised he was now out of bullets.

King sat up. He saw the man standing only fifty feet in front of the speeding Hawkei, eyes boggling, mind racing, searching for some kind of alternative plan.

He had none.

King knew he would attempt to dive clear of the vehicle's trajectory. He kept his muscles loose, his grip poised. He guessed the man would jump right. Most did. He kept his foot planted down and narrowed his eyes, employing tunnel vision. He waited for the man to make a move.

The man dove right.

He wrenched the wheel milliseconds later, aligning the front of the Hawkei with the mercenary's fleeing form. He hoped the women in the back seat were still buried somewhere in the footwell. They would do good not to see what came next.

He felt the crunch as fifteen-thousand pounds smashed into the guy, mid-leap. There was the unmistakeable jolt of metal-against-flesh contact, and then he disappeared underneath the vehicle amidst a tangle of broken limbs.

He would not be a problem any longer.

As soon as the armed mercenary had been dealt with King slammed on the brakes. The Hawkei skidded to a halt directly in front of the canvassed truck, slowing hard enough to throw him against the seatbelt once more. In one fluid motion, he unbuckled his seatbelt and stepped out of the vehicle before it had even come to a halt, M&P already pointed directly at Lars' head.

As far as he could see, both men were unarmed.

Yet Lars' demeanour did not match the predicament.

The man seemed as comfortable as ever, blissfully unperturbed by the handgun aimed at his face. He stood with his hands by his side, smiling at King, as if all was right in the world.

'If you're here that means there's ten dead men back at the dropzone,' Lars said. 'You've still got it, that's for sure.'

'Eleven,' King said, nodding behind him at the mangled corpse of the second-last mercenary. He didn't dare take a look. He kept his eyes locked on the two men in front of him, searching for any sudden movements. 'Where were you taking the anthrax?'

'To another location,' Lars said. 'What do you care? You won, didn't you?'

'Why another location?'

'Well, it's not quite ready yet.'

'Not ready to use?'

'Almost there. I know a guy upstate who will turn the spores I have into aerosol form.'

'A guy?'

'Quite a high-level scientist, actually. Bioterrorism defence expert. Ironic, isn't it?'

'And he's helping you?'

'Everyone has a price. Except you, apparently.'

'Well, I hate to crash the party, but you really should have killed me back in the concrete plant. Then everything would have gone off without a hitch.'

Lars cocked his head. 'What do you mean? Party's still going.'

'You're going to jail for the rest of your life.'

'Oh, am I?'

King felt a slight tremor in his throat, like a small parcel of nerves kicking in. Lars knew something he didn't. No-one was this confident with a weapon aimed at their head.

'Got any weapons on you?' he said.

'No,' Lars said. 'And now neither do you.'

From behind, a pair of hands wrapped around his wrists and tugged hard. The altercation took him completely by surprise. He hadn't heard anyone come up behind him. His heart leapt in shock, loosening his grip slightly, enough for the hands to wrench the M&P out of his grasp. He found himself unarmed for a split second.

Then the assailant fired a single round into his foot. The 9mm round penetrated his all-weather boot and tore through skin and tendons near his toes. The shock caused his legs to buckle and his weight to drop. Before he knew it he lay on the cold surface of the runway, staring up at the barrel of his own weapon, panting from the instant agony that came from such a wound.

It was the person on the other end that startled him most. Officer Kitchener of the Jameson Police Department.

CHAPTER 40

The expression on her face had King confused. Reeling at the sudden change of fortune, it took him a moment to process such a look. It was a mixed bag of relief, angst and fear.

'Good girl,' Lars said.

Keeping her pistol trained on King, she tossed the M4 carbine across the tarmac. Lars caught it and slipped a finger into the trigger guard. Kitchener turned and yanked Kate out of the Hawkei. She fell to the tarmac beside King, staring in disbelief at the police officer. Kitchener wiped her brow and readjusted her grip on the pistol.

'Bet you didn't see that one coming,' Lars said, striding forward in nonchalant fashion.

'Can't say I did,' King said.

'I'm sorry, King,' Kitchener said.

'Sorry?' Lars said, and let out another harsh cackle. 'If you were sorry you wouldn't have shot him. If you were sorry you wouldn't have taken my offer all those weeks ago.'

'Offer?' King said.

‘What did you expect?’ Lars said, pointing at Kitchener. ‘You think a broke small-town cop living from paycheque to paycheque would say no to seven figures? Do you really believe it’s that hard to get people to work for you? Jason, Jason, Jason. You act like everyone who gets swayed by money is a monster. It’s called being human.’

‘That true?’ King said, looking up at Kitchener.

She shrugged. ‘Somewhat.’

‘When did he contact you?’

‘As soon as he landed in the country, last month. I’ve been trapped in this town my whole life. Don’t have the funds to move. Now I’m free.’

‘What about all the people that are going to die?’

‘No-one will know I was involved.’

‘You’re pathetic.’

Her grip on the pistol hardened, and her tone darkened. ‘Am I? Who’s around to say so? Just you and your girlfriend? You won’t be much longer.’

King turned to look at Lars. ‘So she’s been with you this entire time?’

He nodded.

‘Then you’ve been letting me live.’

He nodded again. Another wry, disgusting smile spread across his lips. ‘You’re catching on.’

‘She saved us at the concrete plant.’

'I had a change of heart at the top of the road. Sent her down to help you. I wanted you to tag along for a little longer. Wanted you to actually see me leave with the spores.'

'You killed your own men?'

He laughed. 'Jason, I handled you for ten years. I know *exactly* what you're capable of. You think I sent all my men to kill you at the dropzone with any intention that they would return?'

'I don't follow.'

'I needed to dispose of them anyway. Turns out I had a one-man killing machine conveniently running around behind me. I just fed them to you.'

King saw the plan. 'No witnesses.'

'Exactly.'

With that, Lars turned and swung the barrel of the M4 so that it pointed directly between the eyes of the last remaining mercenary. He was a black man, short and stocky, with wide eyes and a quivering mouth, both recent developments after listening to Lars reveal his true intentions.

'You can't be fucking serious,' he said.

'Sorry, champ.'

Kate let out a cry and averted her eyes from the killing. It only took a cluster of bullets to the temple for the man to tumble back against the side of the monoplane, smacking into its chassis with a dull thud and slumping to the ground a moment later.

Lars turned back to King. 'Where were we?'

'You were explaining your entire plan to me instead of putting a bullet in my head.'

'Ah, so I was. It's hard to resist, you know. The movies make it seem like a ridiculous concept. Why aren't I killing you? The truth is, this is the most enjoyment I've felt in … years. Look at your face!'

'Did you kill Brandt?' King said to Kitchener. 'You killed your co-workers?'

'No,' Kitchener said quietly.

'That was me, I'll admit,' Lars said, raising a hand in jest as if he were a kid in a classroom. 'Officer William Brandt — nice enough fellow — happened to see us carting the spores around the construction site. Kitchener here didn't have the stomach to kill, at least back then. She kindly informed me of his place of residence and I got the job done.'

'Hence the imposter at the police station,' King said. 'You let him in?'

Kitchener said, 'He was one of the mercenaries. I gave him Brandt's uniform when we heard you were in the area. Before we came to arrest you. I didn't want to kill you myself.'

'Oh, so you're a coward as well as a bitch.'

She stepped a little closer to him, barrel locked on target. 'Want to see how I've changed?'

'I saw first-hand at the warehouse. That was a quick turnaround.'

'Money does that.'

King didn't respond. He looked past her, to the tree line on the other side of the runway. The pine branches stirred softly in the breeze. In amongst the darkness of the forest, he thought he saw a slight glint. Like the sun reflecting off metal.

He turned to Lars. 'Want to know the problem with using local help?'

'What's that?'

'They're complete amateurs.'

'Excuse me?' Kitchener said, rattling the pistol in his face.

'You heard me,' he said. 'You see, all this juicy gossip would have been big news if I didn't realise you were working for Lars yesterday.'

'What?'

'Remember when you and Dawes arrested us at the construction office?' King said. 'You took us back to the station and decided to tell me that you'd had a look into my file. You noted that I used to work for Black Force.'

'Yeah…'

'Well, the only way you could have known that was if someone close to me told you. Such as Lars. There are roughly five people on the planet who know what I used to do. And you are definitely not one of them. That division of the U.S. Government doesn't exist. It's a little hard to read a file on it when every single aspect of the program was deliberately kept off the books.'

'You played along, though?' Kitchener said. Now the doubt had begun to creep into her tone.

'I wasn't sure exactly what was going on. It took me by surprise. So I just watched you very closely. And waited.'

'Well it seems you waited a tad too long.'

'Quite the contrary. I made my move last night.'

She paused. 'When you left the factory?'

'I never scouted the town last night. What good would that have done? It's Jameson. Completely useless to wandering the empty streets.'

Silence.

'In fact,' he said, 'I made a few calls. To a few old friends. Turns out one of them was in the country. He had to drive all night to make it here.'

She shot a glance in either direction, keeping her gun trained on him. 'I don't see anyone.'

'That's the point.'

The runway seemed to freeze for a single moment in time. Lars had watched the conversation unfold with growing restlessness, eyes darting left and right, searching for invisible threats. King knew he had unnerved them. Kitchener remained unsure of herself, awkwardly shifting her weight from foot to foot. The type of action that came from sudden discomfort and unease. She'd felt so in control, and now it had all been torn away. Did King really have backup? Was he lying?

The answer came a second later.

CHAPTER 41

A .338 Lapau Magnum bullet sliced through the top of her head, creating a deluge of blood and brain matter. King knew the exact make of the bullet because he knew the round came from a Barrett MRAD sniper rifle, which was the only weapon of choice of the man behind the scope. When the man had one in his hands against a stationary target, missing was something of an anomaly.

The sound of the discharge rang out across the runway shortly after, at the same time that Kitchener's corpse smacked against the tarmac. It caused Lars to flinch involuntarily. He raised his M4 and scanned the tree line, desperately searching for a target. Anything that could possibly resemble an enemy. He found nothing. Just as King knew he would.

Lars had spent the majority of his career behind a desk, which was why he hesitated. The correct course of action would be to unload the gun on the two people in front of him and dive for cover. He did neither of those things, determined to find the sniper in the trees.

It gave King more than enough time to scramble over to Kitchener's dead body, ignoring the throbbing pain in his foot. He snatched up her M&P and had its sights trained on Lars before he even had time to turn around.

'That all changed pretty quickly,' he noted.

Lars turned to him. 'Well, you got me this time.'

'There won't be another time.'

'We'll see.'

'Drop the gun.'

Lars seemed to hesitate for a moment. He didn't respond to the command, which meant he was not co-operating, which meant King's finger tightened on the M&P's trigger, half an ounce of pressure away from hammering the pin and sending a round through his old handler's skull.

Then the man let go of the rifle. Just as expected. It clattered to the tarmac and lay useless.

'Step away from it.'

Lars stepped away from it.

'*All clear!*' King yelled. The words echoed into the forest, audible from hundreds of feet away. On cue, a figure emerged from between two pine trees, previously shrouded in shadow, clutching an enormous bolt-action rifle in one hand, dressed all in black. He stepped onto the runway and headed for their position.

Dirk Wiggins.

They'd spent two years as squad members in Detachment-Delta of the United States Special Forces. King had met with Billy the night before, waking him from a deep sleep in his small living quarters above the post office. He'd used his phone to call dozens of old friends who he'd formed connections with at some point during his military career. Most were halfway across the world.

Dirk was mid-holiday in Sydney.

The man had rented a car and made the eight-hour drive as soon as King had called. Some favours required that sort of commitment.

And King had done Dirk plenty of favours in the past.

'Brother,' Dirk said, striding up to King with an outstretched palm. He stood roughly the same height, but a little stockier. He wore his hair long and dreadlocked, tied back when on the job. In any other setting he would be indistinguishable from a festival hippie. Truth was, he was one of the most accurate marksmen on the planet.

They clasped hands.

'It's been a while,' King said.

'Too long.'

'You doing alright?'

Dirk looked down at Kitchener's nearly-headless corpse.

'I've had better days,' he said. Then he looked up at King. 'So have you by the look of it.'

'I'm a bit of a mess, aren't I?'

'What are you doing in these parts?'

'Recommendation from a friend,' he said, shaking the pistol in Lars' direction. 'Hasn't been a great trip.'

'This your old handler? From that secret post-Delta project you could never discuss?'

'Uh-huh.'

Dirk strode up to Lars, towering over the slight man. He wrapped a hand around his throat and hurled him back into the monoplane's chassis. Lars bounced off the metal and collapsed to the ground, coughing from the sudden violence. He stayed on all fours for a long moment, then spat blood on the tarmac beneath. Then he got to his feet.

'Pleased to meet you too,' he said, just as sardonic as always.

'Shut the fuck up,' Dirk said. A man of few words.

'Glad to know that I'm still smarter than you two idiots,' Lars said.

He brought one hand out from behind his back, revealing a small remote roughly the same size as an car key fob. His thumb rested on its centre, touching a thin circular button. Keeping *just* enough pressure on it so as not to set it off.

'Know what this is?'

'I can guess,' King said, his gut sinking.

'Kitchener might have been useless but she got one thing right. Guess so much has gone on that you haven't had time to check your belt, Kate?'

Kate stared down at her leather belt, frantically searching for something. King watched her out of his peripheral vision, keeping most of his attention focused firmly on Lars. Dirk stood directly beside the man, unmoving, hesitant. Unsure as to the validity of the threat.

Confirmation came a moment later.

'Fuck,' Kate whispered. He thought he heard a sob.

'What is it?' King said, refusing to look away from Lars.

'A small metal cylinder,' she said, voice shaking. 'Clipped to the back of my belt. It looks like some kind of bomb. She must have put it on me last night while I was asleep.'

'That's exactly what it is,' Lars said. 'Heptanitrocubane. The boys at DARPA were experimenting with the stuff, so I grabbed a few on my way out the door. It's a very powerful high-explosive. Your girlfriend will cease to exist if I push this button a few millimetres more.'

King kept the gun locked on target. He didn't move.

'You shoot me and it'll go off,' Lars said. 'You move suddenly and it'll go off. I can't get much closer to setting it off than I currently am.'

Silence.

'I'm leaving now.'

King said, 'No you're not.'

Lars cocked his head. 'Want to test me? Games are over. I'm getting in this plane and taking off and if I see you take a single step towards me I'll blow her up. You're close enough to her that you'll die too. Either instantly, or you'll lose a few limbs and bleed out slowly.'

'That's two of us. If you take off in that plane there'll be hundreds of thousands dead.'

'I don't think you're ready to die yet, King,' Lars said. 'A lot of people say they are, but you're not. That's why you quit. You kept coming too close to death. That's why you came here.'

'So much for that.'

Lars smiled. 'You know, I still can't believe you actually came. All I did was say you should check the area out sometime.'

'I had nowhere else to go. Nothing else to do.'

'Well, I'm glad you did. This has been fun.'

No response.

'I'll be off now. Might blow her up after I take off anyway.'

King tightened his finger on the trigger.

'Go on,' Lars said. 'Pull it.'

'I might.'

'You won't. I know you inside and out. I know how your mind works. You're thinking there's still a way out of this situation. You're thinking of a million different ways to win, as always. But you'll keep standing there, because…'

A flash of movement. A grunt of exertion. Mid-sentence Lars flinched. King made to squeeze the trigger but something made him hesitate. He heard the sound of a small object skittering across tarmac, and he knew the remote had left Lars' hand somehow. It had happened too fast to ascertain exactly what had occurred. Dirk now stumbled past Lars, attempting to correct his balance. He must have swatted the remote away. The action had been blindingly fast, so fast that even King hadn't seen it fully.

All he knew was that the remote had landed somewhere behind Lars.

Dirk stood in between them, blocking a clear shot.

There was no time to re-adjust his aim.

Reacting in a split second, King powered past his old friend and crash-tackled Lars into the runway. They sprawled across the ground, tangled in limbs. Lars wrapped his arms around King's gun hand and wrenched with surprising power. King hadn't anticipated that kind of strength from such a slight man. He lost control of the M&P and Lars' movement sent it spinning away.

King dropped a hard elbow into his stomach. He felt the wheeze of a winded man. Using the same hand he thrust up, fist clenched, driving his knuckles into the bottom of his chin, feeling soft tissue and delicate bone crunch under the power of the blow. Lars' head whipped back and he scooted backwards, heading for the remote. King wrapped a hand around his ankle and tugged him back into range.

He saw the fist coming but couldn't do anything to move away from it. He was stuck lying on his side in an awkward position, one arm pinned under his bulk, chin up, legs splayed. As he saw the approaching shot he knew it would land. He hoped Lars did not possess pinpoint accuracy.

He did.

Spots of darkness swallowed much of his vision as the fist crashed into his head just above his ear. He wasn't sure if it was from the force behind the impact or simply the fact that he had been weakened from such a sheer amount of physical conflict in a short space of time. Whatever the case, he reeled back from Lars, utterly disorientated. To make sure he had the upper hand, Lars kicked out with a steel-toed boot, once again hitting his target perfectly.

King's injured foot.

Searing pain shot up his leg. He let out an involuntary grunt in an effort to manage its effects. The stomp hit him directly above the bullet wound. Coupled with the strike to the head, he knew his body would not respond to his brain's commands for the next few moments.

Which would be more than enough time.

Lars scrambled away, out of reach. He got to his feet and took a couple of short hurried steps and before Dirk could reach him he'd scooped up the remote and had his finger poised on it once again.

'Impressive,' he panted, spitting blood. 'Very impressive.'

King stumbled to his feet, feeling every inch of movement in his nerve endings. As he rose his knees momentarily buckled. He righted himself and assessed their positions.

Now, there was no hope. Dirk and Kate stood behind him, side by side, unarmed. In his haste to disarm Lars, Dirk had dropped his Barrett. Now he stood weaponless, both hands free. Not that a heavy-duty sniper rifle would do much use in this situation anyhow. King saw his own M&P several feet away, far out of reach. Lars stood near the plane's open exit door, a large space built into the side of the fuselage to enable multiple skydivers to leap out at once. It had a rolling cover that was currently locked in place, leaving the door wide open. Inside, King saw the stacked crates of anthrax, tied down with thick leather straps.

With his free hand, Lars wagged a finger in their direction. 'Almost had me, boys. Was worth a shot.'

He paced a few steps to the right and picked up King's discarded M&P. He raised it, levelling the barrel at King's head. King stared at the small dark hole, wondering if it would be the last thing he saw.

Then Lars paused.

'You know what,' he said, 'I was going to shoot you all before I left. But I might just leave you here, King. You'll feel worse when you hear about what I did. When you see the sheer number of casualties. Wasn't that the whole point of this?'

He shook his head, smiling through bloody teeth.

'Where are you going to use it?' King said, his shoulders slumped, his demeanour that of a defeated man.

Lars winked. 'You'll just have to wait and see.'

He turned away from them and stepped up into the P-750. He clambered through to the front. There was no cockpit, just a single pilot's seat built behind the controls to maximise room for jumpers. Keeping them in his peripheral vision, he thumbed a few switches on the dashboard and the front propellor coughed and spluttered to life, creating a whine that echoed through the forest.

King knew that if the plane took off it would be final. With no aerial transport of their own, they would lose Lars forever. As his gut twisted into a knot he battled the urge to pass out.

'King,' Dirk yelled above the roar.

He turned and looked at the man. Dirk stood awkwardly, one hand behind his back, the other hanging at his side. Not a natural position. He was hiding something from sight. As King watched, he brought the hand out into the open. He clutched a leather belt between his meaty fingers. King's eyes darted to

Kate's waistband. No belt to be seen. Dirk must have unfastened it in the few seconds that he had spent fighting with Lars.

He put everything together.

Dirk turned and heaved the belt as far as he could. It soared high in a broad arc and slapped the runway a few dozen feet behind the plane, well out of range. Then he turned back, just as the plane beside them began to roll away, its wheels slowly turning over, picking up momentum. Within a few seconds it had accelerated faster than either of their top running speeds.

They would not catch it on foot.

The P-750's propellor made verbal communication impossible. But two years as brothers on the battlefield meant that words were not always necessary. Dirk pointed a single finger at the Hawkei, its engine still running. King knew what needed to be done.

Head throbbing, foot aching, body screaming for rest, he broke into a sprint for the only vehicle capable of catching the plane before take-off.

CHAPTER 42

As the urgency of the predicament sunk in, King felt his heart beating hard against his chest wall, threatening to break through at any moment. He ducked through the Hawkei's open frame and sat down in the passenger seat.

Ahead, nearly eight thousand pounds of aluminium continued to increase its speed as the P-750 gained traction on the runway. Every passing second meant a higher chance that it would escape.

Dirk shot around the rear of the vehicle and clambered into the driver's side. As soon as he got both feet inside the footwell he stamped down and the tyres spun, screeching against the tarmac. They shot off the mark, accompanied by the familiar stomach drop that came with rapid acceleration. King leant against the head rest and took a deep breath. The next few minutes were the most important of his life.

There was absolutely no room for error.

The Hawkei had a top speed of eighty miles an hour. He wondered if it could reach that before the P-750 did. He looked down and saw the road blurring outside the vehicle. With no door to protect him he would be as good as dead if he slipped and fell out. He guessed death would be preferable in that situation. It beat having to worry about losing most of the skin on his body.

He forced that thought from his mind.

He knew that a leap of faith would probably be necessary if he had any chance of stopping Lars.

They began to gain ground on the P-750. He narrowed his eyes against the blistering wind, focusing on the task ahead. The Hawkei would approach the plane from the left-hand side. Its large entrance door still lay open. Lars hadn't had time to shut it. Just in front and slightly underneath the door, the left wing jutted out from the plane's body.

'Get me as close as you can,' King said.

'You sure about this?'

'Not at all.'

'We can pull up alongside and try to shoot him.'

'It won't work.'

'You sure about *that?*'

King nodded. 'If we don't shoot through the fuselage in exactly the right place it'll be worthless. He'll just take off. Margin for error is way too high.'

'He's close to take-off now.'

King took one last inhale, sucking in fresh air, then zoned in. 'So let's go.'

Now almost parallel with the accelerating plane, Dirk swung the wheel and the Hawkei veered in. Its bonnet came close to crushing into the side of the plane, an event that would significantly hinder take-off. But at the last second the P-750 gained an additional burst of speed and began to pull away.

They blasted down the runway, directly behind the left wing. The open door sat at a diagonal to their vehicle, slightly ahead and to the right. King gripped the armoured frame and swung across the outside step, feeling the wind blasting against his clothes, ignoring the pain racking his system. He got a foot on the bonnet and levered himself onto the front of the vehicle. He tried not to focus on the ground below, speeding by at an unbelievable rate.

One wrong step and he would die.

He knew the Hawkei would reach its maximum speed shortly. Basic physics meant it couldn't go much faster than this.

He braced against the elements and began to assess when would be the best time to jump. He had to time it perfectly. He guessed there was a few feet between their vehicle and the side of the plane.

So perhaps…

Then he saw the front wheels of the P-750 lift off the runway and knew if he did not move now, he would never see the plane again.

He threw caution to the wind and leapt off the bonnet.

Arms outstretched.

For a terrifying beat he thought he wouldn't make it. His back arched, his legs splayed, his fingers reaching for any kind of handhold. It was so close. It was right there.

He began to fall.

His hands slammed into the very lip of the doorway, harder than he anticipated. His grip slipped and his legs dangled in thin air and he started to fall away from the plane. He ignored the sudden numbness in his fingers and locked them tight. They seized the lip. Miraculously, they held.

His stomach dropped into his feet as the plane took off, parting from the ground, ascending fast. He didn't dare look down. He held onto the fuselage by a hair's breadth, clutching the floor of the plane, heart hammering, mind racing.

Straining his forearms, he levered his body up. Bringing his head over the lip of the plane. He took a look inside. Lars sat in the pilot's seat, unaware that King had jumped, concentrating on piloting the aircraft. He battled to control its takeoff, especially in such windy conditions.

King knew he had to act fast. If Lars heard a single odd noise he would turn, see him and put a bullet in his head. He had to get his bulk inside the fuselage and then act with lethal ferocity, making sure he did not come this far for nothing.

He still refused to see how high the plane was. The forest would be nothing than a mountainous blanket of green far below, and he knew the vertigo from such a sight would weaken his limbs, especially with no parachute on his back to save him from falling a thousand feet to his death.

He poised, ready to explode. Both elbows against the plane floor. Upper body inside. Legs hanging out.

Go.

CHAPTER 43

He vaulted into the plane, shaking the fuselage, drawing Lars' attention. But by then it was too late. He got his feet underneath him and took two bounding steps, crossing to the pilot's seat in the blink of an eye. Lars swung a hand up. It contained the M&P. He searched for a good shot, desperate to get the barrel on target.

Not this close.

King smashed the gun with a meaty forearm, sending it clattering away. It came to rest somewhere under the controls. Well out of reach. He looped an arm around Lars' neck and squeezed tight. The move crushed the man's windpipe, eliminating any chance of movement. He held his old handler against the seat for a beat. Waiting for Lars' instinctual struggle to lose steam. When he finally began to tire, King let go and burst forward, ducking into the footwell. He got a hand on the M&P. Before Lars had time to mount any kind of significant attack he peeled away, back into the middle of the fuselage.

Effectively disarming the man sitting across from him.

'What are you going to do?' Lars said. 'Shoot me? I was your boss for years. I know you can't pilot an aircraft.'

King kept the gun trained on Lars. He snuck a look over his shoulder, past the stacked crates of anthrax spores, to the rear of the fuselage. Sure enough, he found what he was looking for. A spare parachute container, kept in the plane in case of emergencies. A Javelin Odyssey, by the looks of it.

Perfect.

'Don't need to know how to fly,' he said.

He retreated to the back of the fuselage, looped one hand around the backpack and stepped into its harness. He worked quickly. Moving with the speed of a man who had thousands of jumps worth of experience.

Lars cocked his head. 'If you kill me and then jump, it'll crash.'

'You're spot on there.'

'You'd risk that?'

'Look down,' King said. 'Nothing but uninhabited forest for miles in any direction. And I recall you saying these spores aren't weaponised yet. They're not in aerosol form.'

'Maybe they are.'

'Backtrack as much as you like,' King said. 'Won't change a thing.'

He clipped the final strap around his waist and strode forward to the open doorway. He aimed the M&P at Lars.

'Now I win,' he said.

Lars let out a primal scream. The type of outcry that came from watching a meticulous plan crash and burn. He ducked low and powered across the final stretch of fuselage in a last-ditch effort. King saw it coming. But he didn't pull the trigger. He saw an opening. He decided to take it.

This way, Lars would at least face unbridled terror before he died.

A gunshot would be too quick.

So he sidestepped, moving to the right. Lars overshot his charge and had to screech to a halt directly in front of the open doorway. Instincts kicked in and he slowed, terrified to fall out of the plane. He reached for a handhold.

A waste of time.

King checked one last time that his parachute was securely fastened, then dropped his shoulder low and rammed Lars in the stomach, lifting off with both feet at the same time. The momentum behind the tackle sent both men tumbling out into open sky.

The wind took them and they spun like rag dolls through the air. King experienced the momentary sensory overload he'd felt a thousand times before, as his brain became suddenly overwhelmed by the sensation of freefall. He let natural reflexes kick in. After more than a thousand skydives, many under dangerous conditions, he'd developed an instinctive response.

He thrust his chin up and arched his back and splayed his arms out on either side. Almost instantly he stabilised in the air.

Alongside him, Lars panicked. He thrashed his limbs, turning over and over. King knew his brain would struggle to process what had occurred. With no form of parachute or means of slowing down, death was inevitable.

He wondered if Lars had accepted that yet. Or if there was still some inkling of hope. Whatever the case, his old handler did nothing but flail as the trees far below grew ever closer.

King estimated that they had exited the plane at somewhere close to five thousand feet. He would have to open his parachute soon, after only a few seconds of freefall. He looked at Lars, who managed to right himself for just a moment.

The two made eye contact.

King saw the man's boggling eyes, pale-white expression, clammy hands.

Now he knew what true fear looked like.

He reached back and tugged the ripcord out of its pouch. There was a moment of delay as the parachute shot out of the pack, still clustered tightly in a ball. The wind did not catch it for a second.

Just enough time to give Lars the thumbs up sign.

Then the canopy billowed out and the shoulder straps dug tight into King's shoulders, slowing his descent. Lars spiralled away, falling at terminal velocity.

King looked up and saw the P-750 far overhead, its nose starting to dip. He analysed its trajectory and figured it would come down somewhere in the valley to the east. The valley held nothing but an uninterrupted wave of pine trees. No towns, no civilisation of any kind. The gamble had paid off. Then he looked down and saw Lars' tiny figure disappear into the trees. The impact zone was obscured, hiding the grisly results.

But King knew there would be zero chance of survival.

Despite being confident in the P-750's landing area, he needed to see the impact for himself. He reached up to the toggles on either side of the harness and steered the chute to the right. His legs swung with the momentum as he corrected course. Now he faced the valley.

It took just over a minute to happen. The plane continued to descend with no-one in the pilot's seat. It bucked and swayed in the wind as it fell. Then it dove into the valley and crashed into the other side, taking down a couple of trees in the process. The violent sound of tearing metal echoed up from the forest, reaching his ears a couple of seconds after the crash. No flames. No fireball. Just a crumpled wreck with a destroyed chassis. The wings were torn off by the impact.

He knew that the anthrax spores would not pose a problem. He'd seen the crates Lars had kept them in. Military-grade, reinforced, designed to withstand the most brutal conditions imaginable. Necessary for such a volatile substance. They wouldn't have torn apart in the crash. Especially with the chassis of the plane protecting them from a direct hit. On the off-chance they had, they would pose no significant risk. They had yet to be weaponised into aerosol form.

He made sure to memorise the location of the crash zone for future reference. The authorities would need to secure the location as soon as they were made aware of the situation. He used the toggles to spin the parachute one-hundred-and-eighty degrees, keeping the movement slow. Staring at the ground in all directions. Getting his bearings.

The runway they'd taken off from lay to the west. He wouldn't make it there. Ahead he spotted the mountain roads ascending up to Jameson, nothing but thin lines from such an elevated position. He estimated he would come down somewhere close to the metal work factory where he'd hid the bodies of eight men. Six of them guilty, two innocent.

It didn't take long for the canopy of branches to rush up at his feet. He guided the parachute into a patch of forest where the trees were widely interspersed. It gave him more than enough room to land. He dipped between a pair of tall pine trees and tugged both toggles down. Flaring the chute. Slowing his descent. It put him at just the right speed to touch down smoothly on the wet grass. Two bounding steps to get his momentum under control and then he was on flat ground.

Perfectly safe.

He stayed upright. Listened to the sudden quiet of the forest, compared to the screaming wind and constant gunfire of the last ten minutes. Then he fell back onto the forest floor, staring up at the clear blue sky above. He sucked in breaths of fresh air. Happy to be alive. Happy that the madness had finally come to an end.

He'd lost count of the number of people he'd seen die over the last three days. Whether it was by his hand, or simply witnessing murder. To anyone else, the sheer volume of horror would be too much to bear. To King, it felt like just another day.

Which was perhaps the worst part.

He had grown so accustomed to violence and death and destruction that the events that had transpired didn't even seem out of the ordinary. It felt like he was back in Black Force, at the tail end of another mission, ready to go for the next one.

This was not a healthy way to live.

He promised himself there would be no next time. He would travel somewhere away from all this shit, somewhere where he could finally stop and take in an ordinary civilian life. He wasn't sure where.

But first there were other matters to attend to.

After what felt like a century of rest he clambered to his feet and got out of the parachute harness. He left it there in the forest, its canopy wrapped around a cluster of branches, flapping gently in the breeze. He wasn't sure he had the energy to cart it back to town.

He moved on. Starting the slow trek through the woods, searching for a main road which would lead him back to the town of Jameson.

Hopefully for the very last time.

CHAPTER 44

It took a little over two hours to reach the town's outskirts. By then, the sun had melted into the horizon. An amber glow permeated through the forest. It created something close to serenity.

King had powered through dense woodland for close to an hour before happening upon a twisting mountain road. He recognised it as part of the connection between Queensbridge and Jameson, and quickly figured out which direction to head. Then it came down to putting one foot in front of the other. Focusing on trying not to faint. If a car passed by he wouldn't bother attempting to wave it down. No-one in their right mind would pick up a bloodied, battered, two-hundred-and-twenty pound stranger, especially in these parts where witnesses were thin.

He knew he looked bad. His swollen cheek had puffed one side of his face beyond all recognition. The other was caked in dried blood that he didn't have the energy to bother removing. His foot had turned numb from the massive dose of adrenalin but as he settled into the trek and the rush subsided he began to feel the mind-numbing pain in every step. His ribs hurt with each breath. He hoped nothing was broken.

And the nearest hospital had to be dozens of miles away.

He passed Yvonne's motel first. At this hour the repair crew were packing up for the day. He noticed they had almost completed their task. Dozens of brand new window panes sat in the sills. The shattered glass had been almost entirely swept up.

He hobbled into the main road and began a short journey past the main shops. Most of the townspeople had returned to their homes. They would be preparing dinner for their families. Without a hint of knowledge as to what had occurred in their town.

Perhaps it would all come out later down the line, after a federal investigation. He doubted it. But it might.

He hoped he would find who he was looking for. With nothing left to accomplish at the airfield, it seemed obvious that Kate and Dirk would return to the town where it had all begun. As he closed in on Jameson Post, he saw two people up ahead. Standing on the footpath in front of a high-powered Ducati motorcycle. Deep in conversation.

They saw him.

Kate closed the distance between them at a lightning pace and they embraced. He held her waist and buried his face into her shoulder. He hoped she didn't mind the blood. It seemed she was too preoccupied to notice.

'You look awful,' she whispered, her voice shaky.

'I've been better. But I'll live.'

They parted. For a long moment they stood there, looking at each other, in mutual disbelief at what they had gone through.

'ASIO's on their way,' Dirk said, approaching them. 'I called a guy as soon as I saw the plane go down. He's bringing a whole team of federal investigators. Word of this has already reached the very top. I imagine they're going to want to interview you for weeks.'

King looked out at the deserted main strip. 'I won't be around to humour them.'

Dirk cocked his head. 'You won't?'

'It's done,' he said. 'Lars is dead. All his men are dead. The threat's eliminated. I could spend months detailing everything I saw, but it's all corporate bullshit. Besides…'

Dirk knew where he was going. 'I'm guessing you overstepped the boundaries of the law just a couple of times.'

'Let's leave it at that.'

'So what do I tell them?'

King shrugged. 'You don't know. You simply happened upon all this shit. The dropzone. The metal work factory out east. The police station. You don't know what to make of it.'

'Where will you go?'

'Haven't figured that out yet.' He paused. 'Somewhere quiet.'

'That's what this place was supposed to be.'

'Exactly. So I'll try again.'

Dirk nodded. King noticed Kate standing off to the side, staring at the both of them, dumbfounded.

'Aren't you in the military?' she said to Dirk.

'Yes, ma'am. On vacation. If you can call it that.'

'And you're just going to let him walk away from all this?'

He exchanged a knowing smile with King. 'I see you two haven't known each other long enough. Kate, when Jason King tells you he's going to do something, there's really not much you can do to stop it.'

'I wish I had the friends you do,' she said to King.

King smiled again. 'No you don't. Because you need to go to hell and back to get the type of friends I have.'

The soft jangle of a mobile phone sounded from Dirk's pocket. He withdrew a slim smartphone. He made a shrugging gesture, as if to say *I have to take this.* King nodded and the man stepped away, speaking in a hushed whisper to whoever was on the other end of the line.

Probably his employers, wanting him back from Australia.

Kate stood across from King. Now the two of them were alone. They let the silence hang for a moment longer.

‘So, what now?’ Kate said.

‘You said you didn’t want to up and leave.’

She nodded. ‘Haven’t changed my mind on that. But doesn’t this feel a little … off?’

He rested a hand on her shoulder. ‘You’re a great girl, Kate. Truly. But you don’t want to spend any more time with me than this. I quit the Force to be alone for a while. I don’t know … I guess I wanted time to digest everything I’ve done in my career. I haven’t had a chance to yet. In fact, this has probably added to the baggage. But it’s going to take its time to resolve. Honestly, I’m not sure if it ever will.’

‘I understand,’ she said. ‘I don’t think I ever thought something permanent would come of it. But we helped each other get through everything.’

‘We did.’

She leant on her tiptoes and pressed her lips to his. He felt the soft touch and pulled her in, savouring their last moments together. When they parted she had a smile on her face.

‘Well, you know where to find me,’ she said. ‘If you ever happen to be passing through again.’

‘Let’s hope when that time comes it turns out less eventful than the first.’

‘Goodbye, Jason. Thank you for everything.’

They hugged a final time. He felt her warmth and held onto that feeling, knowing it might be a long time before he found another girl like her.

Then he turned and approached Dirk, who was finishing up his phone call. The man slid his phone back into his pocket and faced him.

'Just explained what went down to the boss,' Dirk said. 'He wants me to stay. See the whole investigation process out.'

'They'll be flying out their best.'

'I don't doubt it. The conspirator is one of our own. That means the whole process will be messy.'

'And lengthy.'

Dirk nodded.

'I hope you don't blame me for not sticking around,' King said.

'Not at all. It was good to see you again, brother. Even if the reunion was short.'

'You understand why I need to leave, right?'

Dirk nodded. 'When they whisked you out of the Delta Force for some secret project, I knew you'd end up either dead or scarred. I can't imagine the shit you've been through.'

'I came here to heal. Didn't do much of that.'

'Go find some secluded corner of the globe and bury your head in the sand. Can't be too hard, can it?'

‘Knowing my luck … it will be.’ He shot a glance at the Ducati motorcycle, gleaming in the late afternoon sun. ‘Yours?’

Dirk nodded. ‘I shipped it over here a couple of weeks ago. Planned to road trip around the country. Guess that’s not happening anymore. Great bike, she is.’

‘I think I might buy one. Down the line.’

‘How are you getting out of here?’

‘I’m yet to work that out,’ King said. ‘Probably hitch a ride. Someone lent their car to me but I trashed it.’

‘Sounds like you.’

Then Dirk did something that King did not anticipate. He reached into his leather jacket and came out with a small set of keys. He tossed them. King caught the bunch one-handed and shot his friend a quizzical glance. ‘What are you doing?’

‘You need wheels.’ Dirk gestured to the Ducati. ‘There they are.’

‘I appreciate it, but I’ll manage,’ King said. ‘I only need to get to the airport.’

‘First you need to get to a hospital, as fast as possible.’

‘How much do you want for it?’

Dirk shook his head. ‘Remember Mogadishu?’

King flashed back to an earlier time, filled with sand and firefights. He remembered pulling a man from a burning wreckage, seconds away from being burnt alive. He looked across at the same man.

'I remember.'

'So you know I don't want a cent.'

King nodded and held a hand outstretched. 'Thank you, brother.'

Dirk shook it. 'I really hope you find your peace, King. Give me a call when you've settled down.'

'To be honest,' he said. 'I'm finding it hard to believe that will ever happen.'

King threw one leg over the leather seat of the motorcycle and fired it up. He knew how to ride. Before the military, before the special operations, before any of the chaos of the last ten years, he'd spent an uneventful childhood in the small town of Green Bay, Wisconsin. A beat-up Suzuki dirt-bike had been his only method of transportation.

Those were simpler days.

He looked back at Dirk and Kate one last time. Two people he would always remember. He waved. They waved back. Then he rolled onto the asphalt and gunned the Ducati past stores that had just closed and motels that would stay open all night and through to endless rows of forest, thick with vegetation and undergrowth and dark spaces. He left the madness far behind, pressing on through the countryside, passing the low sprawling bar where he'd first had a drink three days before. He recalled what the bartender had said.

Sometimes you need to put all the shit behind you.

He accelerated past the building without giving it a second glance.

Moving.

Always moving.

The only thing he'd ever known.

Read Matt's other books on Amazon.

amazon.com/author/mattrogers23

20843086R00228

Printed in Great Britain
by Amazon